W9-DDP-271

Guerrilla Season

By the same author

Seeing the Elephant: A Story of the Civil War

Open Ice

The Breaker Boys

Guerrilla Season

PAT HUGHES

A Sunburst Book

Farrar, Straus and Giroux

Copyright © 2003 by Patrice Raccio Hughes
All rights reserved
Distributed in Canada by Douglas & McIntyre Ltd.
Printed in the United States of America
First edition, 2003
Sunburst edition, 2009
1 3 5 7 9 10 8 6 4 2

Library of Congress Cataloging-in-Publication Data
Hughes, Pat (Patrice Raccio)
    Guerrilla season / Pat Hughes.— 1st ed.
        p. cm.
    Summary: Two fifteen-year-old boys find friendship and family loyalty
tested in 1863 Missouri, where civilians are caught in the savage conflict
between Rebel guerrillas and Union forces.
    ISBN-13: 978-0-374-40028-6 (pbk.)
    ISBN-10: 0-374-40028-8 (pbk.)
    1. United States—History—Civil War, 1861–1865—Underground
movements—Juvenile fiction. 2. Quantrill, William Clarke, 1837–1865—
Juvenile fiction. [1. United States—History—Civil War, 1861–1865—
Underground movements—Fiction. 2. Quantrill, William Clarke,
1837–1865—Fiction. 3. Guerrillas—History—19th century—Fiction.
4. Missouri—History—19th century—Fiction.] 1. Title.
PZ7.H87374 Gu 2003
[Fic]—dc21

                                                    2002032208

* * *

For Sam, who pushed me onward,
and Scott, who pulled me from the slush

* * *

Guerrilla Season

THE SOUTH	THE NORTH
Guerrillas	Militia
Bushwhackers	Jayhawkers
Partisan Rangers (Partisans)	Federals (Feds)
Secesh (Seceshers, Secessionists)	Yankees
Rebels	Union
Confederates	

Part One

SEASON OF LIGHT
APRIL–JULY 1863

★ ★ ★

1

The dog kicked up the rabbits and worked them through the brush. Matt raised his shotgun to his shoulder.

"Get 'em!" Jesse said.

Right on top of Matt's shot, Jesse's gun went off. Blackpowder smoke burned Matt's eyes. He ducked under it, running to where the rabbit had gone down. When he hoisted it by its hind legs, he was amazed to see Jesse showing him one, too.

"When've you seen *that* before?" Jesse called.

"I would have to say never." It was a quick kill, but not as clean as Matt would have liked. Some of the meat was spoiled, part of the pelt damaged. Before he got to Jesse, he tossed the rabbit into his wheat sack.

Jesse knelt to scratch Patch's head. "*Good* girl! How'd you do that?" He looked up at Matt. "You give me a foot and I'll give you one—but don't say it."

"All right," Matt said, trying not to smile. For a religious boy, Jesse could be mighty superstitious; he didn't like talking about luck. Jesse's rabbit was a cleaner kill, as always. Still, he'd shot only two today. Matt had three—he supposed because he was the one who really needed to bring home food.

Jesse sacked his rabbit. "You getting hungry?"

"I'm always hungry."

They shouldered their guns and started through the cool,

damp woods. Vines, trees, and undergrowth grew a bright green haze.

"April's the best time of year, don't you think?" Matt bounced on a rotting branch until it gave way with a soggy snap. "Redbuds in bloom, birds coming back, the air smells like earth . . . And tomorrow, I reckon I'll start my plowing."

Jesse shook his head. "Matt, you are the only boy I know who *likes* to plow."

At the rocks where they always ate, they shared corn bread and apples from Matt's place, cheese and bread and dried beef from Jesse's.

"So this plowing—you can manage on your own?"

Matt shrugged. "Pa couldn't do much last year."

"Well, I'll help you some."

"Thanks, Jess. But I can do it. And Ben'll help a little."

Jesse grinned. "Oh, yeah. A *very* little."

"I'll make a farmer out of him yet." Matt savored a bite of the tangy beef. "I'm thinking I might put in a bit more corn this year."

"Your pa told you just what to do for this season," Jesse said firmly.

"I don't believe he'd have minded me using my own head a little."

"You have enough fields to worry on, Matt."

"Maybe hogs, then . . . I might go up and talk to Mr. Stone about it."

"Stone." Jesse nearly spat the name. Mr. Stone was Matt's nearest neighbor, and he was Union. He and Jesse's folks hated one another now.

"Don't start about it, Jess," Matt mumbled.

"Well, you ought to watch who you keep counsel with," Jesse said darkly.

Matt looked away.

Missouri was cut to kindling over this war, with hatreds sparking and burning between neighbors, old friends, even within families. The state had tried to stay neutral, but the Union wouldn't allow that. It declared war on Missouri in June of '61, invading with troops from Iowa, Illinois, Wisconsin—and Kansas.

Here near the western border, much of the trouble went back to the grudge Kansas had against Missouri. For two years now, Kansas jayhawkers had been using the war as an excuse to raid Missouri, killing men and boys, burning farms, and stealing whatever they could carry off.

And Missouri's own Union militia weren't much better. They killed only Secessionists, but they robbed both sides blind.

"Look at all that green, Matt," Jesse said, tilting his chin up. "Know what it says to me? Quantrill."

It was Quantrill who roused Missouri men to fight back. He rode out of nowhere about a year ago, collecting a small group of farm boys at first, but gathering force like a summer storm. Soon enough they were raiding just the way the jayhawkers did—striking fast, retreating faster. They killed Union men, fired Union homes, and proved they'd learned another lesson well: stealing from everybody in their path.

They preferred to be called partisan rangers, and they answered to bushwhacker or guerrilla. But the Federals considered them outlaws. If caught, they were given no quarter: they were hanged, or shot. After a skirmish, all wounded were killed. So now the guerrillas did the same to the Feds. The guerrillas had to live in the brush and fight by ambush—and go south in the winter when the bare woods left them nowhere to hide.

"You folks heard from Buck?" Matt asked.

"No." Jesse crunched into an apple. "But I suppose he'll turn up soon enough."

Jesse's brother was riding with Quantrill now. When the war started, Buck was eighteen. He joined the regular Confederate Army, and fought with General Sterling Price to beat the Feds at Wilson's Creek. But Price couldn't hold Missouri, and when he began his retreat Buck was left behind, sick to death with the measles. Federals captured him, made him swear loyalty to the Union, and brought him home.

As the Union was driving Price's army from the state, Quantrill's band started to form. Meanwhile, Buck harvested, planted, and plowed. But last July, the Union's General Order No. 19 commanded every Missouri man to enlist with the Federal militia—to hunt and kill the guerrillas. That was when Buck took to the brush.

Matt's older brother, Clayton, normally didn't speak against either the Union or the Confederacy, but Order 19 made him plenty mad. He said it drove to Quantrill hundreds of men who wanted to keep out of the fight, and boys whose folks had talked them into staying on their farms.

Jesse drew back his arm. "The cottonwood."

Both threw apple cores; only one met the target.

"Got it!" they said at the same time, and then, laughing, "You did not!"

"What time is it?" Matt asked.

Jesse drew his pa's silver watch from his pocket. "Quarter past three."

"Dang!" Matt jumped off the rock. "How'd it get so late?"

"Ah, what's your worry?"

"I got work, that's what." He slung his haversack over his head and under his arm, picked up his rabbits and gun. "You coming or staying?"

Jesse slid slowly to his feet. "I know you've a lot on your mind, but you ought to have fun once in a while, too."

"I'm having fun. This was fun."

Jesse whistled for Patch as they started. "Matt . . . you ever think about girls?"

"From time to time," he replied, frowning.

Jesse elbowed him. "*Which* girls?"

"I don't know." Matt's face felt hot. The only girl he thought about was Susie, but there was no sane reason to tell that to Jesse.

"Well, I've been courting," Jesse announced.

"You *have*?" Matt looked at him. "Who?"

"Martha King."

"No fooling? You gone walking with her?"

"Mmm . . . no. She molds bullets for me."

"Bullets."

"Right. There's this hollow tree by her lane. I ride over and put some lead in the hole. A couple days later, I go back and get the bullets out."

A few steps farther, Matt said, "That's it?"

"Uhhh . . . yeah." Jesse seemed puzzled by his own story.

"That don't sound much like courting, Jess. Sounds more like a business arrangement."

Jesse gave him a push.

"Maybe you ought to sit on her porch when you bring her the lead. Then you could call it courting." They were laughing, Jesse with his head ducked down. "So when you get near her house, do the two of you even *see* each other?"

"Ah, keep quiet." Jesse shoved him again; this time, Matt pushed back.

"And how'd this courtship get started? How'd she find your lead, and how'd she know to mold bullets? She read minds?"

All at once Jesse stopped, swinging an arm out in front of Matt.

"Whoa," Matt said, coming up short.

About fifty yards away, four men watered horses in the stream. One spotted them and called out, "Halt!"

"*Halt.* Listen to him," Matt said under his breath.

"Shhh," Jesse warned, and then to Patch, low and even: "Staaay."

Three men with carbines started toward them; the fourth held the horses.

"Lord." Matt's stomach tightened and he gripped his gun hard. "What in hell are they up to?"

"Don't curse." Jesse gave him an elbow, then stepped ahead of him. "Let me talk."

Jesse was a few months older and a few inches taller, but Matt didn't care to be treated like a child. When the men faced them, Matt saw they were about the same age as Clayton or Buck. He looked them up and down for a clue: militia or guerrillas? Their hair was long and they wore no uniforms, so they could be guerrillas—or else militia trying to look like guerrillas.

"How old are you boys?" one man asked.

"Fifteen," Jesse said steadily.

"Oh, yeah? And *what* are you?"

The answer would be either "Union" or "Secesh," but Jesse made no reply.

"What're you doing here?"

"Hunting."

The man gave a sour grin. "What'd you bag?"

"Rabbits."

"Rabbits! Well, now, looks like we'll have supper tonight after all, boys!"

The others laughed, and Jesse said, "You mean you don't know how to hunt your own supper?"

The leader grabbed a fistful of Jesse's coat, pushing him backward. "You don't want to start mouthing off, boy," he growled.

Let *him* talk, Matt thought. That was surely helpful.

"We're with Captain Quantrill's command, and we take no sass from little boys."

"Well, I see no little boys." Jesse fixed the man with the icy blue glare Matt never wanted on himself. "And how do we know you are who you say?"

"And who are *you* two? Maybe you want to tell me that."

"Maybe I don't."

"All right then. We'll just take your guns and your goddamn rabbits, and you can be on your way." He grabbed Jesse's gun, and another man reached for Matt's.

"Hold on." Jesse's voice took on a pleading tone. "Don't take from Matt. He's got a ma and five brothers and sisters to feed. He needs his gun."

Matt said nothing and looked at no one. When the leader took his hand off Jesse's gun, the other man released Matt's.

"Ah, go on ahead," the leader said, and Jesse turned away without a word.

Matt followed, quietly blowing out his breath—but then Jesse did an about-face.

"If you're with Quantrill," he said slowly, "you might just know my brother."

Matt froze.

"Oh, yeah?" The leader sounded none too impressed. "Who's your brother?"

Jesse told them. The name seemed to echo in the silent woods. Matt squeezed his eyes shut. Should he fall to praying?

"You're *Buck's* little brother?" the man said at last. "I know Buck, the four of us know Buck!"

Then it was all so jolly, with talk about where Buck might be and where Jesse lived and whether militia were around. Jesse would go on about the war for hours given half a chance, and now he had a whole one. Matt wanted to get home and give Ma the rabbits, do his chores, and see Salt. Then he would take these cursed boots off and sit before the fire to warm the chill out of his bones.

"You can have my rabbits," Jesse was saying. "I don't much

care . . . No, wait, let me take them. Ma'll be glad to give you supper. Come by after dark and you can sleep in the haymow, get your breakfast, too."

It was dangerous business, agreeing to feed and harbor guerrillas. The Union had put Missouri under martial law—if you were for the South, you'd better watch your way. Secesh weren't supposed to keep guns, and needed a pass to leave the county. Each town had a provost marshal, whose job was to find out who the Secesh were. In Centerville, it was a man named Ford. He could arrest anybody without giving the reason. If you were lucky, you'd just have to pledge the oath and pay a fat fine. But you might be taken off to work, under guard, for the Federals. You might have to stay in jail. Or you might even hang.

None of it seemed to worry Jesse's ma, though. She did just as she pleased, and she pleased to help the guerrillas. And Jesse was following right along after her.

"What about your friend here?" the man said, surveying Matt from the ground up.

"He's with us," Jesse answered.

"Is that so?" the man asked Matt.

"It is," Matt said.

When he and Jesse were on their own again, Jesse's steps were quick, his manner cheerful. "Well, I guess they'll be out to the house later."

"Your new friends."

"Better than them being Federals. And I see you still got your rabbits—*and* your gun."

"Yeah, thanks, Jess," Matt said, his tone flat.

Jesse bumped him with a shoulder. "You mad now?"

"No, I ain't mad. It's just . . . you're always apologizing for me."

"I ain't apologizing for you. I'm standing up for you."

"I know, I know," Matt said wearily. He stopped and reached into his sack. "Here." He held out a rabbit. "You'll need it more than us tonight."

Jesse hesitated, then took the rabbit. "I'll save the pelt for Molly."

"I appreciate it."

They walked on. A drizzle started to hit through the cover of trees.

"Matthew, what *is* the matter? You been hobbling like a hurt horse all day."

"Oh, I twisted my ankle this morning."

"No, no, that ain't it. Those boots are too small. Aren't they?"

"Boots are fine." Matt pulled his slouch hat down on his forehead. Why didn't everybody keep quiet about his boots? The other day Clayton took it upon himself to tell Ma that Matt needed new ones—said it right in front of everybody— and Matt denied it. They couldn't afford to get him new boots. He would have to make do with these.

"You can't work how you do in bad-fitting boots," Jesse said sternly.

"Boots are fine."

As they reached the edge of the woods the rain came down chill and hard, chasing them up the ravine and onto the road.

Jesse whistled for Patch and tugged his hat, breaking into a run. "See you!"

"So long!" Matt shouted back, and set out in the other direction.

2

"You're late," Ma said when Matt arrived and stood, dripping, in the lean-to shed.

His older sister, Betsy, was cutting turnips. She smirked without lifting her head.

"Sorry, Ma."

Tyler started toddling toward Matt when he heard his voice. But Ben, doing schoolwork at the table with Molly, made believe Matt wasn't even there.

"What kept you?" Ma's hands moved fast, preparing dumplings for rabbit stew.

"Just lost track of time, I suppose, ma'am."

"Hello, Matty!" Molly flashed her lost-tooth smile. "More skins for my cape?"

"Two, Miss Molly, and I'll be real careful with them . . . Come on, Ben, chores."

"Awww," Ben answered.

"*Now*, Ben!"

"Don't shout, Matthew." Ma looked weary, and grimmer than usual in her black dress. She nodded at the rabbits. "Will you get those to me right away?"

"Yes, ma'am." Tyler latched onto him, complaining to be picked up. "I can't, Ty. I got work to do."

"Ahh, ahh, ahh!" Tyler insisted, raising his arms.

"Betsy, will you get this baby?" Matt asked.

"You're not the district commander," she replied.

"Betsy, get the baby," Ma said.

The barn wasn't big enough, but Papa used to say no barn ever was. Up front was the work area: planing bench, tools, plows, and such. At back were the stalls and saddles and other tack, and the haymow and loft were overhead. Matt spread oilcloth on the workbench and picked up the skinning knife. He was done with one rabbit by the time Ben sashayed in.

"A ten-year-old ought to be taking more responsibility around this place."

"I was doing my schoolwork," Ben grumbled.

"Schoolwork's for after supper. Go fetch the animals."

"I don't reckon a little rain ever hurt an animal," Ben said, and didn't move.

"Well, I suppose you could fill the feedboxes first."

"How about *I* skin the rabbit and *you* fill the feedboxes?"

"How about you do as I say?"

Ben continued watching. He was born impudent—those were Papa's words. Pa said he knew they were in for trouble the moment he saw Ben's crop of coppery hair. But he always said it laughing. From the start, Pa, and especially Ma, had let Ben get away with far too much, Matt supposed because they were so happy to have him. Two winters in a row, their babies had died weeks after birth. And then along came Ben.

"That's a fat one. When'll you take *me* hunting, Matt?"

"When you start minding me." Matt began to gut the rabbits.

"Guess what? Tim Hart's aunt got jayhawked. Jim Lane's gang, with Sharp's rifles. She don't even *have* any Negroes! They robbed her horses, chickens, hogs. Took her dang piano! Tim's pa said that's what she gets for flying the Stars and Stripes. Jayhawkers told her, 'You Missouri pukes, you're all Union till we turn our backs.' "

"Don't you have a *new* tale to tell?" Matt asked in a bored voice.

"Yeah, well, that's why I'm Secesh. It ain't right, the way these Kansans do us—"

Matt pointed the knife at him. "Ben, I've told you before: Keep your mouth shut about what you are and what you ain't. Folks are getting killed for mouthing off about being Secesh. And you *know* that."

"Well, they don't kill children," Ben muttered.

"Yeah, well, they sure enough kill children's big brothers," Matt shot back, and Ben turned his head fast. "So keep your dumb little boy's opinions to yourself. Hear?" When Ben didn't answer, Matt kicked his boot. "Hear?"

"Yes."

"Now go and do what I told you."

Ben left the barn without a word.

Years ago, the true Kansas settlers were supposed to vote on whether to enter the Union as a free or a slave state. Instead, abolitionists paid Northerners to move west; they came down the Missouri River by the boatload, pretending to settle in Kansas just to swing the vote. And pro-slavery Missourians swarmed over the border, too—trying to even things up, they said. The Kansans tagged them "border ruffians." Neither side played fair, and there was plenty of fighting and shooting and blame to go around.

Then that crazy devil John Brown got himself into it. In a town called Osawatomie and in the name of God, he murdered five Missouri settlers one night in '56. Matt was only eight then, but he never forgot the gruesome details. Old Brown had pounded on two families' cabin doors. Ignoring the women's tears, he dragged out the men and boys, then chopped off their hands and hacked them to death. After that, the killing never stopped. Bleeding Kansas, the state was called, and the fight was known as the Border Wars.

By '59, the question was settled: Kansas would be a free state. But the Kansans held on to their grudge, and as soon as the war began, jayhawkers under the command of Jim Lane and Doc Jennison poured across the border, hell-bent on punishing Missouri. It didn't matter whether folks were Union or Secesh, whether they owned slaves or not. If you lived in Missouri, they'd kill you smiling.

The barn door creaked, and Clayton came in to do the milking. "Hey, there," he said.

"Hey." Matt didn't look up. He'd finished the gutting, and was carefully digging shot from the meat of that last sloppy kill. Miss a chunk and somebody might end up breaking a tooth.

Clayton leaned on his crutches, watching. He had trouble with his legs—that was how their parents always said it. He couldn't work the fields, but his arms could do like any man's, and he was blessed with more brains than most, Papa had said.

"You seem awfully miserable for a boy who shot two rabbits."

Three, Matt replied in his head. "I'm all right."

Clayton was staring. It made Matt uneasy, the way Clay seemed to know everything. "What?" he asked, frowning.

"All okay?"

"Yeah." He picked up the rabbits and turned away.

After delivering the meat to Ma, he headed to the horse pasture and jumped the fence. Salt trotted to him right away, pushing his nose against Matt's neck. "Hey there, boy, how are you? Ready for some supper? Ready to get dry?" As he rubbed Salt under his halter, Sugar came loping over; he stroked her neck, too.

Salt was five now, and he'd belonged to Matt from the very start. When Matt was nine, he'd gone with Papa to bring Sugar to Mr. Henderson's Morgan stallion. Eleven months later, Papa woke him on a frozen February night, saying Sugar was about to foal. The foal came out steaming, and Matt watched in wonder as Sugar licked him into shape, every inch from head to foot, getting his smell and his taste, and when he struggled to his feet, Papa said, "I'll be darned, I don't believe I've ever seen a foal stand so fast. Matt, it looks like you got yourself a dandy."

And Papa had let him be the one to gentle the foal, to talk to him and hold him so he'd know Matt would be good to him. The foal was chestnut, with a white blaze and white socks and a brown mane and tail—just like his mother. Papa said, "Wait till you know him to name him," and a couple of weeks later he asked Matt if he'd been thinking on it. Matt said, "Well, he looks so much like Sugar, I think I got to call him Salt." Then Papa laughed his head-thrown-back laugh and said, "That's a fine name, Matt, just fine."

Ben brushed by as Matt led Salt and Sugar into the barn. Back at the stalls, Matt saw that Ben had filled the feedboxes. He dried Sugar and picked the stones and mud from her feet. Then he did the same for Salt, and had begun to curry him when Ben returned with the mules, Tug and Tatters.

"I'm done here," Clayton said, getting up from the milking stool.

Ben put out a pan of milk for the barn cats, lifted the buckets, and left with Clayton.

"Don't know when we'll get the chance to ride," Matt told Salt, brushing his coat. "I'll be mighty pressed for a few weeks now. But maybe Saturday or Sunday."

Ben came back and picked up the curry comb. "Sorry, Matt," he said, looking hangdog.

"All right."

"Matt . . . you'll go with Quantrill, won't you? When you get bigger?"

"War'll be over by then."

"That ain't what Bill Keene says. He says the war's nowhere near over, and anyhow, you could fight right now if you wanted to!"

"Well, I *don't* want to." Matt nudged Ben aside and headed for the loft. "Besides, if I went off to fight, who'd run this place?"

"Jesse'll fight though, right?" Ben asked, dogging his steps. "He'll go to Quantrill for sure. And you—"

"Ben!" Matt wheeled on him. "Let's finish up! I'm cold, I'm wet, and my dang—" *feet hurt*, he stopped short of saying. "Pipe down and brush that mare."

Ben turned away, and Matt climbed up to pitch down tomorrow's straw and hay.

"Those rabbits were worth waiting for, Matt," Ma said at the end of supper. "I don't know when I've tasted any so good."

"It's the way you cook them, Ma."

"Well, I appreciate your saying so."

The others thanked Ma for the cooking and Matt for the hunting. Then Ma and Betsy and Molly began to clean up. Ben got his schoolwork out, Matt lay on the braided rug before the fire, and Clayton settled in his chair with a newspaper. He never could get enough of reading. Before Papa got sick, he would buy Clay a book every time he could scrape the money together. Clay didn't get new books anymore, but he studied the ones he had. And Mr. Mead, the storekeeper in Centerville, saved all his old papers for Clay.

It calmed Matt to watch Clayton read, rubbing his chin with

his thumb, his almost-golden hair falling over his face. Clay's hair was the color of summer straw, Papa said, and Matt's was winter hay. Strawtop and Haytop, he'd called them for a time when they were little. Papa had always cut the boys' hair, and Clayton did it now. But Clay didn't like anyone else cutting his, though once in a while he'd let Ma do it. He kept his face shaved clean, and sat out by the pump or in the lean-to most every morning with Papa's razor and looking glass.

Matt wondered when he would start to grow a beard himself. Or grow taller, for that matter. It didn't seem fair—the only part growing was his feet.

After Betsy had cleaned Tyler up, he crawled to Matt.

"What's my name? Can you say 'Matt'?" Every night, he asked those questions, but never got an answer. The baby was more than a year old now. Wasn't it time he learned to talk?

Rolling onto his back, Matt drew his knees to his chest and pulled Tyler onto his legs, pumping them up and down. "It's a wild horse! Look out for the wild horse, he'll *throw* that boy right off!" They were both laughing as he caught the baby, and then Tyler knelt beside Matt, pulling his hair, yanking his ears.

"You oughtn't to let him do that," Ma scolded. "He'll think it's all right to hurt people."

"He's just playing, Ma." Right then, Tyler slapped him in the face.

"Tyyyy-lerrr," Clayton said, low and stern.

Tyler looked at Clay, then at the floor. He began to cry.

"Aw, Clay, you made him sad." Matt sat up and held the baby, stroking his curls.

"You'll spoil him, Matt," Clayton said.

"He's only a baby."

"Babies spoil easier than anybody," Ma put in.

Matt didn't care. He felt sorry for Tyler, who would never even remember Papa. Born into illness and this dreadful war, Tyler deserved to be a little bit spoiled.

"Here, Ty. Don't cry. Here." He sat the baby on his knees. "This is the way the lady rides," he sing-songed, gently jouncing him. *"Dee-dee-dee, dee-dee-dee."* Tyler giggled. "This is the way the cowboy rides. Giddup! Giddup!" He bounced him faster and harder, and Tyler shrieked with glee. Then Matt bumped him from one knee to the other, as if about to let him fall. "And this is the way the Kansan rides—"

"Matt!" Clayton and Ma said sharply.

"What?" He looked from one to the other.

"Stop," Ma commanded, her voice tight.

"It only means—"

"Stop!" she said, louder, reaching down to take the baby.

"—they're all from up North and they don't know how to ride." Ben finished Matt's sentence fast.

But Ma ignored Ben and said to Matt, "I won't have it. Is that clear?"

"Yes, ma'am," he said, staring into the fire.

Ma went off with Tyler.

Clayton turned back to the newspaper, shaking his head with disapproval.

Matt couldn't believe he'd been so stupid. The song was funny enough when Jesse sang it to little Johnny, but by no means was this house anything like Jesse's.

Right from the start, Ma and Pa had said that this family

would take no side. Ma was raised in Philadelphia, and after twenty years that still would tell in her speech and in her ways. And Pa was the South, in everything from his manner to his music. He had been sick a good two years before the war even started, and Matt suspected another reason they agreed to stay neutral was that they had so much else to worry over—and better ways to spend their time together than arguing over politics.

But over at Jesse's house, they talked about the war all the time. The North only wanted power, Jesse told Matt, and tariffs—taking the South's money to run the North's cities. If they had their way, they'd crush the South, turning the farms into factories just as they'd done up there. They'd have the government telling everybody what to do about everything.

Some pretended this war was about the slaves. But Jesse's ma said the only reason the North didn't have slaves anymore was that they no longer needed them. The North, she said, had a kind of slavery all its own: putting thousands of foreigners to work in filthy mills for paltry pay.

At the start, President Lincoln came straight out and said he had no intention of interfering with slavery, and no right to do so. It was only after the fighting had dragged on a year and a half, with no end in sight, that he issued his Emancipation Proclamation—trying to get England and France behind him, Clayton explained.

Matt had been at Jesse's place last September when his pappy came in with the paper announcing it. Susie cried, thinking they'd lose Aunt Lotty and Aza. But Mrs. Samuel read it close and said, "Hush, goose, it means nothing. He claims he'll free only those he *can't* free, the ones in the Southern states." In the Union states—and Missouri still was one, according to the Feds—folks could keep their slaves. "Just think," Mrs. Samuel crowed, "if I manumitted Aza and Lotty, I could rightly say I freed more slaves than Old Abe!"

Then there were the so-called abolitionists from Kansas. Only a fool could believe *they* cared about the black folks. When Jim Lane—U.S. Senator Jim Lane—led the jayhawkers to raid Osceola, it was murder and plunder and liquor on their minds. The jayhawkers shot nine Missouri men dead, stole a million dollars' worth of property, and burned the town to the ground, leaving three thousand people without homes. Hundreds of drunken jayhawkers had to be carried back to Kansas in wagons. They carted off a parcel of slaves, too—just more Missouri loot, to them. Contrabands, the Northerners called Negroes. Didn't that say it all?

Still, why in the world did he mention Kansas? Ma would know that came from Jesse. Sometimes he thought Ma only let him go around with Jesse because he'd lost Papa. If he started to repeat the Samuels' notions about the war . . .

Matt poked at the fire, thinking about the guerrillas in the woods. How did Jesse figure who they were? Right now they'd all be crammed into the dining room—Susie, too—eating supper together. The Samuel family always had strangers at their place. Matt preferred being home with his own family, when they weren't finding fault with him.

Ma returned from her bedroom, where she and Tyler slept.

Papa had built the log house as one big room with a loft. After he and Ma were married, he'd added their bedroom and the lean-to, which was connected to the back of the house. It was used for storage and washing up—Ma's barn, Papa called it. Then he'd made the loft into two rooms, for the children they expected to have. He always said he'd put a parlor on the house someday.

"It's still raining, Matt," Ma said gently, picking up her sewing.

"Yes, ma'am." He looked at her, and she smiled. "I meant no harm, Ma."

"They spoil easier, and they learn faster," she answered.

"Yes, ma'am." He frowned at the fire, then got up to add wood.

"Clay, shall we have some music?" Ma said cheerfully.

"Sure, Mama." Clay put the paper aside. "Ben?"

Ben fetched Papa's mandolin, Molly pulled her little stool nearer to the fire, and Betsy took up her sewing next to Ma.

Clayton began tuning up. "What shall we have?"

" 'Old Dan Tucker!' " Ben said right away, sitting beside Matt. Clayton began:

> "Old Dan Tucker was a fine old man,
>   Washed his face in a frying pan,
>   Combed his hair with a wagon wheel,
>   And died of a toothache in his heel."

Matt wasn't in the singing mood. He watched Clayton play as the chorus began:

"So get out the way, old Dan Tucker,
You're too late to stay for supper,
Supper's over and breakfast is cooking,
Old Dan Tucker stands there looking."

All at once Ben leaped up, yelling, "I got one!" Papa had started the family tradition of making up verses about one another.

Clayton kept playing. "Go on, then!" he said, and Ben jumped in:

"Old Matt Howard, boots too tight,
Cries in his bed most every night.
Ma would buy him another pair,
Matt says, 'Mama, I don't care!'"

The others laughed through the chorus. Ma, Betsy, and Molly applauded Ben. Matt pulled him to the floor and pretended to pummel him.

"That was a fine one, Ben," Clayton said, ending the song.

"Do you *really* cry, Matty?" Molly asked, hugging his neck and looking worried.

He swung her around onto his lap. "No, Miss Molly, I do not."

Soon it was bedtime for the younger ones. Matt took them to the privy; then they brushed their teeth at the washstand in the lean-to.

Before Ma went up to hear their prayers and tuck them in, she said, "Matthew, truly, I do want you to go to Liberty."

Matt said, "Really, Ma, the boots are fine."

3

Clayton kept plucking at the mandolin strings, Betsy hummed along as she sewed, and Matt sat before the fire, thinking of Susie. When he fetched Jesse today, she'd come outdoors holding her little sister, Sally. Matt had felt tongue-tied, and it only now occurred to him that maybe she'd been shy, too. Maybe she'd come out wanting to say hello. But what foolishness—how could Susie care for him? She was nearly thirteen and a half now—and looking older every time Matt saw her. She kept getting prettier, too, with her fetching smile and shining black hair, and eyes as black as Jesse's were blue. And Matt was just her brother's friend, who'd spent much of her life helping Jesse devil her.

Once they chased her through the corn rows with a milk snake, saying it was a copperhead. She went yelling to her ma, but Mrs. Samuel just said, "You puzzleheaded girl! If it was a copperhead, how could *they* be holding it?" Then Susie sent Buck after them, and he gave them both a few good cuffs . . . When did she stop wearing short skirts? When did he stop seeing her as Jesse's tagalong little sister?

"Well, children," Ma said, returning to her seat. "We won't have many more evenings by the fire, will we? Soon we'll be on the porch, if God wills it."

She sighed deeply, then cleared her throat. "I've hesitated to bring this up. But it's been on my mind . . . You all know that since your papa left us, we've taken some . . . losses. Due to . . . the war."

Matt turned to Clayton, who was looking carefully at Ma.

The Federals had raided their smokehouse and chicken coop in the winter, and militia often knocked at the door demanding meals. The Union issued an order that let them take whatever they wanted, wherever they found it. For two months Matt chopped and hewed timber to rebuild fences the Feds had pulled down for firewood. Normally that was beaver-trapping time—he sold his pelts, and they sorely needed the money. Instead he had to mend the fences or else pay the devil when the corn came up and animals got in.

"I was up at the Stones' today," Ma went on. "Mr. Stone heard that the bushwhackers are returning."

Matt held every muscle to keep Clayton from reading his face.

"I'm frightened, children," Ma said. "The things that go on . . . I'm frightened for all of you." Now Matt knew what she was about to say: "I must consider leaving here." The mantel clock ticked into the silence. Nobody moved. Ma finished quietly. "And I'm thinking of writing to my parents."

That he never would have guessed. Ma had not heard from her folks since she married Pa. He had gone with a friend to Pennsylvania, and met Ma at a church social—love at first sight, they both said. But Ma's folks hated Pa because he was not book-educated and he was poor. "Folks *will* judge unfairly at times," Pa said, and Ma's parents were the proof. They didn't want to know him, they just forbade Ma to see him. So

Pa and Ma met in secret until the time came for Papa to return to the farm. She was eighteen, Papa twenty-one when they ran away.

"Does anyone care to speak?" Ma's voice was barely a whisper.

Clayton said, "Mama, what are you hoping to hear from your folks?"

"That's a good question, Clay. I'm hoping when they learn how things are for us . . . that they'll forgive me. And ask me to bring you children home."

Home! Matt's face was burning; he didn't think he could tolerate another word. Move North? Stay with people who despised his pa?

"Missouri's our home, Ma," Clayton said. Matt wanted to jump up and hug him.

"Well, Clay, I know that, don't I?" Ma said peevishly. "But Missouri is not a safe place right now, is it?"

"No, ma'am."

"Perhaps," Betsy said in a small voice, "perhaps, if they'll have us, after the war we could come back. Or those who wanted to . . ."

That was pretty. Leave it to Betsy to sell out first, Betsy with her notions about living a town life and wearing nice clothes. She'd fit right in with the Northerners.

"Well, yes," Ma said. "After the war, we would come back. Presumably. If everything—" She took a deep breath. "I don't know if my folks would even answer me. I wrote once before . . ."

"You did, Ma?" Clayton asked.

"When I was expecting you, Clay. I wrote that I was sorry, but I was well, and happy. I received no reply."

That was a glimmer of hope, anyway. Maybe they'd ignore her again. But the news about Pa could change everything. They'd kill the fatted calf and welcome her home. *Forgive*, Ma said. As if she'd committed a sin marrying Papa.

"Matt!" Ma said sharply. "You haven't said a word! And don't frown so at me. Tell me your thoughts."

He considered, then slowly said, "I could work harder. Maybe raise some hogs."

"Oh, Matthew!" Ma paced impatiently. "How much harder could you possibly work? You're still a boy."

It seemed he was always too young or too old, depending on her convenience. And why force him to talk if she was only going to yell? He hunched himself up with his chin on his knees and watched the flames dance.

Ma sat, and everyone was quiet. "It's bad enough you had to stop school. Papa would have hated that, you know it. If you—" She cut herself off. "All right, children. I'm sorry to mention all this. I'll have to decide what to do." She wound the clock Papa had brought from his home in Kentucky. It was the last thing she did every night.

Clayton shut the mandolin case, Betsy put away her sewing, and Matt banked the ashes.

"Now, don't mention this to the younger children. All right? Matt?"

Why single him out? Was *he* the one she had to tell twice?

"Yes, ma'am," he answered, and walked to the lean-to. He climbed down to the root cellar for Salt's carrot, then went to lock up. Before the plundering, they never locked the barn. And he knew anybody who wanted to could get in. Still, locking up made him rest a little easier.

The night had turned clear, stars speckling the sky. Tomorrow should be perfect for plowing, the ground soft but not too wet. But now tomorrow was spoiled. Why put in a crop he might not be around to harvest? No! Of course he'd stay here, on his own if he had to. He could take care of himself. He had no cause to fear Quantrill, and when the time came, with the rest of them gone, he'd decide whether to fight or not.

He used the privy on his way back. At the lean-to, he and Betsy passed without a word or a glance. Matt brushed his teeth, and when Betsy returned, he held the door. Betsy said good-night to Ma and climbed the stairs.

"All in," Ma said to him. "Good night, Matt."

" 'Night, Ma." She went to her room, and he bolted the doors. He took Papa's Kentucky rifle from its pegs above the front door. Pa's father used it in the War of 1812, fighting with General Andrew Jackson when the American boys—mostly Southerners—crushed the British in the Battle of New Orleans. Matt checked the rifle and replaced it, then felt for the bullets and caps he kept in a tin box.

Clayton was already in bed with Ben. "You all right?"

"Yes." Matt changed into his nightshirt and put his clothes on the window seat Papa had built for Clayton to read in.

The room was small but comfortable, with a chest of drawers, a nightstand on Clay's side, and a blanket chest at the foot of the double bed, which was covered with a colorful patch-work made by Pa's ma. The bed was plenty crowded. Luckily Ben slept the still, deep slumber of a dead man, or it would have been pure misery. In winter it was good for keeping warm, but in summer they pulled the old straw-tick mattress from under the bed, and Matt or Ben slept on it by the window.

Matt lay on Ben's other side, and Clayton pinched out the candle.

"Matt . . . out in the woods, did you and Jesse see anybody?"

"No," Matt said, then turned away.

Would Ma really write her folks? He knew Ma's family had some money and lived in town. Their name was Bennett, the name Papa gave to Ben, saying it was Ma's name as well as her folks', and it was Ma he meant to honor. She had only one brother. Hard to imagine, with all the brothers and sisters around this place. Matt didn't know how his grandfather made his living. *Grandfather*, that was a strange thought. Pa's folks were both dead when he met Ma, and his brother and sister had died young. At Jesse's house, there was always kin visiting after harvest. He seemed to have a hundred cousins. Did Matt have cousins in Pennsylvania?

"Clayton?" he said into the quiet. "You reckon she'll write that letter?"

"Yes," Clay said. "I believe she will."

4

Matt was up before the rooster, prickly and restless and ready to move. By the time Ben came to muck out the stalls, Molly to gather eggs, and Clayton to milk, the plow was in the barn lot.

"I think you ought to face the day with more enthusiasm," Clay deadpanned sleepily, and Matt had to laugh.

After breakfast Matt was glad to be at the barn with Tug and Tatters instead of at Pleasant Grove School with Ben and Molly and a dinner bucket. The day was cool and clear, just right for fieldwork, if not for these blasted boots and— He pushed Ma's letter out of his mind. As for the boots, the only remedy was to plow barefoot. But the soil was hard and rocky still; he could cover more ground in boots. So he tolerated a fair amount of discomfort, watching the plow turn the cold earth up to the sun, inhaling the dark, rich smell.

When the dinner bell rang, Matt unhitched the mules. He rode Tug and held Tatters's reins, relieved to be off his feet. Recalling Ben's song, he laughed to himself. He would have to give in and get new boots.

Ma gave the blessing; last night's conversation hung over a quiet meal. Then Clayton, who could see out the front window, said curiously, "Here's Jesse."

Matt turned. "Why's he coming around?" He would have been alarmed, but Jesse looked calm enough as he looped

July's reins over the fence post. Matt met him at the lean-to door.

"Hey." Jesse was holding a grain sack. "You having your dinner?"

"We're about done. Come on in."

Jesse stepped inside, taking off his hat. "'Afternoon, Mrs. Howard, Betsy." He ran his hand back through his dark hair. "Hey, Clayton."

"Hey."

"Hello, Jess." Betsy's voice was much more pleasant than usual.

"Hello, Jesse," Ma said. "Is everything all right?"

"Yes, ma'am. Sorry to barge in."

"You're always welcome here."

"Thank you, ma'am, but I know it is a strange time to show up."

Ma smiled, waiting for an explanation. He didn't seem about to give one.

"Uh, Jess?" Matt prompted.

"Ma'am, I was wondering, could I talk to Matt outdoors?"

"Of course," Ma said with forced ease.

Matt picked up his hat and pushed Jesse out, shutting the door behind them. "What in the *world* are you up to?"

Jesse led the way to the barn. Inside, he pulled the rabbit pelt from his sack.

"Thanks." Matt draped it on a nail. Later he'd tack it to the barn wall, where the others were curing. He waited.

Jesse handed him a rabbit foot, which Matt put in his pocket. "Well?" Jesse said. "You got mine?"

Matt tossed the foot from the workbench. "And that's why you came?" he asked, shaking his head.

Jesse laughed and turned the sack over. His boots tumbled out. Matt looked down; Jesse was wearing a different pair.

"Last night, I couldn't shake the thought of you plowing in those doggone boots," Jesse explained. "I dug up this old pair of Buck's, and they fit just fine. And I want you to have mine."

"Jess, I can't—"

"Lord, Matt, try them on. Nobody's coming up behind me but Johnny, and he's thirteen years away from those boots. Ma said it was all right."

"For sure?" Matt said, eyeing the boots.

"For sure. Now hurry up, or your ma'll think we've run off to join Buck."

Jesse laughed while Matt tugged hard at his boots. "Oh, yeah, boots are *fine*."

"Shut up." Matt stood in Jesse's boots. They were more comfortable than his own had ever been. "Whoa," he said, walking a few steps. "I don't know what to say, Jess." He shrugged. "I appreciate it."

Jesse gave a sharp nod. "I know. All right, then, I got to get home." They headed for the house. "Ma said go, but don't tarry. Me and Aza are plowing, too."

"Well, mine'll go a lot better now."

At the gate, Jesse unlooped the reins.

"Hey, Jess? Yesterday. How'd you know who they were?"

Jesse's darting eyes searched his. "You think Federals would've left your gun and rabbits just because I asked?" He punched Matt's shoulder and jumped up on July. "Only Southern men would do that." Waving, he trotted off.

Matt closed his hand on the soft rabbit foot, watching till Jesse left the lane. "Luck," he said, and went for the mules.

5

"Visitors, Ma," Clayton said solemnly, tilting his chin toward the window.

Matt turned in his chair. Four men in blue coats were riding from the woods at a walk.

"What kind?" Ma asked.

"No telling."

They could be bushwhackers disguised in Federal blue. Treat them well and they might burn you out, and kill any men on the place for being Union sympathizers. And sometimes it was the other way around: soldiers came in civilian clothes, or in guerrilla overshirts embroidered by mothers or sweethearts. Feed *them* and you'd suffer the same punishment, for they would be Federal militia, wearing shirts stripped off dead guerrillas.

Occasionally, the visitors were exactly who they looked to be. You just never knew whether things were as they seemed or whether somebody was trying to trick you into showing loyalty to the wrong side. These men had long hair, but blue coats. Who were they?

Whenever men came, Ma made it clear she was neutral. Normally that wasn't tolerated, but it had worked for them . . . so far. Clayton said perhaps that was because of their situation— a dead pa, a grown boy who had leg trouble, a woman alone with six children. And because Ma carefully tailored her talk.

The men were dismounting. When Clayton reached for his crutches, Ma went to the door, with Matt following.

"Hello!" one man called.

No visible weapons, but surely revolvers were under their coats.

"Good morning," Ma said, stepping into the dooryard.

"Ma'am." The man lifted his hat. "Your husband home?"

"My husband's dead, sir. You see by my dress. Illness took him last spring." She always let them know right away that Pa had not been murdered.

"I'm sorry to hear it, ma'am. We wondered if we could get some breakfast, and feed for our horses."

"Well, sir, I don't know who you are, but I'll fix something if I must."

"Thank you, ma'am."

Three men followed Ma indoors; Matt and the fourth led the horses to the barn. The horses were well brushed, but rawboned. The man was clearly older than the partisans in the woods. His black beard and mustache were bushy, like his hair. But was that part of the disguise?

"*You* look old enough to fight," he said.

"I reckon." Matt's pulse raced in his throat.

"Question is, what side?"

"Question is," Matt said, "who's asking?" He was surprised by his own words, surprised again when the man laughed and pushed past him. Matt trailed him to the house. The children had been sent outdoors; they crowded around Matt when the man went in.

"I'm scared, Matty," Molly whispered.

"It's all right." He patted her cheek. "They just need their breakfast."

"Bushwhackers!" Ben said. "You see their weapons? I want to come, Matt!"

"No. You stay right here and mind these two," he warned, and headed for the house.

"My husband was a Southern man," Ma was saying as Matt entered. "You can tell by my talk that I'm from the North, but I don't claim a side." She was wiping plates and forks, returning them to the table. "We do our work and mind our business."

Matt leaned against the wall, folding his arms. Clayton looked grim in his chair by the hearth. Betsy laid a plate of corn bread on the table; the men didn't waste a second grabbing for it. Matt wanted to laugh at her disgusted face as she turned back to the cooking. Ma went to her side to help.

"You seen any Federals around?" the leader asked Matt.

"Not unless you're them," he said steadily, and Ma whirled on him, startled.

"This one's got a mouth on him, ma'am," the bearded one said with a mean grin. "He better watch who he backtalks with it."

"Matthew," Ma said.

"Boy," the bearded one continued, "you seen bushwhackers around here?" And he locked eyes on Matt.

"Sir." Ma came to stand between him and Matt. "I'll thank you not to take that threatening tone with my son. If you'll not identify yourselves, that's your business." Ma's voice was shaking, her breathing fast. "But why you frighten people half to death even when they show respect and hospitality, I do not understand!"

"Aw, am I frightening you, boy?" the bearded one asked.

"No," Matt said, narrowing his eyes.

"Well, sir, you are frightening me!" Ma said, and Betsy burst into tears.

"Dang," the leader said.

"Ah, shut up now, Jim," another man muttered.

The one who looked to be the youngest kept quiet.

Ma put her arms around Betsy. "Hush. It's all right. Go outdoors."

Clayton gripped his chair.

"No, Ma, no, I can help." Betsy wiped her eyes with her apron.

"Ma'am," the leader said, "I'll have you know we're partisans with Captain Quantrill, and proud of it. Our apologies for scaring your daughter and yourself. I've got a ma myself, in Jackson County, and things are hotter there. I realize you folks never know who's at the door. But understand—we never know who's behind it."

"Yes," Ma said quietly.

The only sounds to follow were of cooking, serving, eating.

Matt looked out the window. Ben was chasing Tyler, who ran with unsure steps, shrieking and giggling. Molly was jumping rope, singing:

"My papa has a horse to shoe
How many nails do you think will do?
One, two, three, four, five . . . "

The youngest man went out first. When Matt followed the rest, Ben was with the young one at the pump. "Ben," Matt said sharply. "Come here."

Clayton came up behind Matt. "What is it?"

Ben skulked over, and Matt pulled him toward the porch. "What in the world are you doing?"

"Nothing!"

The young bushwhacker was shaking his head and frowning as he spoke to Clay, who only nodded. At last the man joined the others, and they were off. Clayton looked madder than Matt had ever seen him.

"What in God's name did you say to that man?" Matt mumbled.

"Ben!" Clayton yelled, and Ben took off. "He's got to be whipped, Matt, and I want you with me." Clayton might as well have been breathing fire. "Do you know what he told that baby bushwhacker? *Do* you? 'The rest of them are neutral, but me and Matt, we're Secesh.' "

Matt flinched as though dirt had been thrown in his eyes.

"And what in *hell* does that mean?" Clayton hit his crutch hard against the ground. "Is that what you two talk about? You tell him you're Secesh?"

"No! I swear, Clay!"

"I've got to have some brush boy come in my house and tell me how to raise my little brother?" Clayton dug his crutch into the grass. "Cut me a switch, Matt, and make it a good one. Then find him and bring him to me."

Matt turned away, sick with dread. Clayton was far too angry to give a fair whipping, but Matt would have to deliver Ben—would have to watch, even. He reached the cherry tree beside the house. Clayton would send him back if the switch was too small. If it was too big, there was no telling how bad Clay might hurt Ben. Matt changed his mind several times, then grimly hacked a switch with his Barlow.

"You're so dumb!" he hollered at Ben, huddled up and sniffling in the loft. "I told you to keep your mouth shut, and you *promised*! And now you got me in trouble, too!"

"I'm sorry," Ben sobbed.

"Sorry ain't enough! Now quit sniveling and get on your feet—Clay's waiting. Here, you carry your own switch." He kicked Ben's boot sole. "You best take it like a man, too, and let me get on with my work."

Ben looked forlorn.

"Don't you give me that face, Ben. I'm about as mad as Clay," Matt lied.

Ben shuffled behind him to the woodshed, where Clay, no calmer, sat on a stack of wood. The sight of him started Ben crying again. "I'm sorry, Clay . . ."

"Quit that," Matt snapped. "Aren't you ashamed?"

"Yeah," Ben said, but he kept on crying.

Clayton took the switch. "Let's get it done," he said through clenched teeth.

Ben dropped his pants. Matt looked away. He heard the whoosh, the sharp crack, Ben's breath catching. Clayton hit once, twice, three times. Each time Matt felt tighter, like the spring getting wound in Papa's clock. Again. Again.

Matt expected Clayton to whip four times, maybe five, but when he didn't stop at ten, Matt jumped between Ben and the switch, only to get hit himself, across the legs. It stung straight through his pants. "Enough, Clay!"

As soon as the rhythm broke, Ben fell.

Clayton's face was twisted and ugly. "You stay out of it!" he yelled.

"It's too much!" Matt shouted back.

Clay brandished the switch. "You think *you're* too big to whip?"

"Just go ahead and try it."

Ben was up and off like a jackrabbit.

"Don't *ever* come between him and me again!" Clayton roared, getting to his feet.

"I will, if you do him like that!" They were hollering in each other's faces so hard, Matt felt his eyes popping.

"It's my responsibility—"

"It's rage!" Matt interrupted. "Papa said never hit a boy with rage!"

"He put us all in danger!"

"But you don't fix it that way! He's just a boy!"

"There are no boys around here." Clayton fell back onto the woodpile and dropped the switch.

Matt heard the swishing of Ma's skirts. "Boys! Why all the shouting? Where's Ben?"

Matt pointed at Clay. "He was whipping him too awful. I had to stop it."

Clayton held his head in his hands.

"Oh, Clay," Ma said sadly.

"Excuse me, ma'am," Matt said, and slipped past.

Ben would never let himself be found now, so Matt headed for the mules. Poor Ben, he wouldn't be able to sit for a while. Well, all the more reason to push a plow. Matt would give him the morning to feel sorry for himself. After dinner he'd put Ben to work.

But it was Clayton Matt couldn't get off his mind, Clayton's wild eyes and hard face. He had just sat there while Ma and Betsy cooked for the guerrillas, sat there while Matt mouthed off, sat holding tight to his chair. And then he had to take it all out on somebody, and Ben was the somebody who gave him the chance. Clay was always so calm and controlled, knew what to do, knew what to say. That he couldn't manage some things had never meant much to Matt; it was just the way it always had been. But now Matt felt he was understanding for the first time what it was to be Clayton.

When the dinner bell rang, Matt was weary and achy and fiercely hungry. By the time he washed up, everyone was at the table except Ben. He questioned Betsy with a look; her reply was a small shrug. Ma gave the blessing and they ate mostly in silence, Matt and Clayton avoiding each other's eyes.

"I'll just take Salt and have a look around," Matt told Ma quietly on his way out, and she nodded. But once in the woods, he decided to ride first. It was spring and it was warm—the plowing would keep. Salt needed to run, and so did he.

On the prairie, he had only to hit his heels against Salt's sides for him to take off at a keen run; for miles Matt leaned into the speed and freedom. At last he reined up, taking off his hat to let the wind cool his hair. Purple dewflower peeked above the breeze-blown grass, and white clouds puffed like gunpowder smoke in the deep blue sky. Prairie chickens strutted, hawks soared and swooped, and there was a haylike sweetness to the air. Papa said that when he found this place, he knew he'd never leave. Other men stayed awhile, then stopped at the out-fitter's in St. Joe before heading west on a wagon train. But Pa decided to make his life here, and Matt was glad of it. He couldn't imagine a better home.

He found Ben lying in the creek, his head propped on a rock. Riding into the creek bed, Matt stopped himself from laughing. "Hey. What're you up to?"

"I'm cooling my backside," Ben growled.

Matt dismounted and tied Salt in the brush. He sat on his heels and tossed a stone so that it splashed Ben's face. "Well, you got to come home now. I'm tired of plowing on my own. You don't get a holiday for getting whipped."

Ben turned his face. Matt splashed him with another stone, then another.

"Hey. Don't make me come get you." This time he threw a rock.

"Quit that!" Ben hollered.

"Come on out."

"I hate Clayton! I'll never talk to him again."

"You will, though."

"He had no right to whip me like that!"

"He sure did."

"Then why'd you stop him?"

"I shouldn't've done that."

"Then I hate you, too!"

"I guess that explains why you'd go and tell a perfect stranger I'm Secesh."

"I knew who he was," Ben muttered.

"No, Ben, you did not," Matt said firmly. "That's why you keep your mouth shut. And I thought I already crammed that through your thick head." Ben didn't answer. "Now Clay's asking *me* why you say those things. What is it *I'm* telling you?"

"Tell Clay I got a mind of my own!" Ben said, defiant.

"Yeah? Well, next time tell your own mind to keep from speaking my name." Matt stood up. "All right, Ben? All right?" He untied Salt, then let him drink from the creek. "Let's go."

Ben blew out his breath, carefully rolled onto his side, got to his feet, and sloshed out of the water. Matt mounted and set off, and Ben trudged alongside. After a while Matt stopped and reached down. Ben took his hand and hopped into the stirrup with a grimace, getting in front of Matt and practically lying down, his face on Salt's head.

"I hope to never get another whipping like that. Who'd you get your worst whipping from? Papa?"

Matt pondered. "No . . . a schoolmaster. He was a mean one,

we didn't have him but a while. It was over some devilment of me and Jesse's. I don't even recollect what. But I recall the whipping just fine."

"And I suppose you didn't *cry*, right?" Ben grumbled.

"Well, I didn't—but I wanted to, believe me. Just I was always having to show Jess how tough I was."

They rode in silence for a while. Then Ben said, "I never get to have any fun."

"Excuse me?" Matt said in disbelief.

"All I ever do is go to school and do chores."

"All *I* ever do is chores and more chores."

"You're the farmer. That ain't the same as choring. Anyhow, you and Jesse go hunting and fishing, you go riding. You have since you were Molly's size. With school out now, I never even *see* my friends, because Ma doesn't let me go to Tim's or Bill's or anywhere."

"School lets out in April so boys can help with the plowing, not play with their friends," Matt grumbled, and Ben didn't reply.

But Matt felt ashamed. When he was young, Papa was always taking him out, teaching him. And it was true he'd had a lot more freedom at Ben's age—but these were different times. "Well, I'll go fishing with you. Or hunting. Or riding."

"Will you, Matt?"

"If you behave better."

"I will, I promise."

They dismounted at the pasture. "Go on up and get something to eat," Matt said. "Then come down to me."

Clayton sat on the barn lot bench, mending harness. He

didn't acknowledge Matt's approach. Matt stood, uneasy and hot, shifting the tack and his weight. Sweat rolled down his face. "Clay," he finally said, "let's don't fight that way again."

Clayton looked up with a peaceful face.

"I'm sorry I interfered."

"You were right to stop me," Clayton replied. "I'm just sorry you had to." He reached for his crutches and stood. "I'll speak to him. But I've something to say to you, too."

Matt's jaw tightened up.

"About this Secesh business."

"Clay, I never told him—"

Clayton cut him off. "I'm not saying you did. What I *am* saying is this: Until such time as we are forced to take a side, we do not have one. You understand that, Matt?"

Matt stared at him, face burning, heart pounding.

"Do you understand?" Clay said sternly.

"I do."

Clayton gave a curt nod and went to the house.

6

Ma said Matt and Betsy must go to see the Stones. They were getting on in years, and both their daughters had married and moved to Kansas long ago. Ma liked to check on them now and again. Matt would talk to Mr. Stone about farming, the way Pa used to. Betsy was to visit Mrs. Stone, and help her bake her light bread.

No sooner were they on the road than Betsy started in: "Why must *I* be the one to go? Molly's seven now. She's old enough to do it."

"It's good for young people to think about others." Matt repeated Ma's words with a smirk.

"Oh, hush."

"What in the world are you carping for? You're the one who's always jawing about wanting to get away from the house."

"When I say get away, I mean do something *interesting*. See a friend, go to town."

"You just went to town with Clayton the other day!"

"Centerville!" she snorted. "Mr. Mead's store, to buy a bit of sugar and a paper of pins! I mean a *real* town—like St. Joe. Heavens, even Liberty would do! *You're* happy going a mile down the road to Jesse's."

Matt couldn't dispute that, so he didn't reply. Why had he even answered her to begin with? This last year or so, it seemed they argued more than talked.

At the Stones' dogtrot porch, Betsy put on her cheerful, friendly act, kissing Mrs. Stone. Mr. Stone led Matt right to the fields.

"You getting your land in order, son?"

"Yes, sir." Matt followed him along the furrows.

"Now, you know you don't want to plant too deep."

"Yes, sir, I know."

"Inch or two is all. And not too thick. Don't crowd it all in."

"Yes, sir."

"Lot of work for a boy alone. But you're strong. Like your pa."

"Yes, sir. Is there anything I can help you out with, sir? Long as I'm here?"

"Weeeelll, I piled the rocks in the barrow, now I can't move the barrow!" Mr. Stone chuckled, pressing his hand to his back. "Gettin' old, boy. And there's more down there a piece. Rocks just grew in these fields over the winter."

"Seems like it, sir, doesn't it?" Matt commenced hauling.

Afterward, Mr. Stone fixed him with watery eyes and asked in a gruff voice, "Want to see my hogs?"

"Yes, sir." As they started for the barns, Matt said, "I was thinking about raising hogs myself. Ma said no."

"She's right. Why bother? Raise 'em so the damned bush-whackers can kill 'em right under your nose?"

Matt said nothing.

"Your ma says some were over to your place. Had no choice but feed 'em, eh?"

"Yes, sir."

"Goddamn bushwhackers. County's crawling with 'em now. Hunt 'em and shoot 'em! No quarter, that's the law I like! String 'em up on the nearest tree!" He searched Matt's face. "What do you think, boy? Eh?"

"Well, uh, they say they're just defending their homes, sir."

"Nonsense!" Mr. Stone slapped his thigh. "Don't you be-lieve a word of it, boy! They're devils, bandits playing at being heroes! Desperate men, Matt! Cutthroats!"

"Yes, sir."

"Our own neighbors, some of 'em! You know who's one? Zerelda's boy, Buck!"

Mr. Stone knew Matt and Jesse were friends. So what kind of answer did he expect to hear?

"And the mother, that big, loud-mouthed Rebel, she makes no bones about it! And the younger boy, he'll be coming right up behind his brother! Don't you go that way, Matt! They'll come to a bad end, every one. They'll die like the dogs they are."

Matt wished he could speak up. But if he said anything, even admitted he knew what Buck was, Mr. Stone might tell Ma . . . or someone else.

Matt followed Mr. Stone into the hog barn. They leaned on a pen rail, watching an enormous sow suckle way too many piglets. "That's my prize sow," Mr. Stone said, calmer. Seeing her seemed to put him in a better mood.

"She sure is big, sir."

The sow kicked at a piglet that ran all over her, trying to find a teat.

"They raise hogs, too." Mr. Stone jerked his head toward the door. "Down the road . . . Everything's changed, Matt. Everything. When Zerelda came here, her and Robert, what a nice young pair! Zerelda always outspoken, though. Always. But Robert, good man, good preacher. If he was alive, I wonder would he let his boys go to bushwhacking."

Matt stayed quiet.

"Reuben's a good man, too. But he lets that woman rule the

roost." Mr. Stone started, as if he'd forgotten Matt was there. "You help me with my butchering this year, boy?" he said abruptly, heading out of the barn.

"Yes, sir."

"Did a good job last time."

"Thank you, sir."

The arrangement had stood for many years: Pa helped with the butchering in exchange for meat. Matt's training started when he was nine. Last fall, he and Mr. Stone did the job on their own. Maybe this year, Ben would learn.

"Never did get your pa to start raising his own hogs."

"No, sir." Matt smiled, remembering. He kicked at the dirt.

In the kitchen, Mrs. Stone served cider and cookies. "Oh, Matt, you're growing taller and taller," she gushed.

Matt rolled his eyes at Betsy, not wanting her to think he believed it.

"And don't you resemble your papa more every time I see you! Isn't it so, Bill?"

"What!" Mr. Stone roared.

Matt and Betsy both jumped, then looked at each other.

"I said, doesn't the boy favor Dave more each time we see him!"

"Why, in the field, I swear for a moment I thought I *was* with Dave! Walks like him. Talks like him. Looks like him."

"Same soft brown eyes," Mrs. Stone said. "Same mischievous smile. Recall the day we met Dave, Bill? Oh! He was the dearest boy."

"Come to me for advice. Just on the land, and he made his farm from *scratch*!" Mr. Stone slapped the table.

"Spring of '41," Mrs. Stone said, nodding.

"No, '40."

"It was '41, Bill!"

" 'Forty, I say!"

Again Matt's eyes met Betsy's, and again each looked quickly away.

"Listen, you old fool!" Mrs. Stone counted on her fingers. " 'Forty-one, Dave came here! He worked the place two years before he went off and came back with Carolyn. December '44, Clayton came along. I should know, I helped birth him!"

"Well, maybe you're right," Mr. Stone allowed, scratching his neck.

"Of course I'm right!" Mrs. Stone took Betsy's hand. "Oh, how I wanted your papa for one of my girls! I was always having him to supper, hoping to instigate something. He went off with that friend of his, after harvest of '43, said he wanted to see a little bit of something else. What was his name, Bill? Bill!" She leaned in and slapped her husband's head.

Matt dared not look at Betsy.

"What?"

"Who was the boy went to Pennsylvania with Dave?" Mrs. Stone nearly shouted.

"John Robertson!" he called back.

"John Robertson, that's right! A nice boy, a Yankee. Full of romantic notions about homesteading."

"He didn't know *what* the hell he was doing!" Mr. Stone

roared merrily. "Your pa took him in and worked him like a hired hand one year. And they went off on that visit, but your pa comes back with a pretty bride and no John Robertson!"

"Weren't *we* surprised!" Mrs. Stone raised her eyebrows, giving Betsy a nod. "And wasn't I disappointed! Oh, but we loved her dearly, right from the start. She never *had* cooked or cleaned, or sewed one thing—well, maybe a pretty sampler. The girls and I taught her carding, spinning, soap-making, everything! She was a quick study, a true farmer's wife in no time."

"Good trade, I called it!" Mr. Stone hollered. "John Robertson for your ma!"

"They were awfully sweet together. He was patient with her trials and errors—they certainly had plenty of laughs," Mrs. Stone said. "And when Clayton came along, they were terribly brave."

Betsy dabbed at her eyes with her handkerchief.

"Oh, goodness me. Oh, Betsy, I'm sorry, dear."

"No, no," Betsy said, sniffling. "I love hearing about it, truly."

"Went to that damn doctor in St. Joe, recall?" Mr. Stone thundered. " 'This child will never walk!' he said. Pompous windbag! Your pa never said, Oh, yes, he will walk. Took Clayton as he was. Said, 'Well, if he don't walk, he'll do other things.' "

"But by the time you were walking," Mrs. Stone chimed in, turning to Betsy, "so was Clay, with little crutches your papa made."

Mr. Stone chuckled. "Then your pa taught him how to climb the stairs on those things—imagine!"

"Yes, your papa wanted all the children to be together upstairs, just as he and his brother and sister were in his own boyhood," Mrs. Stone explained. "At first your ma was worried Clay would fall, but, my gracious, he was so proud of himself when he learned! It was just around the time Matt was born." She looked at him warmly. "Oh, now, Matt, *there* was a beautiful baby! And, oh! How your papa came right in when I called out 'It's a boy!' He would *not* wait until it was proper." She threw up her hands. "Walked straight in and took that baby. Matt was hollering and kicking. But that's what your pa wanted to see, the kicking. Then he put you down on your ma's breast and near about fell on her, the two of them crying and crying."

Matt pressed his knuckles to his mouth, holding his breath and concentrating mightily on the whorled wood of the table.

"Matt?" Betsy said. He raised his eyes. "We ought to . . ." She glanced toward the door.

"Yes," he said quickly, and stood.

"Weeell, I got to slop the hogs," Mr. Stone said, stretching and shuffling to his feet.

"Bring some cookies to the others." Mrs. Stone rushed to get a tin.

"Thank you, ma'am," Betsy said.

"They're mighty tasty, ma'am," Matt said, trying to smile. "Thank you."

"Oh, you're quite welcome, dear." Mrs. Stone patted his cheek. "It is a joy to see you both. And don't mind my old-lady ramblings."

As Matt and Betsy walked down the Stones' lane, she said, "I *do* love stories about Ma and especially Papa, don't you?"

"Mmm," he answered.

"I never heard that before, about your birth. Did you?" she asked quietly.

"No." He pulled his hat low over his eyes.

She slapped his head. When he turned to yell at her, she called out, "It was '41, you old fool!"

"What!" Matt hollered. " 'Forty, I say!"

" 'Forty-one!"

"Ah, go slop the hogs!"

Now all their choked-down laughter came pouring out, and they were still shouting and swatting at each other when they entered their yard.

7

For weeks Matt had been out at first light, plowing before sunup. Ma cooked his favorite breakfasts—corn cakes with molasses, eggs fried with potatoes and onions—and always bacon or sausage to go along. When he wasn't too tired, he plowed in the moonlight until Clayton hollered him in. Papa had told him not to plant the north field: *It might be just a little too much for you.* But this year Matt plowed it. They would need every row he could raise—who could say how much would be stolen?

One morning Ma walked all the way to the lower field, and

when Matt called a halt to the mules, she asked, "Which is the field Papa said not to plant?"

He felt betrayed: Pa had shared their plans. In silence, he pointed.

"You've plowed it," Ma said with a frown.

"I can do it, Ma. We'll need the corn."

"You're to do as Papa told you," she said firmly.

"But I can manage, Ma. Please."

Her face softened, and she touched his shoulder. "Last spring, after you and Papa made these plans, he lay in bed snickering. He said, 'Carrie, you'll have to keep an eye out. When I'm gone, he'll try planting that field.' So I'm respecting Papa's wishes. And I'd like you to do the same." She gave his hair a tousle and walked away.

As April drew to a close, Matt fretted about when to plant. Every farmer had his own way of telling when the ground was ready to take the seed. But if you judged wrong, your crop suffered. Or if it hailed after planting, you might have to start right back over again.

Saturday was the second of May, and he was still skittish. So he said he'd just go down the road and see when Dr. Samuel was fixing to put in his crop. Ma said he should ask Mr. Stone about it. Matt agreed, but said he valued Dr. Samuel's opinion, too.

In truth, he valued the possibility of seeing Susie as much as Dr. Samuel's opinion. And when he dismounted and tied Salt, Susie was the first one in the yard. "Hello, Matt," she said, barely glancing toward him, then smiling at the sky.

"Hello, Sue." He touched his hat, and already his face felt

hot. He had never touched his hat to Susie—and she could not help but notice.

"You want— You and Jesse going riding?" she stammered, and Matt was relieved when Jesse came from the house.

"Well, really it's your pappy I'm here to see."

"Pappy?" she repeated.

"Crops, Sue," Jesse answered, and grinned at Matt. "Right?"

"Right."

Jesse nodded toward the back door. "Come on in."

Mrs. Samuel was cordial enough, asking after Ma and the others. Jesse's ma had always treated Matt well. Still, he'd been a little scared of her as far as he could recall, more so since the war.

When Matt, Jesse, and Dr. Samuel went out to the porch, Mrs. Samuel didn't join them. Of late it seemed she was never around when Matt was. That made him uneasy, but Dr. Samuel was so kind and helpful, Susie so attentive, and Jesse's mood so sunny, Matt felt he could stay all day.

"Pappy, don't they say plant when the oak leaves get the size of squirrels' ears?" Jesse asked.

"That's certainly one method," Dr. Samuel said thoughtfully.

"How in the world do I judge that?" Matt replied. "Carry a squirrel up a tree and hold his ear to a leaf?" He liked their laughter—especially Susie's.

Matt and Dr. Samuel talked so long, Jesse got up and shook Matt by the shoulders, barking, "Soil! Furrows! Plows!" before he walked off the porch. Susie giggled, but stayed where she was. Jesse rounded up the little ones and played Old John

Brown, chasing them in the shade of the big coffee bean tree.

Finally Mrs. Samuel called Susie in, but Susie came out once more with lemonade and ginger cakes. When she handed Matt a glass, their hands touched, and he knew it was no accident on either part. But he kept his eyes down, and she hurried indoors.

"What way did your pa use, Matt?" Dr. Samuel asked at last, leaning close.

Matt smiled to think of Papa kneeling in the field, head bowed, eyes closed. "Well, sir, he'd just work his finger into the soil, and one day he'd say: It's time."

Dr. Samuel nodded. "If it worked for your pa, it'll work for you."

And on the sun-filled, clear-skied fourth of May, when the apple trees bloomed a blizzard and wisteria crept up the front windows, Matt said at breakfast, "I reckon we'll put the corn in today."

Papa had always liked everyone to come to the fields and plant a little. Clayton took his time and got there when he got there, refusing all help. Matt gave Tyler some seed, too—kept him from popping it into his mouth, showed him what to do with it. When Tyler caught on, Matt told him, "There. Now you've planted corn on your farm."

After a while the others went away, except for Ben—who claimed, as the morning wore on, to feel weak with fatigue, heat, and hunger. Matt told him he ought to be ashamed of trying to dodge such important work. Ben kept scowling, but he kept planting.

That evening Matt built a fire outside the barn, melted down his lead, and molded bullets for the Kentucky rifle. Papa had always hunted with that gun, and Matt loved to do the same. But he was afraid to bring it to the woods now—someone might take it from him. He'd have to content himself with using it to shoot at crows, scaring them away from eating the corn before it pushed through the soil.

For days he and Ben stalked the fields, Ben with his shotgun, which used to be Papa's. Matt did all the loading, owing to his speed and experience. Sometimes he'd let Ben shoot the rifle. This was work Ben took a shine to, so he stuck with it cheerfully from first light to sundown.

Matt had seen corn come up in five days, and he'd known it to wait two weeks. So he knew he shouldn't be alarmed when a week had passed and the fields were still brown. But he lay awake anyhow, thinking what he'd do if the corn just refused to grow. One night his fears spread like fire on a dry prairie until he had to wake Clayton and say: "What if the corn won't come up?"

"Matt. Of course it will. Go to sleep."

Clay's weary boredom was a comfort. Still, Matt said, "But what if it doesn't?"

"It's only been a week—"

"Eight days."

"—and it's been a bit cool and dry. The corn'll come up. Go to sleep."

But in the morning, Matt was disappointed again.

Matt went in for breakfast and found Ma in blue calico. He stared as if at a circus freak. She looked embarrassed and happy and sad all at once. "It's a year today," she explained. "The twelfth of May. Papa said he didn't want me in black one day past, so here I am."

He'd lost track of the date, and couldn't say a word. After the funeral, when they were alone together at last, Ma had picked up her sewing as if nothing had happened. *Well, children, I've heard it said when someone you love passes on, the first year is the hardest. They say once you've been through every special day and every ordinary day without him, the sorrow becomes easier to bear.*

"I thought we'd take a picnic to Papa's grave at noontime," Ma said. "I believe he'd like that."

All morning in the fields, Matt brooded. He hadn't been to the grave since they'd laid Papa in it, and he didn't want the others along his first time. Likely Ma was right, a picnic would please Papa—but he still couldn't abide it. When the whole family trooped past with blankets and baskets, he quietly asked, "Would it bother you, Ma, if I didn't go?" She did look bothered, and hurt, so he fumbled out, "I just don't think I could—"

"It's all right," Ma said. "I'll tell the others you're staying with the corn."

He walked along the furrows, eating the food she left, searching for one sprig of green, thinking how right it would be for the corn to show itself on Papa's death date.

But it kept him waiting two days more. Then, at sunup, it was one bright mass, forward-marching perfect and straight like a vast green army, rows turning right-face here and left-face there as he walked and then ran joyfully through them. And when he had inspected every last regiment, he went to the house to give his report.

8

Early on Sunday mornings, Matt hitched up the wagon and drove Ben and Molly to the Methodist church for Bible school. Back at home, he did whatever chores couldn't wait and polished his boots with tallow. Then he had to put on his good clothes, including the white shirt—along with the collar he suspected Betsy overstarched, knowing how it itched him— and the black necktie. And every week Ma told him to comb his hair, but it just refused to take a part, and five minutes later she would tell him again.

At 10 they went to service, where Ben and Molly joined the family. It was pure torture, sitting still in uncomfortable clothes as the pastor droned on and Matt thought about all that needed doing at home. Afterward he saw boys he knew—not Jesse, his family was Baptist—and they'd ask Matt to go riding or fishing. But he always found an excuse. He'd had time for other friends when Papa was well. Now, when he could get away, he'd rather be with Jesse.

Today he had to stay in Sunday clothes after church, because the Stones were coming to dinner. He felt useless and stiff, wandering the yard with the younger ones.

Clay had just gotten a stack of papers from Mr. Mead. He would be in that rocker now for hours at a stretch, frowning at the war news, rubbing his chin. Matt never asked about it, and

Clayton rarely told. Matt figured he learned from Jesse what he needed to know about the war, and besides, the Union had suppressed the Missouri papers. If they printed anything that showed sympathy for the South, Federals would raid them, steal their press, and scatter their type. *So much for freedom of the press* was what Jesse's ma said.

"Matt!" Clayton called, signaling him to the porch.

Matt kicked at stones as he went.

"Sit a minute, will you?"

He rested on the rail.

"Ma wrote that letter," Clay said, studying his face. "And mailed it."

Matt looked toward the woods. "Maybe they won't write back. Maybe they'll say, like Pa: You made your bed, now you got to sleep on it."

"Matt—"

"I don't want to hear it, Clay!" He swung his legs over the rail, jumping down. "Don't tell me any more!" He left the yard, passed the vegetable and root gardens, and kept walking, past the cornfields, up to the apple orchard. Carefully, so as not to tear his clothes, he climbed the topmost tree as high as the branches would hold him.

There was his corn, growing about an inch a day. There was the hay meadow, the little field of wheat, and the north field, the thorn in his side. There were his fences and the pastures, the cows and horses and mules peacefully grazing. There were the sheep, huddled stupidly. The barn and the house, smoke drifting out the chimney. The timber woods, and beyond that, though he couldn't see it, the prairie. "What'll I do, Papa?" It chilled him to talk, for the first time, as if Pa were alive. But then he said again: "What'll I do?"

Remembering the Stones, he made his way down. Ma would expect him to greet company. But they were already there when he reached the yard, and she scolded him with her eyes.

"Hello, Mrs. Stone," Matt said, lifting his hat. "'Afternoon, sir."

"Well, Matt, I've got something for you, if your ma agrees to it." Mr. Stone nodded toward a box at his feet. Two fat pink piglets poked their heads up, wondering where they were.

Matt turned to Ma, who said, "Oh, Mr. Stone. It's too much, we couldn't—"

"They're so sweet!" Molly said, and Ben scratched their heads.

"Well, now, Carolyn, what's two piglets, more or less, to me? The boy has a mind to raise hogs; why not let him try his hand?"

"Ma?" Matt asked.

"Well . . ." Ma said in her giving-in tone.

"All you do is build a pen," Mr. Stone said. "They eat most anything, that's the beauty of hogs, and they just grow fat!"

"Well, all right," Ma agreed. "And thank you, both."

"Much obliged, Mr. Stone. And Mrs. Stone," Matt said. "Thank you, Ma."

"Matt and I'll start on a pen tomorrow," Clayton said.

"The worst thing about hogs, Clay, you got to make sure they *stay* in the pen," Mr. Stone told him. "They can cause a lot of havoc, is all. But if it doesn't work out, why, Matt knows how to butcher," he finished, and they all laughed. Mr. Stone clapped him on the back. "Come on, boy, show me your corn."

The meal was pleasant. Matt was grateful that the talk didn't turn to war or Papa. But when Ma was serving Mrs. Stone's cake, someone knocked at the back door.

Trying to look calm, Ma went through the lean-to, with Matt at her heels. When he saw it was Jesse, he was relieved—and horrified. Jesse didn't even say hello. His eyes darted to the Stones. Matt sensed a stir behind him.

"Jesse!" Ma said with a nervous smile. "How are you?"

"Uh, hello, Mrs. Howard. I, um . . . I didn't know you had company."

"Come in," Ma said.

"No, ma'am." Jesse stepped back, twisting his hat in his hands, red in the face. "No, I—I thought maybe Matt could go riding, but, um . . . I'll be going now." He was blinking fast. Ever since they were little, that was how Matt could tell when Jesse was upset.

Now Jesse mumbled, "'Afternoon, ma'am," and turned away.

"Ma?" Matt asked, and she shooed him out. Jesse was making tracks for July. "Jess!" Matt caught up.

"Matt." Jesse stopped short, pivoted, and nodded at the house. "That shouldn't be."

Matt had never seen Jesse look so grave. "I can't tell my ma who to invite for Sunday dinner. And anyhow, they're good folks. He even brought me two piglets to get me started with hog raising."

"Maybe he's trying to buy you for the Union," Jesse said with a mean grin.

"Jess, you know they're old friends."

Jesse gave his head a determined shake. "Southern man can't be friends with a Federal. I got to go. I won't be seen where that man is."

"Damn, Jesse!"

"Don't curse," Jesse said, and swung up into the saddle.

"Well, maybe I'll come by after they leave."

"That won't do, Matt. I don't want you seen at my place after he's been to yours."

Matt was stung, but he just shrugged.

"So long," Jesse said.

"See you," Matt replied, and watched him kick up dust in the lane.

Indoors, the air felt thick. Ma and Mrs. Stone were chatting about gardening, but there was a falseness to it. Mr. Stone was glowering, eating his cake with concentration. When Matt caught Clayton's eye, Clay raised his brows. Matt took his seat, but even though he was partial to cake—and this was spice cake, with icing—he could barely swallow a bite.

It seemed a day and a half before Mrs. Stone said, "Well, I think it's time we were getting on." She began to rise.

"Oh, must you?" Ma stood, too, and so did Clayton, Matt, and Betsy.

Mr. Stone got up. "First I'll have a word with the boy. About those pigs, Matt."

Matt and Clayton swapped looks again, and with dread Matt followed Mr. Stone to the barn. The piglets were asleep on top of each other.

"Feed 'em anything," Mr. Stone said, his voice harsh with

anger. "Potato skins. Carrot tops. Corn. Table scraps. Pretty much anything."

"Yes, sir." Matt could barely hear his own words over the sound of rushing blood.

There was silence, then Mr. Stone muttered, "Didn't know you were friends with Zerelda's boy."

Matt drew in a careful breath. "Didn't you, sir? Jesse and me've been doing everything together since we were about seven."

"Didn't know you were *still* friends with him."

"Sir?" Matt braced himself. "I have no reason not to be."

"Matt, those people are Secesh!" Mr. Stone pointed a trembling finger toward the road. "And that boy's brother is a goddamn bushwhacker! The Union, Matt!" He pounded his fist into his palm. "The Union has got to be preserved!"

"Well, sir, I don't know what Buck is or isn't," Matt said slowly. "But it seems to me the partisans are no worse-behaved than the jayhawkers and the Federals."

Now he was certain Mr. Stone would hit him, so certain that he took a step back.

"If your pa was alive—" Mr. Stone scowled.

Matt folded his arms to keep his heart from jumping right out. "If my pa was alive, sir, he'd tell me to go my own way." His knees were shaky and he could feel the sweat on his neck, under his arms. He looked straight into Mr. Stone's eyes. "Jesse's been my friend forever, and no war'll pull us apart. I mean no disrespect, sir, and if you want to take back your pigs, I understand."

Mr. Stone was the first to turn his head. "Just like your pa." He waved his hand. "Couldn't tell him anything, either. Go your own way, then, son. But go careful."

"Yes, sir."

"And no, I don't want those pigs back. I got too many as it is. Let the damned bushwhackers steal 'em from *you*."

"Yes, sir," Matt said as they walked to the house.

The others were on the porch. Mr. Stone took off his hat and scratched his head. "Well, Carolyn, this is quite a boy."

"Isn't he?" Ma said, but her smile was uneasy.

"Dave's boy," he mumbled. "Dave's boy every inch of the way. Come on, Mary. Let's go home."

9

Jesse didn't come around, and Matt didn't look for him. There was plenty to keep him busy: he and Clayton built the hog pen, and he had to climb each apple tree to thin the fruit—and there was the hoeing. Day after day he was in the fields, keeping the weeds from choking the corn. Every row, every acre must be hoed until the corn was strong enough to hold its own.

And then there was Ben-wrangling, which sometimes seemed the hardest work of all. Every time Matt turned his head, Ben disappeared and Matt had to hunt him down or holler him back. In the evenings Matt could barely stay awake through supper, and went to bed with the young ones. It rankled him that Ben saw this and still didn't willingly help, that Matt had stuck his neck out for Ben with Clayton, but Ben wouldn't lift a finger for him. It was nearly time for first haying. How would he manage if Ben didn't pitch in? But he didn't complain to Ma or Clayton, and he wasn't quite sure why.

One morning Ben piped up, "Ma, Matt never took me hunting like he promised."

"Did you promise, Matt?" Ma dished him some sausage.

"I *said* if you behaved better," Matt growled.

"And he hasn't?" Ma asked.

Matt glared at Ben, who gave him a bright smile.

"Matthew? I asked you a question."

"He's tolerable," Matt said evenly.

"Well, might be if I could go hunting or riding or *anything* once in a while, like a boy named Matt did *all* the time when he was my age, then I'd be more tolerable still."

Bargaining for good behavior—Matt could barely believe it. If he had ever talked that way to a parent, he'd have been slapped, at the very least.

To make matters worse, Ma said, "Well? Can you find the time to take him hunting? What about after dinner?"

"All right, Ma," Matt said, and Ben gave one triumphant clap.

After breakfast, Matt went to fill a water jug. Ben was at the pump soon enough, asking, "What'll we go for, Matt? Rabbits?"

"You'd best work like a mule this morning." Matt thrust the jug at him. "Or the only thing I'll be going for is you."

Ben did work, though he was silent and sullen. That suited Matt fine—he wanted to be left in peace. He'd much rather go hunting with Jesse. He had been working it over and over in his head, whether Jesse had the right to be mad. And who should offer the peace pipe. Jesse was the one who rode off in anger. *I don't want you seen at my place.* As if anybody would be so foolish as to think Jesse would swing over to the Union side. But Matt was still smarting over those words. Would pride pull them apart before the war had a chance?

At dinner Matt said nothing but "please" and "thank you," and Ben not much more. Afterward, Matt said, "Well, let's go," and Ben scrambled out to the barn.

"Matthew." Ma took his arm. "I don't appreciate the scowling. If you can't take your brother hunting with a charitable spirit, perhaps you oughtn't to go."

"Yes, ma'am."

"When Papa took you anywhere, he always did it cheerfully and gladly."

And I always helped Papa cheerfully and gladly, Matt thought. *Nobody made me promises to get me to work and behave.* But he said again, "Yes, ma'am," and she let him go.

Ben was waiting, with Papa's shotgun slung over his shoulder. "I loaded yours, too," he said, handing Matt the bored-out, shortened-down musket that had been Papa's when he was a boy.

"You probably did it all wrong," Matt replied, grabbing it. "Don't touch my gun again." He picked up the powder flask and shot bag he'd made from deerhide, then fetched his haversack, with caps, corn husks, and the cow-horn measures for powder and shot inside.

They walked a long time, Matt's steps big and fast, Ben lagging behind, then trotting to catch up. Matt couldn't shake his anger and bitterness. He knew well enough that he didn't measure up to Papa—he needed no reminders from Ma. Then he was ashamed of feeling sorry for himself. If there was one thing Papa had well and truly hated, it was folks feeling sorry for themselves.

The brush got denser. It was a windless afternoon, close and damp. In a blackjack thicket, Matt stopped to roll his sleeves. Ben did the same. Matt took out two caps and offered one to Ben.

"Mine's already on," Ben said.

Matt looked down at Ben's hammer. "You fool boy! You don't go stomping through the woods with your gun half-cocked!"

"Why not?"

"Why not? Because if you trip, you're liable to shoot yourself. *Or* your hunting partner, which I might not take too kindly to. That's why, and you ought to know that at your age." Matt shook his head, pulling back the hammer to put the cap on.

"Well, I forgot," Ben said in a small voice.

"Sit down. Now, you remember the most important rule of hunting?"

"I thought you just told it to me," Ben said sulkily.

"Stay down and stay quiet. You think you can manage that, Ben?"

Ben didn't rise to the bait. "Will you give me first shot?"

" 'Course I'll give you first shot. Just watch and wait. When a rabbit's close enough, I'll whistle. He'll stop to see where the sound came from. Aim for his eyes. Then you get a clean shot and you don't spoil any meat. You bring home a nice pelt and Molly keeps warm next winter."

"All right."

"When he stops, you have about a count of three to fire. Rabbit won't sit there and say his prayers while you get a bead on him."

"Okay."

Matt didn't want to beat the brush, as Ben would never be able to shoot a rabbit on the run. But they waited so long, he thought he'd have no choice. Then here came a rabbit, hopping right toward them. Matt jogged Ben with an elbow, and Ben raised his gun. Matt stuck two fingers in his mouth, letting the rabbit get closer and closer. Then he whistled. The rabbit halted just as if following orders—and Ben did nothing.

Matt nodded, but still Ben didn't fire. "Shoot!" Matt said in a fierce whisper, but the rabbit was off at a zigzag. "Now!"

Ben fired. Matt ducked the smoke. He raised his own gun, but it was no go. The rabbit was gone.

"What in the world were you doing?" Matt hollered, lowering his gun.

"I couldn't—"

"You had a clear shot, a perfect shot!"

"You confused me! What was all the pushing and nodding?"

"What do you want me to do, read out a general order?"

"Are you telling me a rabbit'll hear you whisper thirty yards off?"

"Well, you just have an answer for everything, don't you?" Matt pushed the flask and shot bag at him. "Load up!"

Ben pushed them right back. "No!" His voice broke. "I'm going home!" He started off, rubbing his eyes with the back of his hand.

"Ben!" Matt called, but Ben kept walking. "Dang." Matt sighed. He pulled back the hammer to work the cap off, then ran to catch up, resting his hand on Ben's back. "Ben."

Ben whipped around. "What're you so mad at me for?" Tears poured down his face. "I want to go home and I want Papa!" He dropped his chin to his chest and covered his face with his arm, sobbing.

Now all Matt's anger seemed petty. Papa would have been disgusted with him. But he said, "Quit crying, Ben. You're always crying." He was surprised to hear the words. He surely had not meant to say them.

"I'll cry if I feel like it!" Ben dropped his gun and pushed Matt with both hands. "And I don't care how rough you or Jesse or anybody was when you were ten or seven or two!"

Matt held him off, biting back laughter. He turned Ben around by the shoulder. "Come on. Let's go down to the pond. See if we can't bag ourselves a duck or two. Rabbits are hard to shoot."

"You got two last time," Ben said, sniffling.

Three, Matt thought. "Well, I'm five years older than you. And I had a much better teacher. And anyhow, Jesse and me had Patch."

"When can we get a dog again?"

"When times are better."

They walked in companionable silence this time, Ben sticking close by Matt's side. At the pond, they got down in the duck blind Matt and Jesse had made.

"Go ahead and load up," Matt said.

Ben measured the powder and carefully poured it down the barrel. He wadded up some corn husk and rammed it in, then pulled the rod out again.

"No, keep going with that," Matt said. "Jam it down good and tight."

Ben did as he was told and glanced at Matt, who nodded approval. Ben poured the shot, then rammed down more husk. He turned to Matt again.

"You're doing fine. Just be sure you jam it all in tight. You leave any space down there, I'll be taking you home with a few less fingers."

Ben laughed.

"And you know who Ma'll blame." Matt handed him a cap, and Ben looked him a question. "It's all right, we'll be here a while."

"Don't you have a duck call, Matt?"

"I do, but best not try it, I reckon. Jesse says it scares the ducks off. But you should've heard Papa's. Ducks'd come from miles around just to admire it." It felt good to get Ben laughing this way. Matt lay down, facing the sky. "Take off your boots. Like as not you'll be going in after your kill."

"Hunting sure is a lot of waiting," Ben said, tugging at the boots.

Matt judged by the sun: "I reckon they'll be along soon."

Ben played with a salamander he found under a rock, and at last the ducks skimmed across the water.

Matt pushed Ben's head down. "Let them come in close. Unless you've a mind to go swimming."

Ben grinned, raising his gun. The way the birds were all flocked up, Matt knew Ben could get two or three at once. But he said nothing. If he shot when Ben did, they could get even more. But then Ben wouldn't have the pleasure of knowing which ducks were his.

"Any time now," Matt whispered. Ben fired, and Matt jumped up to take a shot at the birds on the wing. They were still low, and now over land. He aimed, fired, and watched one tumble.

"I got two!" Ben shrieked. Matt went for his own, then turned. Ben was knee-deep in the pond, holding up a pair of dead ducks.

"You did it! Just look at that!"

"Tonight you'll all be thanking *me* for supper," Ben said proudly.

Matt told him it was best to draw out the innards right there, but Ben wouldn't hear of it. He wanted to show Ma those ducks just the way the Lord had made them.

On the way home, Ben kept running ahead, then stopping and bouncing on his toes, calling, "Hurry up, hurry up!" When the barn came into view, he took off at a dead run, leaping the fence.

By the time Matt reached the lean-to, Ben was near the end of his story:

"—and Matt got one on the wing, he's a crack shot, Ma, you should've seen that bird fall out of the sky!"

Ma smiled at Matt. "So it went well."

"Yes, ma'am." He presented his duck. "I think I'll take it up to the Stones. For the pigs."

"That's very thoughtful, Matt," she said gently.

In the Stones' dogtrot, Matt knocked at the kitchen door.

Mrs. Stone yelped in surprise. "Who is it?" she asked, voice quavering.

He shut his eyes tight. "It's Matt, Mrs. Stone."

"Oh. Matt." She unbolted and opened the door. "Hello, dear."

"Sorry I startled you, ma'am," he said, touching his hat.

"Well, that's all right, dear. I just— I wasn't expecting any-one, and Mr. Stone isn't here." She peered anxiously toward the yard.

"Ben and I went hunting, and I thought you might like a duck."

"Why, Matt! How sweet of you. My, that's a fine one! Just leave it right there on the shelf. Oh, come in, dear, do come in."

"No, thank you, ma'am. I've got an awful lot of work. But, well . . . give Mr. Stone my regards, and tell him those pigs are doing fine."

"All right, Matt, I'll be sure to. And thank you, dear. Thank you."

"You're welcome, ma'am."

She shut the door and bolted it again. As Matt turned, he noticed Mr. Stone's riding horse in the pasture, and the wagon by the barn. Walking down the lane, he had the unsettling notion that he was being watched.

10

Matt cut the hay grass, and the next day he and Ben raked it into windrows. Two days later, it was dry enough for storing. Clay drove the wagon while Matt pitched the hay up to Ben, who spread it in the hayrack and trampled it down. Back at the barn, Matt and Ben pitched it into the mow.

When all that arm-breaking, thirst-making work was done, Jesse still hadn't turned up. It had been more than three weeks since the Stones came to dinner. Now Matt decided he'd rather have his friend than his pride. He told Ma to plan on catfish for supper, and set out with his line, hooks, and gun.

From the road he saw Jesse and Dr. Samuel talking while they hoed corn. The sight called Papa to memory and tugged at Matt's throat. He measured their crop against his leg as he walked. It was not quite knee-high. His was taller. "Afternoon, Dr. Samuel. How're you, sir?"

"Well, hello, Matt! I'm just fine. Your corn coming along?"

"I'm pleased enough with it, I suppose. And much obliged to you, sir, for letting me go on about it that day."

"I enjoyed our talk," Dr. Samuel said warmly.

"Hey," Jesse said.

"Hey."

"Looks like you've a mind to do some hunting, Matt," Dr. Samuel said.

"Catfishing, sir, and I was wondering if Jesse wanted to go. If he could."

Dr. Samuel nodded. "Go on, Jess."

"You sure, Pappy?"

"Go, boy." He patted Jesse's shoulder. "We're far enough along here."

The little ones played in the yard, where Aunt Lotty was washing clothes by the pump. Susie was weeding in the vegetable garden. When she looked up, Matt hesitated. Should he call to her? Just wave? She bent to the weeds again, and he turned away.

Aza was pitching hay into the mow.

"Howdy, Aza," Matt said.

"'Afternoon, Matthew."

"You care for a catfish supper, Aze?" Jesse asked.

"I care for it, but I bet I won't get it," Aza replied.

Laughing, Jesse fetched his haversack. With all the horse-stealing, they'd stopped taking Salt and July catfishing more than a year ago. The creek was deep and wide where they fished, bordered by high rocks. If they left the horses, they might never see them again.

As they started for the road, Mrs. Samuel hollered from the house, "You, Jess! Where are you off to?"

"Fishing!" Jesse called, picking up his pace.

"Who gave you leave?" She was in the yard now.

"Pappy!" he answered, then muttered to Matt, "Come on."

"Jesse!" his ma yelled. "Reuben!"

They ran across the road, laughing as her shouts faded.

"Why's your ma so bridled up?" Matt asked when they were back at a walk in the woods of Jesse's neighbor, Mr. Askew. "Your pap said—"

"Oh, you know Ma. She always wants to be the one who says."

Matt considered before he spoke up. "I don't believe your ma cares for me coming around your place anymore."

"Ah, it ain't you, Matt. It's this dang war. Ma can't countenance it, you folks—"

"Being neutral," Matt finished when Jesse stopped himself.

"You can't do that way forever," Jesse mumbled. "They won't let you."

"I'm cognizant of that," Matt said slowly. "And it ain't me, anyhow. I'm no half-and-half."

"I know where you stand."

"Mr. Stone? He said not to go around with you, but I told him I would."

"Oh, yeah? Then why didn't you come by?"

"You told me not to. You recall?"

"I recall. And I meant that *day*, not the rest of your life."

"Well, I didn't know that, did I?"

"Sure you did. You just got all up on your Matt Howard high horse, and I had to wait for you to come back down."

Matt looked away, trying not to smile.

"*Isn't* that right?" On the first word, Jesse gave him a shove.

Matt didn't reply.

"You get your hay in?" Jesse asked.

"Yep."

"My Lord, the way Pappy jerks that wagon. I kept falling over, and Aze was down there laughing at me. I said, I'd like to see *you* keep on your feet with him driving!"

Shouldering his gun, Jesse started a left-right soldier's march and sang:

> *"Oh, they chaw tobacco thin in Kansas,*
> *Oh, they chaw tobacco thin in Kansas."*

Matt matched his step, singing along:

> *"They chaw tobacco thin,*
> *And they spit it on their chin,*
> *And they lap it up agin in Kansas.*

> *"Oh, they say that drink's a sin in Kansas,*
> *They say that drink's a sin in Kansas,*
> *They say that drink's a sin.*
> *So they guzzle all they kin,*
> *And they throw it up agin in Kansas."*

They crashed hard on the last line, laughing, trying to knock each other down. It was good to be with Jesse again, acting like a pair of fools where no one could see to tell them they were.

They stopped to dig crawlers. At the creek, they climbed the rocks and set to work, tying lines to overhanging branches.

"Jess?" Matt asked. "You thinking about going?"

"You *know* I am, Matt."

"I mean now. This season."

Jesse took a deep breath and blew it out. "I'm praying on it."

It seemed peculiar, Jesse being a prayerful boy, even though he always had been. A favorite story at Jesse's place was how he stood right up in church when he was six and asked the congregation to pray for Buck's soul. He had his own Bible, won at a Sunday school competition, and he'd memorized plenty of it. Matt supposed that because his real pa had been a minister, religion was a way for Jesse to keep him in mind.

They baited the hooks and set the lines in silence, then sat. Jesse said, "Missouri needs every last man."

"Only you ain't a man."

"Be sixteen on the fifth of September."

"I know your birthday, Jess."

"And you'll be sixteen next February."

"I know *my* birthday, Jess."

"There's plenty of boys like us fighting."

"Well, I can't say I'm keen to *be* one."

Jesse seemed not to hear. "Those partisans who knew Buck? They told Susie and me there's a couple of *girls* riding with Quantrill."

"No, sir!"

"They swore to it. But not pretty little girls like Susie, they said. The girls with Quantrill are a mighty rough lot."

Matt didn't care for the idea of those bushwhackers sitting in the Samuels' dining room calling Susie a pretty little girl. Did she like that sort? Probably, since Buck was one, and she adored Buck.

Jesse said, "I laughed when they were telling Susie she was

pretty. And she hauled off and *hit* me. You think she's pretty, Matt?"

Off his guard, he stammered, "Uh, well—no—well, she's tolerable, I suppose."

"Tolerable!" Jesse hooted, enough to scare every catfish in the county. "Oh, won't she like that!"

"Don't tell her," Matt mumbled, turning his face.

"I sure *will*! Ha! Those boys had her all puffed up. Tolerable. That'll take her down a notch!"

"Jesse, don't you tell her I said that." Matt stood to busy himself with his lines.

"Matthew . . . ? You *do* think she's pretty, don't you?"

Matt hauled a line up, as if he thought something was on it.

"There's no use," Jesse said gleefully. "You can't get out of it now! You're sweet on my little sister!"

"Just keep quiet about it, Jess, all right?" Matt said, pointing a warning. If Susie was to hear how he felt about her, he wanted her to hear it from him.

"I won't tell, I won't!" Jesse held up his hands. "But how'd I miss that? Matt, are you getting all sneaky on me?"

"Just keep your mouth shut. Will you do me that one little thing?"

"All right," Jesse said in a humoring tone. He lay back and shut his eyes. "Mmm, that sun feels good. Better to be lying in it than working in it, huh?"

"Yep." Matt's line dipped, then dragged. He pulled it from the water. "Got one," he announced, dangling the flopping fish over Jesse's face.

Jesse sputtered, rubbed his eyes, and looked. "Big one, too."

Matt unhooked the cat, strung it, then lowered it back into the water. He rebaited and set the line again. Jesse slid his hat over his face, and Matt snickered.

"What're you cackling at?" Jesse said.

"You. You reckon you'll catch a fish that way, laying there not paying any mind?"

"Since when do you have to mind a fish to catch it?"

"Jess, he could eat your bait, toss the hook back, and ask for more, and you wouldn't even notice."

Jesse laughed under his breath. "Recall what your pa said when we built the raft?" he asked, sitting up.

Matt turned fast. "What?"

"He said, 'Jesse works hard, and then he rests hard.' "

"Well, he pegged *you*," Matt said, grinning. It was like a little present, hearing a memory of Papa that he'd forgotten.

"He was a fine man, Matt," Jesse said quietly. "And you're fortunate to've known him so well."

Matt made no reply.

"I wish I could recall my own pa. They say the day he left I cried and took on so, he nearly changed his mind." Jesse took out his watch and rubbed the glass with his shirt. "Ma says that's when he gave me this, and asked me to hold on to it till he could get back to us. 'Kiss Jesse for me,' that's what he wrote in his last letter home."

Every time Jesse told the story, Matt listened as though he'd never heard it before. When Jesse was just two, his pa had gone with the gold rush, hoping to get enough to educate the three children. He'd died a few weeks after reaching California.

"Still"—Jesse slipped the watch back into his pocket—"I don't suppose I could have a better step-pa than Pappy."

"I don't suppose *anybody* could," Matt agreed.

But Jesse wasn't so lucky the first time. When he was five, his ma married old Mr. Simms. Folks said she believed Buck and Jesse needed a firm hand. It turned out that Mr. Simms's particular hand was a little too firm. He didn't like her children at all and couldn't bear to be around them.

Jesse had told Matt about the time Simms insisted on leaving the children in the care of Aunt Lotty while he took Jesse's ma to his farm in Clinton County. She was gone for a long time, and Jesse was scared she'd never come back, just like his pa. At last she did return, but without old Simms. Jesse said his ma was planning to divorce the man, so he died rather than give her the satisfaction. Soon after, she met Dr. Samuel, who was practicing medicine near Liberty. She married him when Jesse was eight, and Dr. Samuel became more farmer than doctor.

"Got another." Matt hauled out his line. This cat was even bigger.

"What was that?" Jesse said sharply.

"What?"

Jesse was sitting straight up, blinking fast, brow furrowed. Just as he grabbed for his gun, someone yelled, "Get 'em!" and one man pounced on Matt, two on Jesse. Matt caught glimpses of blue as the men dragged them down the rocks. His head was pushed forward so that all he could see were cavalry boots. Then the man shoved him to his knees, jamming his head into the mud.

Water sloshed. They were forcing Jesse into the creek.

"Jess!" Matt yelled.

"Matt!" Jesse shouted back.

"Where's your brother?" one man hollered; then Jesse was fighting for air.

"I don't know!" There was another splash.

"Jesse!" Matt called, struggling.

"Shut your mouth, boy, or you'll be next," the man holding him snarled, grinding his face harder against the stones.

"Don't know or ain't telling?" came a voice from the creek.

"Both!" Jesse choked out, and they put him underwater once more.

Why'd he have to say that? Why couldn't he stick with 'don't know'? Now these Federals would shoot them for sure.

Then a fourth man shouted from the woods: "All right, enough!"

Matt was jerked to his feet, arms pinned behind him. Would his body be found, so he could be buried next to Pa? Jesse stood doubled over, hands on knees, coughing water. Matt tried to go to him, but the man in the woods yelled, "Stop!" and the one holding Matt yanked him back.

Jesse straightened up, and the woods man stomped toward him. Paralyzed, Matt felt his throat would burst. Then the man took off his hat, and he was in the creek—but Jesse was splashing right to him. Had he lost his senses? What was he planning to do?

Just as Jesse reached the man, Matt figured it out.

"Buck!" Jesse hollered, and leaped into his arms. Buck held him off the ground, then put him down and ruffled his wet hair.

"Damn," Matt muttered, spitting mud. He turned to face his oppressor—no man, after all. Overgrown, but only about seventeen. The boy released him, shrugging an apology.

Jesse and Buck jabbered in joyous reunion as Matt climbed the rocks.

"I barely recognized you!"

"I know!"

"Wasn't till you took off your hat and I saw those ears!"

"That's why I took it off!"

Matt cut his lines, got the cats, and packed his haversack.

"Pappy tell you where I was?"

"No, Aze."

"You coming home?"

"Can't stay but a day or two."

"What the *heck* you do all this for?" Jesse laughed.

"Ha, ha, ha," Matt said under his breath.

"I had to. I had to know what you'd do."

"Doggone it, Buck, you should know!"

"I knew what you *thought* you'd do. I had to see what you *would* do."

Matt climbed down and started off.

"Whoa, there!" Buck called to him. "Where *you* going?"

"Home."

"He's steamed up." Jesse had noticed him at last.

One side of Buck's mouth turned up, halfway between a sneer and a smile. "Hey, Matt. When you coming out with us?"

"Hey, Buck," Matt said, but chose to ignore the question. He hadn't seen Buck since he'd gone to the brush. Buck looked bigger and rougher than before. He didn't quite have a beard, but his face was unshaven. And he wore his hair long, just like every other guerrilla Matt had seen.

"Jess, is he safe?" Buck asked, and Matt wished he could punch him.

"He's fine," Jesse said.

"Maybe you better ask him."

Jesse fixed his eyes on his brother's. "It's Matt, Buck. I've no need to ask him."

Buck nodded. "You can go."

Matt turned away. *You can go.* Who did Buck think he was, royalty?

"Hey!" Jesse caught up and walked alongside. "You want to ride Sunday?"

"You still be here Sunday?"

"I reckon so."

"All right, then."

Jesse ran back to the others. "Did Susie see you yet? She's been pining for you. Buck, Buck, Buck. It's like living with a chicken!"

Their laughter died as Matt walked off. How could Jesse be so cheerful? Just minutes ago, he must have been sure he was drowning. But he hadn't seen Buck for a long time. *He'll turn up*, Jesse had said, nonchalant, but likely he was thinking Buck could be dead. Now they would all go to the Samuels' place, and Susie would be in Buck's arms. And more guerrillas would be fussing over her. And Matt had to go home and act like a happy boy with his fat catfish. Pretend nothing had happened, and not tell anybody.

11

"Didn't expect to see you so soon." Clayton sat down on the barn-lot bench, where Matt was gutting catfish.

"Jess had to get home."

"Normally you two clean your catch by the water."

Matt ignored the comment. "When you expect to shear those fool sheep, Clay?"

"I was thinking wash Thursday, shear Friday. That suit you?"

"I reckon."

"Everything okay, Matt?" Clayton asked after a time.

"Yep." Matt got to his feet. "You going up soon?"

Clayton studied him. "In a bit."

"Mind taking these to Ma? Think I'll deal with those weeds awhile."

"All right."

"Ben's down there, I hope?"

"Your hope is as good as mine."

Matt was astonished that Ben *was* there—and working, until he saw Matt and ran to him. "Matt! You been to the house?"

"No."

"Something's up with Ma. She's *happy*!"

The words punched him in the stomach. A letter had come, for sure. Why hadn't Clay told him? Matt stared at Ben.

"After you left, Mrs. Stone came by. Then, after that, Ma was *happy*!" Ben said, as if accusing her of a crime. "I don't get it. Do you?"

"No." Matt began to hoe with a vengeance.

"Well, I sure wish I knew. I ain't seen Ma so cheerful since *way* before Papa died."

"Come on, Ben, back to work."

"Oh, all right for *some* folks. Do a little fishing, do a little hoeing—"

"*Don't* work, then," Matt snapped. "But quit your jawing and leave me in peace."

Ben turned away. "What's *your* problem?" he grumbled.

The only reply was the *chunk, chunk, chunk* of Matt's hoe hitting weeds.

"Well, Matthew, this is a fine feast, and I thank you for it."

"It wouldn't be so fine if you didn't cook it so good, Ma."

"*Thank* you, Matt."

"You're welcome, ma'am."

Across the table, Ben silently mocked him. Ben had made no mistake about Ma's mood. And surely they were about to learn the reason for it.

"Children, I have some news. The Stones were in town to-day, and they brought me a letter from the post office."

"A *letter*?" Ben said. "Who from?"

"Well, Ben . . ." Ma fixed him with a plastered-on smile. "I wrote to your grandparents, in Pennsylvania. And they wrote back." Ben's eyes jumped to Matt's; Matt looked away fast. "Clayton's seen it. And I'll read it now." As she withdrew the letter from her apron pocket, Matt stared at his plate as if nothing could be more fascinating than catfish bones. "It's dated the twenty-seventh of May," Ma said, her voice high and nervous. "A bit less than two weeks in transit. That seems quick, for these times."

She read:

> *"Dearest Carolyn,*
>
> *Words cannot express the joy your mother and I felt upon receiving your letter. We have always prayed to hear from you, but we did not believe we ever would. I must tell you first that we never received the letter you speak of having written those many years ago. How can you begin to imagine that we would not have responded? We love you now, as then, with all our hearts, and our disapproval of your marriage could never change that."*

Matt gripped his legs so tight it hurt. If he moved, if he breathed, he would have to jump up and run.

> *"Had we but known how deep your feelings were for the young man—that it was more than a girl's fancy— we would never have taken the course we took. A description of the scene when we found you had gone, and the emotions in the days and months following, I will leave until another time. Suffice it to say, we never could have dreamed that two young people would be able to disappear so quickly, and so thoroughly, despite our searching and inquiries."*

Ma cleared her throat, paused, and continued:

"We are truly saddened to hear of your husband's death, and desperate with worry over the situation you describe. We have read of the Missouri problem, but we take it more to heart now that we are certain you are there.

"At the same time we are overjoyed to learn we have been blessed with six wonderful grandchildren. We read your descriptions of them repeatedly, and are becoming accustomed to speaking all their names, as if we know them. This, of course, we wish very much to do.

"Carrie, we want nothing more than for you to come home to us, at least until this horrible war is behind our nation. As you see by the address, your mother and I moved out of the city, though I still own the house. You and the children will want for nothing. Our home is quite large enough to hold all of you, and the children will attend the best of schools. Will has enlisted with the 26th Pennsylvania. Therefore we were unable to tell him the news in person, but we have written it to him and only regret that we cannot see his face when he reads it."

Again Ma's voice broke, and she waited.

"We imagine you'll be quite surprised to hear whom Will married: Sarah Huggins. They have two children. Dan is 15, and Lucy is 9. They live quite close by, and we see them nearly every day.

"Darling Carrie, I shall stop now. Though writing help me feel I am with you, and I am loath to part, I want to be certain to get this into today's post. Please write as soon as possible with your intentions. We long to hear more of you and the children.

"Mother asks me to say her letter will be along, with a package she is getting together with presents for all, but she sends her best love through this one. She also wonders if the children would like to write to us. We should be delighted to hear from them, also. Please, dear, tell us what to do next. I would board a train tomorrow, but I wait to hear your wishes.

"Your loving Father"

It was so quiet, Ma's folding the letter sounded like firecrackers. Matt's ears started ringing. Still he could not move, or raise his eyes, or think.

"Children?" Ma said softly. "Would anyone like to speak?"

Ben leaped up so fast his chair clattered to the floor. Tyler began to bawl. Ben pointed at Matt. "You knew! And you didn't tell me!" His voice quivering with rage and tears, he turned to Ma. "I won't go! I'll run away just like you did! Only I'll *never* write again and you'll never *ever* find me!" He dashed upstairs and slammed the bedroom door.

Matt sat back, covering his mouth and shutting his eyes.

"Well," Ma said. "That's one opinion." And she went after Ben.

"*I* want to go," Molly chirped as Betsy lifted Tyler from his chair. "They don't have war in Pennsylvania. They have pretty bonnets."

Matt shot Betsy a look. "You *told* her!"

"What of it?" Betsy snapped back.

"Ma said not to tell them!"

Betsy was jostling the crying baby. "I knew Molly wouldn't say anything."

"That isn't the point, Betsy," Clayton said evenly.

"It ain't fair, Clay," Matt protested. "Ben was the only one who didn't know!"

"Oh, what do *you* care?" Betsy said. "You're always shouting at him anyhow!"

Matt took Tyler from her. "I care plenty, you imbecile!"

"Matt!" Clayton said.

"I've a mind to tell Ma what she did, Clay!"

"Go right ahead, Matt, you don't scare me!" Betsy answered.

"Why are you mad, Matty?" Molly asked. "Don't you want to go, either?"

"Hush, Molly," Betsy said quietly.

"Oh, you fine fool." Matt was seething. "First you fill her head with nonsense, then you tell her hush."

Betsy marched right up and shook her finger in his face. "You shut your mouth, Matthew, about what's nonsense and who's a fool. Maybe you're not afraid, but I *am*, and I don't want to stay!"

"All *right*, you two," Clayton warned.

"You'd leave Papa out there all by himself?" Matt jabbed a finger toward the orchard. "This house he built, leave it to get burned down by who-knows-who?"

"I keep Papa right here, Matt," Betsy replied, pressing her fist to her heart. "I've no need to live where people are killing each other, to keep my memories of Papa. You think he's out there under the ground? Well, then, what did *you* learn in Sunday school?"

Matt wheeled around and left the house, Tyler's cries piercing his ear. "Shhh," he whispered, kissing the baby's temple. "Shhh. Look!" Matt pointed at the scythe-shaped moon. "See that? Look. Moon. Can you say 'moon'?" His brother was calming down. "Can you say 'Matt'? What's my name? Who am I, Tyler? Who am I?"

Matt headed for the barn. "Want to see the horsie? What's my horsie's name? Can you say 'Salt'?" Salt nickered and tossed his head. "See? He knows me. You want to pet him? Soft. See?" He pressed the baby's hand to Salt's hide, his own face to Salt's neck. "You think you'll ever ride a horse on our farm, Ty?"

He locked the barn and carried the baby across their land. "Here's our pastures . . . There's our sheep . . . That's Ma's kitchen garden . . . That's our root garden . . . And this is my crop." He tapped his chest. "Matt's corn. Matt's crop." Tyler ran his hand over Matt's face.

Matt kept walking and walking. "See all the corn? And over yonder's our orchard. And way up there—" He stopped. "This is our farm, Ty. *Your* farm."

"*Mah,*" Tyler said, and Matt hugged him close.

"You said my name. How about that? You know my name."

"Maaaa—thew!" Ma's voice sounded miles away.

"Uh-oh," he said to Tyler, and hollered, "Coming, Ma!"

When they got to the yard, Tyler was laughing from the run.

"What on earth are you doing?" Ma demanded.

"He was crying. I just started walking. I wasn't thinking . . ."

Ma took the baby and heaved a deep sigh. "Ben's terribly up-set, Matt. Clay's with him. Are you all right?"

"Yes, ma'am."

She started for the lean-to. "Come indoors."

"I'll just be a minute."

Matt sat on the porch step, clasping his hands behind his neck. Ma's father wouldn't even use Papa's name. *Young man*, he wrote, *your husband*. Ma had told her folks all about them, but they knew nothing about her folks. Her brother. He had a cousin his age. Jesse's age. What was that boy like? A town boy. A rich boy, it sounded like. A Northern boy whose father was fighting for the Union. What did he think about the war? Living up there where men marched off to invade Southern soil, his cousin would have no clue what it was like here. Had he even heard of bushwhackers? Jayhawkers? Jim Lane? Quantrill?

Ma was so pleased with that letter. His feelings didn't matter. All she cared to hear was "yes, ma'am," so that's what he gave her. Her parents wanted them to write. Would Ma force them? Presents. Her mother was buying presents. A quite large house, the best of schools. It was too much to think about. Could it be that just a couple of hours ago, Buck's friend was feeding him mud?

Clayton opened the door. "Come on in."

"No."

With a thump, Clay sat on the rocker.

"Why didn't you tell me she got the letter?"

The rocker creaked mournfully. "I believe you have more secrets than I."

Weary, Matt rubbed his face with both hands. "What'll Ma do, you think?"

"Matt, what do *you* think?" Clayton said in his best annoyed voice.

"I don't believe I'll go." Matt more heard his words than said them—and instantly regretted them.

"Well, if that's the way of it, you'll have to tell Ma. Because I surely won't be the one to."

After a time, Matt said, "She's so happy. That's what galls me."

Clayton made a sound of exasperation as he got to his feet. "Matthew, you've got some growing up to do. Now come on indoors."

"No." Matt could barely see through his anger, and defying Clayton seemed his only comfort.

"When I go in, I bolt that door behind me."

"Good, Clay. I'll sleep in the mow."

Clayton stabbed his back with a crutch. "Mama's got enough on her mind without you adding to it. Now get inside or I'll lay you flat."

Matt hesitated, then obeyed, brushing past Clayton and up the stairs. The girls were giggling behind their door. It made his blood boil. Ben was asleep, or shamming, breathing in that still-crying way. Matt undressed quickly, pulled the straw tick to the window, and lay facing the wall. Clayton was getting a little too high-handed lately, threatening him, whipping Ben. He wasn't their pa, and he'd better not get to thinking he was. It wasn't fair of Clay to challenge him that way. He knew Matt could beat him in a minute—but never would.

Clayton tapped on the girls' door, saying gruffly, "Go to sleep." Matt heard him change and get into bed. " 'Night, Matt," he said after a while, but Matt didn't answer.

Ben's catching breaths were irritating. Matt pulled his pillow over his head. Ben could cry and holler as much as he wanted. He was still a child. He would have to go to Pennsylvania.

But Matt could go to Quantrill. He supposed he was tall enough in the saddle. He was a better rider than most boys, and about as good a shot—and he could get better. He wouldn't make a fuss. He'd keep quiet and do his work. But when the time came, he'd just say he was staying behind. And there was nothing Ma or Clayton would be able to do.

12

Even in the best of times, sheep-shearing was the worst of chores. This year there was neither banter nor laughter. Matt talked to Clayton only when necessary, and Clay returned the favor. Matt tried to joke with Ben, but a blank stare was the reply. Then Matt limited his remarks to "get the dang thing" and "hold the fool animal."

Adding to his misery, it was brutally hot for the second week of June. That was all right when they were in the stream, washing the creatures. But when it came to holding them while Clay did the shearing, Matt felt the wool would smother him.

He had no love for the stupid sheep, with their empty eyes and unhappy mouths. When they got ornery, he had to force himself to treat them right—and to remember they were the reason he had clothes. He preferred to butcher with Mr. Stone; dead hogs put up a lot less fight. After the job was done, Molly and Tyler jumped into piles of soft fleece, and Matt and his brothers cooled off in chilly silence by the pump.

When Jesse rode into the lane on Sunday, he was a more than welcome sight. Matt started walking from the barn lot as Jesse tethered July and opened the gate, calling, "Hello, Clayton."

Clay was on the porch with his papers. "Jess," he said.

"What's the news?" Jesse asked in a jovial way.

Matching his tone, Clayton answered, "I'll wager you know better than I."

Jesse laughed and pushed his hat back, leaning on the porch rail. "Well, anyhow, I reckon I know better than those censored papers of yours, Clay."

Clayton pretended to read. "Let's see . . . hmmm . . . Lincoln's still president."

"Not in my country. But I reckon he's still on his throne in that big white castle."

"Watch it, Jess," Clayton answered.

By the time Matt reached them, they were both smiling—but neither was happy.

"Your turn," Matt said when they were in the lane.

"The cave," Jesse answered. They started at a trot, but Jesse slowed to a walk at the Stone place. "That's odd. Your neighbor does her wash on Sunday?"

Two bright coverlets hung on Mrs. Stone's line. "I don't know. Maybe she's just airing them out. Ma does that sometimes."

"On a Sunday?"

"No . . ."

"Huh." Jesse patted July. "So, you two reckon you can beat us today?"

"Giddup!" Matt answered, and Salt was off.

"Cheating!" Jesse yelled.

As they left the road, leaping the fence, July raced ahead. She was a Morgan, too, bay-colored with a white star and a black mane and tail. Jesse got her when she was grown. She was a fine mare, but she couldn't compare to Salt, and Matt always thought the one thing he had over Jesse was that he'd broken and trained Salt on his own, from Papa's instructions.

In the woods they were neck and neck. Where the path was only wide enough for a single horse, Matt always had to be the one to drop back to keep them from colliding. Then the branches were so low they were lying flat on the horses, July still in the lead. But when they came out onto the prairie, Matt had only to give Salt the reins and watch him speed ahead. Behind him, Jesse was giving a howl that was part Comanche, part coyote, just the way he said the bushwhackers yelled going into a fight.

Back in the brush, Salt was well ahead, and Matt had already dismounted before Jesse got to the cave. "What kept you?" he said casually.

"That's one sleek animal, boy."

Matt's pride welled up in his chest. "Yeah, well, watch out

you don't kill him one day with your antics on the wood path," he said, and Jesse laughed. "Because if you do, I might have to kill *you*."

"Listen to that mouth," Jesse said, knocking Matt's hat off. "And on Sunday, too." He retrieved the hat and jammed it over Matt's eyes, then unstrapped his saddlebag. "I've something to show you."

They had found the cave years ago—no other boys knew where it was. When anybody tried to track them, they always caught on and led the others to the river instead. The best part about this cave was how the sunlight slashed between two boulders. When they squeezed inside through a narrow opening, it was almost as bright as the day.

They sat, and Jesse pulled out a shiny, long-barreled revolver.

"Whoa," Matt said.

Jesse held it out; Matt looked at him. "Take it," Jesse urged.

Matt had never held a revolver before. He hefted it in his palm. A whole lot heavier than he'd expected—still, much lighter than a shotgun.

It was one fine weapon, with a walnut grip and a brass trigger guard, the rest of it smooth blue steel. Matt examined the scene engraved on the cylinder: ships in a battle. "Colt's Navy?" he asked. That was what the guerrillas carried.

"Nope. A .44-caliber Army," Jesse announced.

"Army? Why's it got ships on it?"

"Don't know. Go on, Matt, hold it like a *gun*."

Matt shifted his hand to the smooth, warm grip. "Not loaded," he said more than asked. Jesse shook his head. It took Matt a fair amount of strength to pull the hammer back with his thumb. When he heard a click, he thought he was done.

But Jesse advised: "Keep going. That's only half-cock."

Matt pulled harder, embarrassed by his trembling hand. A louder click, and the hammer stopped. "Buck give it to you?"

"Yep."

Matt looked up. "Where'd he get it?"

"Off a dead Federal," Jesse said steadily.

Aiming at the cave wall, Matt squeezed the trigger. The hammer fell. "You'd better have ammunition," he said, turning to Jesse.

Jesse snickered. "Matthew, you surprise me." He raised the saddlebag over his head, overturned it, shook it. Cartridges rained down.

Matt shut his eyes tight, then opened them wide, making Jesse laugh more. "Where in the world did you get all these?" Matt asked, picking one up.

"Made 'em," Jesse said proudly, pulling a tin of caps from his pocket. "Spent two nights helping Buck and them. They left me some for practice. All right, now. Watch." Matt handed over the gun. Jesse held it in his left hand, muzzle pointing up. "Set it on half-cock; now the cylinder will turn." He picked up a cartridge. "See this paper tail? That's the powder end. Tear it off with your teeth before you push it in. Poke the ball end in with your finger. Ram it home with the loading lever. Do that for all six chambers." As he talked, he worked fast, spitting paper. "Then you turn it to fix the caps, on this notched side here." He pushed one on and turned the cylinder till it clicked. "Do all six. Then you just turn the whole cylinder, slow, all the way around, so you're sure everything's in right and nothing'll hitch." Nothing did.

"Damn," Matt said in admiration.

"Don't curse, Matt." They piled the ammunition back in the saddlebag. "Let's go," Jesse said, pulling the hammer to half-cock.

"Hang on." Matt scrambled to his feet. "You carry it like that?"

Jesse signaled him closer. "Look here. This gun can't fire at half-cock because the hammer's locked. You can pull the trigger hard as you want—see?—and the hammer won't fall. Now watch close." Slowly he pulled the hammer farther. "As you bring it to full-cock, the cylinder turns and lines up the cap with the hammer. *Now* it'll fire."

Matt stared in wonder: "Well, *that's* just sheer genius."

"And *that*," Jesse said with a wink, "is Mr. Colt." He set the hammer back to half-cock. "Too bad he's a doggone Yankee."

Matt slung the saddlebag over his shoulder and followed Jesse out.

"See that dogwood?" There was one about fifty yards off. Jesse raised his left arm.

Puzzled, Matt asked, "What're you doing?"

"Quantrill wants his men to shoot just as well with both hands. He'll drill you and drill you on that, they said." Jesse shot fast, pausing only to re-cock. He made it look mighty easy. They ran to the slender tree. Every ball had met its target.

"You do *any* farm work since Buck came?" Matt said.

"Buck claims he shot a Federal off his horse a hundred yards away at a keen run. I said I reckoned I could do that. He laughed at me. But I bet I could."

"Well, come on out to the prairie," Matt deadpanned. "You can try it on me."

Jesse shook his head, befuddled. "What?"

"That was a joke," Matt explained.

Jesse laughed uneasily and blushed hard. "I really wanted one of Buck's Navys," he said. "They're even nicer. They feel *so good* in your hand. Make a neat, round hole where they hit a man, Buck says."

Matt felt sick to think of them inspecting their work as if they were hunting rabbits.

"He's got *five*," Jesse went on, "but he wouldn't part with a one. I begged and begged—I wasn't proud. He says he needs every one. Know what they do, Matt?"

"What?"

"Before a fight, they load all their guns. They start out one in each hand, two in their belts, and if they have more, they keep them in a saddle holster. When a gun's empty, they just drop it and pull out the next. Half the time the Federals are fighting with a carbine and a bayonet. So the partisans get off about thirty shots to every one or two of the Feds'. Then they win the field, go back, and pick up all their Navys. *And* the carbines and the bayonets and everything else." Jesse began to load again.

"Don't the Feds catch on?" Matt asked. "Why don't they fight the same way?"

Jesse shrugged. "They're fools. Hey, this was supposed to be your turn."

Matt knelt beside him, taking the gun. Jesse gave him a cartridge; he tore it with his teeth. His hand felt shaky, his fingers thick as he pushed it into the chamber.

"Steady," Jesse said. "Just think of it as no big thing. Keep cool, that's what the bushwhackers say. Before a fight, Quantrill rides up and down the line and tells them: *Keep cool. Stay low. Fire when you get loaded.*"

Matt looked up. "That *would* be the time to fire, I suppose," he said, but Jesse wasn't amused. Each time Matt swung the loading lever down to push a cartridge home, he felt more confident. But trying to place the caps, he fumbled again.

"There," Jesse said, guiding his hand. "And there. Now you." Matt did one alone. "Again. Once more. And turn," Jesse said, and the cylinder did turn. "There you go!" They stood. "Try with your left."

"I will not," Matt said irritably. "I'll be glad to hit anything with my right."

"Come on, Matt!"

"No! I'm just learning, Jess. I'm not getting into some contest with you!"

"All right, all right, don't get surly," Jesse said, laughing.

Matt pulled the hammer back. "I'm trying for that sycamore," he announced, as if daring Jesse to comment. It was considerably closer than the dogwood—and considerably fatter. He aimed; it felt peculiar not to have both hands on the gun. When he fired, the gun kicked up. He re-cocked, re-aimed, fired, and lowered his shaking arm.

"Go on. You got four more shots."

"I can count, Jess," he said, and aimed again. How did they do it, shot after shot after shot, firing left and right, tossing down guns, riding with the reins in their teeth?

After the fourth shot, Jesse came to stand beside him. "Here.

Hold your left hand under the butt, like this, to keep it steady . . . That's good."

Matt fired the last two shots and let out his breath. Jesse trotted off to inspect the sycamore. With dread, Matt followed. "You hit it twice. That ain't bad."

"And it ain't good."

"Times you hit were probably those last two."

"I reckon."

"You just need practice."

"I prefer to shoot food," Matt replied, and Jesse looked shocked, as if Matt had taken the Lord's name in vain. He shrugged, handing Jesse the gun. "Sorry."

Jesse went back to his saddlebag. Matt sat beside him and watched as Jesse loaded, then held out the gun. "Try again."

"I don't care to."

Jesse fixed him with a chilly gaze.

Matt raised his eyebrows. "Is that supposed to scare me?" he asked, though he *was* unnerved. He made a sound of disbelief and shook his head. "Don't give me that look, Jess. If I don't want to shoot the gun, I won't shoot the gun."

Jesse turned and fired all the rounds with his left hand. He put the gun away. "You want to ride?" he mumbled, buckling the saddlebag.

"I do."

On the way to the river, Matt thought of the games they'd played when they were younger. For Pony Express, they pretended one of them was Johnny Fry, who made the famous first run from St. Joseph on the third of April, 1860. For Wounded Man, one lay in the tall prairie grass and the other rode up at full speed to rescue him, leaning way out of the saddle, pursued by invisible, tomahawk-toting Apaches.

Now here was Jesse, talking about shooting Federals off their horses. Another kind of game. And another competition with Buck, as half his life had been. If he thought it was all so fine, why hadn't he just gone ahead with Buck? And why was it that in all these stories, there was never a dead guerrilla?

All week Matt had waited for this afternoon away from the silent anger at home. But this was even worse.

Jesse kept ranging up to Matt, then falling back, as though wanting to say something, then deciding against it. At the river they let the horses drink, then rode upstream and tied them out of sight in the brush, where thick vines hung from the trees.

"Wasn't trying to *scare* you," Jesse said at last.

"All right." Matt grabbed a vine, swung out over the water, and jumped back to the bank. He did it twice more.

Jesse sat on his heels and trailed his hands in the water. "So, you and Clayton aren't talking. What's that about?"

"My ma got a letter from her pa," Matt said, sitting beside him.

Jesse turned. "She what?"

"You heard."

"I thought she—"

"Well, she wrote to them," Matt interrupted. "And they wrote back. And now they're wanting her to take us to Pennsylvania."

"Pennsyl*va*nia!" Jesse repeated.

"Yep. She told them about Pa, and us, and all this mess. And they said they don't hate her and they want us to come."

Jesse scrambled to his feet and flung his hat. "Well, that's the dod-dingus thing I ever heard!" he hollered, and Matt almost couldn't keep himself from laughing. No matter how mad Jesse got, he would never curse. He wouldn't say "damn," he wouldn't say "hell." When he said "dod-dingus," you knew he was furious—and you'd best not tell him how foolish it sounded. Jesse kicked the hat and then the dirt. "What'll you do if they go? Could you stay on your own? No, you'd stay with us! I'll ask Ma. I'm sure she'll say all right—"

"Jess, don't go telling your ma about this."

Jesse fired a stone into the river.

"My ma wouldn't even like me talking about it. So *don't* tell yours. Hear?"

"I hear," Jesse muttered. "But Ma and Pappy'll take you in. And we can help each other get our crops in. Then we'll go to Quantrill together."

"So that's the plan. You go after harvest."

"Nothing's sure," Jesse said, staring across the water. "Buck's got a squad all picked out for me, though. Leader's named Taylor. But it's not decided when I'll go."

"Not *decided*?" Matt shook his head. "How does that work? Who's making the decision, anyhow?"

Jesse started blinking fast. Then Matt wished he could take his words back, change the whole mood of this day.

"You're doing it." He gave Jesse an elbow. "The thing with your eyes."

Jesse turned his face. "I can't help it. And you're not perfect, either."

"Oh, I know *that*. They never quit telling me."

They sat in silence until Jesse mumbled, "Lord, it's hot."

Matt jumped up. "We can remedy that." He stripped down, grabbed hold of a vine, and took a running leap. The river wasn't too deep, but it was fast. It tugged him under, then bobbed him up; Jesse was way behind him already. "Come on!" Matt called.

Jesse pulled his shirt over his head, and Matt let the current carry him away.

13

"Let's cut your hair, Matt," Clayton said as he headed out through the lean-to the following evening.

Matt fetched Molly's stool. Ma, washing supper dishes with the girls, handed Matt the scissors as he passed.

"This is fixing to be one long summer," Clayton said, straddling the bench near the pump. "And if you and I are miserable with each other, it'll be longer still."

Matt set the stool down and sat with his back to Clayton. "I don't especially want to be miserable with you, Clay."

"Nor I with you." The scissors went *scritch, scritch, scritch.* "I have a lot of time to sit around and think, Matt. And what I do sometimes, I try to put myself in someone else's place. Can you imagine what it was like for Ma, writing that letter? When she believed her folks hated her so much, they didn't even answer when she wrote to say she was about to have a baby?" Clayton stopped cutting. "Do you think she'd humble herself that way, if she didn't believe her children were in danger?"

Matt clenched his teeth, swallowing hard.

"And how do you imagine she felt when she read their answer? To learn that all those years, they were praying for word. That they want to welcome her back, and make her children safe. It's like a darn fairy tale, Matthew. Why *shouldn't* she be glad?"

"I never said I didn't *understand* it. I'm not a fool. But it pains me, Clayton, all right? She'll take you ones and go up there and forget about this place and——" He leaned over, elbows on knees, pressing his hands to his forehead.

"She'll never forget Papa," Clayton said quietly, touching his back.

Matt shook his head.

"Speak to her, Matt, will you? Tell her what's on your mind."

He made no reply.

"Sit up." Clayton tapped Matt's head with the scissors. "Come on."

Matt straightened himself, and Clay started snipping again. "Did she write back?"

"Why don't you ask her?"

"Well, dang it, Clay, I'm asking you!"

"Yes, she wrote. But she said nothing definite. She isn't keen to take Ben away against his will, and she knows where your loyalty lies."

Working on his courage, Matt finally asked, "Do you want to go?"

Clayton barely hesitated. "Yes. I believe I do."

The house tilted, then righted itself. "But how *can* you, Clay? Papa named you after this county. How can you leave here and go to a Northern state?"

"Matt, look at me," Clayton demanded. "I mean it, look at me." Matt turned and Clayton touched the point of the scissors to his own chest. "I'm a cripple."

"No, you're not!" Matt said fiercely.

"Yes, I am, and Mama and Papa putting a good name on it does not change the fact. I'm a cripple, and there's nothing here for me. You think I want to spend the rest of my life reading newspapers and milking cows? You tell me about Jesse going courting. Don't you reckon I think of such things? Of a girl who'll take me as I am? Do you suppose I'll find her here?" He gestured at the woods.

Matt was embarrassed to hear Clayton speaking of it, and ashamed he'd never thought of Clay that way before. Clay was the one who shaved, who had a man's voice and hair on his chest. Why wouldn't he think about girls?

Clayton gave a bashful laugh. "I guess this is what you and Papa'd call feeling sorry for myself."

"No, Clay, you don't ever feel sorry for yourself," Matt said quickly.

"I do, though. But I don't think there's anything so terrible in it." He cut carefully around Matt's ear. "You know Papa meant for me to go to college. You know he wanted to make a life for me away from here. Remember the last night, when he called us in?"

Of course Matt remembered. Papa knew he wouldn't make it till morning, and one by one, he had them in to say goodbye.

"Well, do you know what he said to me, Matt?" Matt didn't want to hear, but Clay went on. "He reached up and put his arms around my neck. And I laid my head on his chest and he said, 'You'll find a way, Clayton. Somehow, you'll find a way.' "

Matt ground his teeth together. He didn't think he could bear one more word.

"So I have no doubt Papa would approve of my leaving," Clayton said. "And I don't feel he'd bear any ill will about my going to the North, either. And stop doing that with your teeth, it makes my skin crawl. Turn to face me, so I can do your front."

The last thing he wanted to do was face Clayton, but he did as he was told.

"Now, what about you?" Clay said.

"What *about* me?"

"What's Jesse have a mind to do this year?"

"I thought this was about me."

Clayton cut across his brow. "Sometimes it seems to be almost the same thing."

"Don't cut too much and make me look like a fool."

"I believe you're avoiding my question," Clay said pleasantly. "Matt." He laid the scissors down. "Will you make me a solemn promise?"

"Tell me what it is and I'll tell you if I will."

"If he talks you into going off to Quantrill, you give me one last chance to talk you out of it."

Matt looked into his brother's clear gray eyes. "You have my word, Clay."

They shook hands. "One other problem," Clayton said.

"What's that?"

Clay nodded toward the porch. Betsy and Molly were carding wool, but Matt knew they weren't the problem. Ben lay on the floor, his legs propped up on the wall.

"I don't know what to do about that problem," Matt said.

"Well, if he thought *you* thought going to Pennsylvania was all right, likely he'd feel the same."

"I won't lie to him, Clay. And I don't think it's fair to ask me to."

Clayton handed him the scissors and reached for his crutches. "All right, Matt."

"Besides, he's got no choice. He's ten years old, he goes where Mama tells him."

"What if he *does* run away?"

"Run away? Where to? Down to the stream to catch a cricket frog?"

Clayton didn't answer.

"Believe me, Clay, that boy will not be leaving his mama."

Clayton seemed uncomfortable. "Try to put it right with him, would you?"

"All right."

Ma was on the porch when they reached it. "Hmm . . ." She

appraised Matt, fists on her hips, head tilted. "Clay did a fine job, I'd say."

"Yes, ma'am," Matt said, combing his hair with his fingers. "This ought to be a bit cooler out in the fields."

"I think he looks dumb," Ben grumbled, and Matt seized the opportunity to hoist him by the ankles so his head was inches off the floor. "Put me down!" Ben yelled.

"Oh, Matt, do be careful," Ma said.

"No, Mama, I don't take to such insults from pestiferous varmints," Matt said solemnly. Tossing Ben over his shoulder, he started down to the barn lot.

"Let me go!" Ben hollered, pounding Matt's back and struggling mightily.

Matt dumped him into the hog pen. Ben scrambled furiously to his feet as the piglets rushed from their shelter, squealing. Matt hung on the rail, laughing. "Teach you to sass your elders."

Ben lunged for his neck.

"Whoa!" Matt held him off. "Hey! If you strangle me, I can't take you riding tomorrow."

Ben halted. "And if I don't?"

"Then I might could," Matt said, and a grin took over Ben's face.

Sometimes it seemed like any other June. They did their work, ate their meals, spent the long evenings on the porch with the mandolin. Matt showed Molly how to taste honeysuckle nectar, and helped Ben catch fireflies in a canning jar.

But now, when he locked the barn, he heard the woods crackling with campfires, and horses whinnying, and men's voices—near, far, shouting, laughing. Every night he checked Papa's rifle, even though he knew it was loaded, and felt for the caps and bullets in the tin box, even though he knew they were there.

Every morning, when Molly went to gather the eggs, she counted the chickens. Occasionally, one would be gone. But Matt knew if all they lost was a few chickens, they could count themselves almost too lucky.

Matt took to keeping his own gun under his bed, and one night he woke in a cold sweat, certain he'd heard someone outside. He grabbed the gun and crept downstairs and out the back door on shaky legs. "Who's there?" he said, chilled by the thick, hollow sound of his own voice. What would he have done if someone had answered?

Another night the noises were inside the house, and he was surprised by Ma, sitting at the table reading the Bible. She started when she saw him. "Oh! Matthew, you oughtn't to prowl around like that."

"Sorry, Ma. I was thinking the same about you."

She smiled softly. "Come, sit with me a moment."

He hesitated, but had no choice. Propping his gun against the wall, he sat across from her. He almost never saw Ma with her hair all the way down. It was longer than he would have thought, and prettier, too, shining almost red in the flickering candlelight.

"I've been thinking, Ma. Maybe you and Tyler ought to take our room, and we should move downstairs. It doesn't seem right, you and the baby down here alone."

Her kind eyes warmed him. It had been a long time since he'd felt such affection for her.

"Oh, Matt. That is awfully thoughtful. You can't know how I appreciate it. But I couldn't think of leaving Papa's and my room. And besides, if anything were to happen, it's best for me to be first to the door."

"Yes, Ma."

She meant they wouldn't kill a woman—neither side would. That remained the only civilized part of this whole mess.

"I've been reading the Psalms," Ma said. "They speak a great deal to our situation."

"Is that so?" he asked politely, but he was uneasy, knowing where this would lead. He was like Pa, upright—at least he tried to be—but not religious. Like Pa, he couldn't tolerate much Sunday school or Bible reading or pastors' sermonizing. When he felt the presence of God, it was in green shoots of corn pushing up through warm earth, or in an astonishing blue sky, or when he was flying across the endless prairie on a speeding horse. He held no prideful notion that these thoughts were original to him. He knew he had come to them from his time outdoors with Pa.

Ma bowed her head:

"My heart is sore pained within me: and the terrors of death are fallen upon me.

Fearfulness and trembling are come upon me, and horror hath overwhelmed me.

And I said, Oh that I had wings like a dove! for then would I fly away, and be at rest."

When she looked up, Matt looked down. He didn't want to have this conversation.

"It'll be a new month before we know it," she said. "I keep delaying my decision, hoping things will improve."

He said nothing.

"Matthew," she said softly, "if we leave here, what will you do?"

"Whatever you say, Ma," he mumbled.

"Do you mean that?"

He nodded, keeping his head down. Could she possibly believe him?

She closed her hand over his. "Is there anything you want to say to me, darling?" she asked, and he thought he must be the worst boy in the world, to lie in the face of such a good ma.

He swallowed hard. "No, ma'am."

"If your papa were here—"

"Please, Ma." He pushed his chair back fast, standing. "Please don't." Their eyes met and tears coursed down her cheeks. He turned away and picked up his gun. "Good night, Ma," he said, and went upstairs.

14

Ma turned on him the very next day. After dinner, she had taken the girls to town—there was talk of fabric and dresses, likely for going up North. Well, Matt told Ben, I reckon if they can buy fabric, we can go fishing.

Matt caught two bass, Ben one. They went for a swim. When they were by the pump with Clayton, cleaning fish while Tyler played, Ma came into the yard at a clip. She nearly jumped from the wagon, heading straight for Matt.

"Matthew Howard." Her face was flushed, her breathing ragged. "I heard something today and I want you to tell me if it's true."

Betsy and Molly looked woebegone. Matt felt his brothers standing close.

"Were you and Jesse in the company of Buck and other guerrillas?" She gripped his shoulders and shook him. "Think before you answer! Don't you dare lie to me!"

Matt said, "Well—I—"

"Yes or no?" She was rattling his brains. *"Yes or no?"*

"Yes," he said, and Ma slapped him hard across the face.

"Mama!" Molly shrieked, hiding her eyes. Ma had never hit a child.

"But Ma—" Matt began.

She hit him again. "Go indoors! Go upstairs and stay there. You'll have no supper! Oh, it's too much, it's too much," she said to no one, and knelt to take Molly in her arms.

Matt hesitated, then went inside and slammed the door, climbed the stairs and slammed the bedroom door, too. To think that last night he had felt so kindly toward her, and she had pretended the same. The first chance she got, she attacked, without even letting him explain. Damn this war! A person couldn't do one thing without somebody finding out and telling somebody else. What would she hear about next? The dead Federal's revolver?

You'll have no supper. Did she think he was twelve? He was the one taking care of them all. He was far too old to be sent to his room. So why had he gone? Why hadn't he just walked out of the yard? Why not do it now? Pick up his gun, go to the pasture for Salt. What was stopping him? But he couldn't, and that made him more furious still.

The only thing that would soothe this anger was pain, so he punched the wall until his hand was numb. Papa had told him, *It scares me, the way you're quiet and quiet, and then you go off.* But if Pa was here, he'd understand. *Now, Carrie, don't be irrational,* Pa sometimes said—and he'd say it now, Matt knew. Irrational and unfair.

He rubbed his raw, swollen knuckles. What was he to do now, shut up in this room? Standing at the window, he took deep breaths. His brothers and sisters were in the yard, at the barn, choring. With the sun beating on the roof, it was almost unbearably hot. If he took the chinking out of the walls, the breeze could come through. In fall, he would replace it. He opened his knife and began prying the clay from between the logs.

Quick, light steps on the stairs, and then a knock.

"Come in, Molly."

With a bright smile, she peeked in. "How'd you know it was me?"

"Just smart, I guess."

She held out the Bible. "Mama said you're to read the verses she marked," she told him solemnly, and his bitterness rose again. Ma just had to keep punishing him, and to keep letting the others know it.

"Thanks, Moll." He placed the book on the window seat.

Molly stared. "Did it hurt when Mama hit you?"

"Go along now, sweetheart," he said, patting her head. "Close the door."

As she left, he smelled his bass cooking—for them. Well, that was all right. Jesse said the guerrillas sometimes went days without food. He could stand it for one night. He closed up his knife and looked at the Bible. Last night he'd had enough, and now here it was again. Jesse ought to be in his spot. This wouldn't be punishment for him. He probably knew these verses already, and could tell Matt what they meant. Matt had a mind not to read them at all. But if Ma questioned him and he hadn't read the verses . . .

The first passage was in the book of Isaiah, the verse that went:

> *And they shall beat their swords into plowshares, and their spears into pruninghooks: nation shall not lift up sword against nation, neither shall they learn war any more.*

He understood that one all right, he'd heard it plenty. But why was she having him read it? Did she imagine he enjoyed this war? That he'd prefer fighting to plowing? He flipped to the second bookmark—those Psalms again:

Deliver me, O Lord, from the evil man: preserve me from the violent man;

Which imagine mischiefs in their heart; continually are they gathered together for war.

They have sharpened their tongues like a serpent; adders' poison is under their lips.

Keep me, O Lord, from the hands of the wicked; preserve me from the violent man.

Matt recalled Buck's peculiar grin: *When you coming out with us?* But just because they weren't on Ma's side didn't mean they were evil. If Ma thought the guerrillas were wicked, what Bible verses did she have for Jim Lane and his murdering Kansans?

The verse went on and on. "The proud have hid a snare for me, and cords; they have spread a net by the wayside . . . Let burning coals fall upon them: let them be cast into the fire . . ." Now Matt understood: Ma believed the evil men were setting traps for him by the roadside, and she wanted those men in hell.

Hot with anger, Matt shut the book and rubbed his eyes. The room was growing dim, and he was no longer accustomed to reading, especially such tiny print. Why would Ma think he needed to read all this nonsense? Was he not doing everything she told him, everything Papa told him? Was he not working as hard as he could? In return, she only shouted and hit him and threw her Bible. *Talk to her*, Clayton had said. But how could you talk to a mother like this? No. He'd just continue on his way, try to be pleasant and polite. When they went North, he would go to Jesse's.

He lay on his side to get at the chinking close to the floor. In time came another knock, and he steeled himself to face Ma. Betsy carried in a plate heaped with bass, fried potatoes, green beans, and a big chunk of Ma's good corn bread. He was beyond hungry, but he said, "Ma said I wasn't to have any supper."

"Well, she told me to bring you this." Betsy set it on the window seat.

"Then you can take it right back. I'm not hungry."

For a moment their eyes met. "Matt . . . don't," she said quietly.

"Please take it away, Betsy."

"Fine," she huffed, and shut the door hard as she left.

When it grew too dark to see the chinking, he settled in the window.

"All right, I'm coming!" Ben was hollering back to Clayton as the barn door swung closed. Matt felt resentful again: Ben should not be doing that work.

He had a powerful need to pace, but Ma would hear him, and he didn't want her to know what was in his head. Just below, Tyler fussed as he always did before sleep. And then Matt heard Ma singing:

"*Me and my wife and my wife's pap,*
 We all live down in Cumberland Gap.
 Cumberland Gap, Cumberland Gap,
 Way down yonder in Cumberland Gap . . ."

It was Papa's song—he sang it to them all when they were babies. Matt was never in his room when Tyler was going to bed, so he hadn't heard Ma sing it before, her voice muffled by the floorboards. He couldn't bear to hear it, yet he desperately wanted to. He lay on the floor to get closer to the sound, pressing his ear to a crack. With such longing, he recalled Papa tucking him and Clayton in while singing the last lines:

Lay down, boys, and take your nap,
Fourteen miles to Cumberland Gap.

He lay quiet, still swallowing his sadness, when Ma stepped in without notice. She just barely smiled, placing the lamp on the blanket chest. "What are you doing on the floor?"

He wasn't sure his voice would hold, so he didn't answer and didn't move.

"Betsy said you're not hungry."

Sitting up, he cleared his throat. "No, ma'am."

Ma dropped on the bed, looking like the weariest woman in Missouri. "Buck and the others, they're hunted under a black flag. Do you understand that?"

"Yes, ma'am," he mumbled. Of course he understood. Did she think it was news to him?

"No quarter. If they're caught, they're killed. And no one will stop to sort the guilty from the innocent." She leaned toward him and said urgently, "Do you fully understand that, Matthew? If the wrong people find you where Buck is, you will die right along with him and Jesse."

That's why I left, he wanted to say. *That's why I got away as fast as I could.* But she didn't ask his side, so he wasn't about to tell.

"Do you understand?" she repeated.

"Yes, ma'am."

"Do you know the name Jim Vaughn?"

"No, ma'am."

She raised her eyebrows. "You ought to look at Clay's newspapers on occasion. Jim Vaughn was a guerrilla, captured by soldiers in General Blunt's command. It's said Quantrill tried to negotiate an exchange of prisoners. General Blunt refused. He would rather have his own men murdered by the guerrillas than negotiate with them. *That's* what 'no quarter' means. Jim Vaughn was hanged on the twenty-ninth of May, and thousands gathered to watch."

Well, here *was* news—news nearly a month old—and he was ashamed not to know it. What, he wondered, happened to Quantrill's prisoners? He would ask Jesse. It felt so peculiar, Ma telling him war details.

After a time, Ma said, almost to herself, "Honestly, I'd like to know what goes through Zerelda's mind. How *can* she place her other children in the way of such danger?"

For Ma or Pa to speak in front of children about someone else's folks was beyond peculiar. It was unheard of. Matt sat still, hoping she'd go on.

But she came to herself and looked at him. "Sit with me, Matt," she said, patting the bed beside her, and he began to worry. Feeling foolish and young, he did as he was told. "When Buck turns up at the Samuel place, he endangers the entire family. And when you're seen with Buck, you endanger our entire family."

Matt traced a pattern on the quilt.

Then she said slowly, quietly, "Matt . . . I'm wondering if it wouldn't be best . . . if you didn't see Jesse any longer."

A strange calm came over him. He folded his arms and frowned at the floor and finally said, "Ma, please don't ask that of me."

"And if I did, would you obey?"

Her grim, determined face told him he must placate her now. He gulped down his pride. "Ma, you never even asked how I came to be where Buck was."

She looked surprised and flustered, but tried to hide both with a cool voice: "Will you not tell me?"

He had gotten the upper hand. That had never before happened with a parent, and it sure felt good. "If you want to hear it, ma'am."

"Certainly I want to hear it."

"Well, Jesse and me were fishing, and they just turned up. Buck hadn't been home for a long while, and Jesse *was* glad to see him. But I got away as soon as I could, Ma, and said no more than two words to Buck."

Ma searched his face. "Is that so, Matt?"

"Yes, ma'am, it is. And Buck won't be going back there again this season," he went on, talking fast. "I'm sure of it."

"Yes. Too busy burning railroad bridges, I suppose."

They were quiet awhile, and then Ma said, "I'm glad you walked away from it. That lets me rest a bit easier." She gave a short laugh. "It reminds me—" She cut herself off.

"What's that, Ma?"

"Oh, never mind. Something Papa said about you."

"What was it?"

She seemed doubtful. "Last night you didn't want to hear about Papa."

"Please, Ma. Tell me."

"Well . . . He said, 'Matt's not so good at spotting trouble, but he's awfully good at getting out of it.' "

He felt his face tighten up. "What'd he mean by that?"

"Oh, he meant it to be a compliment," she said quickly. "Truly. He said it proudly; you know that proud, laughing way of Papa's."

Matt knew it well enough. Still: *Not good at spotting trouble?* Did Papa think he was stupid? *But good at getting out of it.* Did Papa believe he ran from trouble instead of facing up to it? Now here was another whole piece he had to fit into his puzzled head. He sorely wished he hadn't asked.

"Truly, Matt, I wouldn't have told you if Papa meant it mean."

He forced a good-boy smile.

"Oh, I *am* glad we had this talk." Ma sighed as she stood. "It's eased my mind somewhat . . . Light the candle, Matt."

He brought the bedside candle to the lamp. "Ma? Can I go check on things?"

"Ben's taken care of all that."

"But Ma, he—"

"No, Matt," she said firmly, and he sat back on the bed. She walked to the door, then turned again. "Answer me one more question."

"Yes, Ma?"

"When you and Jesse are together, do you ever talk about going to the brush?"

He didn't hesitate. "No, ma'am."

"Good night, Matthew."

" 'Night, Ma."

Then Matt heard Ben tearing up the stairs.

Ben dived onto the bed. "You *saw* Buck?" Candlelight gleamed in his eyes. "What kind of weapon did he have?"

"You feed everyone?" Matt asked.

" 'Course I did. Who was he with? What did he say? Did he—"

"You give Salt his carrot?"

"Yes, yes, and I ain't—"

"You lock the barn?"

"Yes, and I ain't saying one more word till you tell me about Buck!"

"You put the key on the hook?"

Ben pressed his lips together and shook his head.

"All right, Ben, I'll tell you just how it was," Matt said, lying beside him. " 'Cause I want you to know I didn't *try* to be with him, and I didn't *want* to be with him."

"Tell me!" Ben said, but just then Clayton started making his way up. "Awwww." Ben groaned and flipped onto his back.

"Shhhh." Matt rolled off the bed and began to undress.

"*Aww* what?" Clayton said, closing the door. "*Shhh* what?"

"Matt was just about to tell me about Buck," Ben admitted as he got up to change. "But he won't do it with you here!"

Clayton gave a sharp laugh and sat on the bed. "Get my nightshirt, Ben, would you?" He dropped his crutches. "Go ahead, Matt, tell it."

"All right, I will. Then you'll *both* know it wasn't my fault, nor Jesse's either. It was the day I caught those cats—"

"I knew it," Clayton said. "I knew something was up when you came home."

"We were just sitting there fishing, and all of a sudden the devil's coming down on us. Two men drag Jesse into the creek. Another pushes my head down so I can't see. But I can *hear* them, asking Jess where Buck is, holding him under till he chokes, and then doing it again."

"Jesse tell?" Ben's eyes were wide.

"Blast it, Ben, Jesse doesn't know where Buck goes."

Clayton studied him with knitted brows. "What were *you* doing?"

"Eating dirt, that's what. I'm calling to Jess, he's calling to me—"

"And then Buck came to the rescue?" Ben said eagerly.

"Sure, Buck came all right. Came out of the woods and told the rest that was enough. He was trying Jesse out, see. To find if Jesse'd tell anything to Federals."

"Ah!" Ben threw up his hands.

"That Buck," Clayton said, deadpan. "Always the joker. So what'd Jesse do?"

"Sloshed out of the water and jumped up in Buck's arms."

Clayton shook his head, smirking.

"And that was the whole of it, Clay. Here's the words I said to Buck: 'Hey, Buck.' Here's the words Buck said to me: 'Hey, Matt.' And I picked up my catfish and came right home and no, Ben, I did not see his weapon, nor anyone else's."

"Awww."

"And I did not tell Mama this whole story. You hear me, Ben?"

"Yes, I hear. You think I'm deaf?" Ben climbed over him and got into bed.

Clayton was rubbing his chin. "You said Jesse doesn't know where Buck goes."

"That's right."

"Then why would Buck see the need to have him roughed up that way?"

Matt didn't answer.

"Truth is, you have no idea what Jesse knows and doesn't know. Do you?"

Still he said nothing.

"Jesse's on the grapevine, Matt," Clayton said in an ominous tone. "Don't fool yourself about that."

Matt wished he'd never told a word of it, and he couldn't believe Clayton was saying all this in front of Ben. Then Clay gave Ben a nudge. "And you'd better know by now to keep to yourself what you hear in these four walls."

"Yes, Clay," Ben said, his voice ghostly soft.

Clayton pinched out the candle and lay down. Matt sat a bit longer, pondering Clayton's words. His stomach growled loud and clear, and they all laughed.

"Matt, you were so dumb not to eat that supper," Ben said.

"I know," he admitted, and his stomach complained again. "Uh, I guess I'll sleep on the tick." After a while he asked, "Clayton? Ben asleep yet?"

"Yes."

"She oughtn't to have done it, Clay. Put me in my room like that. I'm too old. And Ben doing my work, it ain't right. Papa told *me* to close up, he said it's *my* responsibility. She oughtn't to treat me like a little boy."

"You tell Mama all that?" Clayton asked.

"No."

"Am I the one who put you in your room?"

Matt made no reply.

"You're so grown up, why don't you learn how to talk to her?"

Matt turned to the wall, the breeze cooling his face. By the time he spoke again, he wasn't sure Clayton was still awake to hear: "Well, I don't believe I'll stand for it again."

15

"What do you think, sir?" Matt called out.

Approaching through the hip-high stalks, Mr. Stone raised his arms above his head. "What do I think? Boy, I think you do your papa proud!"

Matt was so pleased he wanted to laugh. "Yes, sir, it's not a bad start, is it?"

"This is no *start*, boy! It's a crop, and it's a fine one!"

"Thank you, sir. But isn't the corn generally taller by the tag end of June?"

"Every crop is different, son, every growing season its own. You can't compare them one to the other. We had a late start this year, and it's been a bit dry."

"Yes, sir, it has."

"You have plenty of plowing yet to do."

"Oh, I know that, sir." Matt surveyed the fields, nodding.

"But you've done it, boy. You've done it!" He slapped Matt's back. "Now come on and show me those pigs!"

In the barn lot, they leaned on the pen rail. The pigs were asleep, one atop the other. "They're looking good, too," Mr. Stone said. "Big and fat."

"Yes, sir."

"Imagine your pa, all those years, not raising any hogs! *Stubborn* man, your pa!"

"Yes, sir." Matt was smiling so hard his face hurt. He stepped up on the lower rail and jumped down, again and again.

" 'Dave, for the love of God, why don't you keep hogs?' I'd say. 'Don't like 'em,' he says. 'You don't *have* to like 'em, just *raise* 'em!' I'd say. 'Don't want 'em,' he says."

Matt was laughing now. Papa had told it about the same way.

" 'Raising hogs is the cheapest and simplest thing on a farm!' I'd say. 'What better way to get your corn to market than wrapped in pigskin?' And he says, 'Don't like 'em, don't want 'em on my place.' "

" 'Just like to eat 'em,' " Matt finished, and they laughed together. "But I don't suppose Pa'd mind my having them."

"Nor do I. Because he'd want you to go your own way. Right?"

"Right, sir," Matt said, nodding slowly.

"Well, boy, I'll leave you to it." They started up the lane. "Your ma's up to my place drinking tea, so I thought I'd walk down and throw you my two cents."

"I'm always glad to have it, sir."

"The woods," Mr. Stone said after a while. "They're alive at night."

"I know, sir. I see the fires."

"A hundred circling camps," Mr. Stone muttered. He patted Matt's shoulder. "Go careful, Matt."

"Yes, sir. I will."

Mr. Stone waved, and Matt watched him go. How strange it seemed to be so old, and walk so slow, and see the world through such bleary eyes. But Mr. Stone was still sharp enough, though a little hard of hearing.

Matt walked back to the house. "Betsy!" he called from the lean-to.

She rushed toward him, hissing, "*Shhh!* If you wake Tyler, you'll look after him!"

"I will not," he said cheerfully, following her out. "Where's everybody?"

"Molly's with Ma, I have no idea where Clay is, and Ma let Ben go to Tim Hart's." At the outdoor oven, Betsy slid a loaf onto a breadboard.

"I thought I'd go hunt up some supper. What do you care for, Betsy? Fowl? Fish? Squirrel?"

She eyed him suspiciously. "Are you feeling all right?"

"I'm just dandy. No preference, then?"

"Mmm . . . fowl."

"All right. A slice of that bread for a promise of fowl?"

"Well, you'd best enjoy it," she said. "It's the end of the flour, with no money for more, Ma said." Holding a cloth on one end of the loaf, she cut him a chunk. Steam rose, followed by the mouthwatering aroma of fresh light bread.

"Thank you, miss." He waved the bread to cool it, then held it in his teeth as he headed to the pasture for Salt.

On a day like this, the sun so bright and the crop so fine, he could almost forget there was a war and the threat of leaving home. As for flour, who cared? Ma's corn bread was just as good.

Matt thought he would shoot for a prairie chicken, but out there nothing was moving but the tall grass, its bright red haze of Indian paintbrush rustled by a light breeze. He kept Salt still and looked around. There was no point in getting down. Then he heard shots and saw three figures way down at the edge of the woods.

They were boys, not soldiers, but who? When he got to their horses and saw July, his mood darkened. A little closer, and there were Scott Moore and Sam Wright.

Matt had never been able to get along with those two. They thought they were rougher than everybody else. They talked louder. They were always playing the fool. And they wanted to be best friends with Jesse.

Still, they and Matt had managed to stay somewhat civil over the years. But ever since the war started, Scott and Sam would light into him whenever they got the chance, because he wasn't allowed to take sides.

He told himself to turn right around, but instead he rode up.

Jesse and Scott had shotguns, and Sam was holding the dead Federal's revolver.

"Hey, Jess," Matt called.

"Hey." Jesse walked to him with a guilty-looking grin. "What're you up to?"

"Hoping to bag supper, but you three scared it all away."

Jesse laughed uneasily and scratched Salt's neck. "They came for me to shoot target practice. I'd have come by your place, but"—he shrugged—"*you* prefer to shoot food."

Matt nodded, looking away.

Jesse tugged at the stirrup. "Come on down."

Slowly Matt dismounted, took his gun, and tied Salt.

Sure enough, Sam started right in: "Better quit talking about the war, Scott."

"Why's that, Sam?" Scott asked, making believe he didn't see Matt.

" 'Cause look who's here."

Scott turned. "Oh! It's Jesse's little half-and-half friend."

"Matt Coward," Sam said, and they brayed like a pair of jackasses.

"Shut up," Jesse said evenly, taking the revolver. "Don't call him that." He fired into the woods.

"Don't call him what?" Scott said. "Coward, or half-and-half?"

"Or little?" Sam added, laughing more.

"I said, shut your mouth." Jesse turned slowly, leveling the gun right at Scott. Matt didn't so much as breathe. The very first time Pa put a gun in his hands, he said you never, ever, loaded or not, aim it at a person unless you're fixing to shoot him.

"Don't point that goddamn thing at me, Jess!" Scott hollered, striding up to the muzzle. "What in hell are you playing at?"

Jesse let his arm fall. "Ah, I was only fooling."

"That ain't no way to fool, so don't do it again," Scott said, coming still closer to Jesse, whose whole face stormed up.

"Don't tell me what to do, Scott," he said with his steely glare. "I don't much care for it."

"I'll tell you whatever I want!"

Jesse dropped the revolver. Matt let his gun fall, and so did Scott. Just as Jesse threw a punch at Scott, Sam pitched into Matt, bringing him down with a bone-jarring crash. Matt couldn't even swing once before Sam was kneeling on him, crushing his head and punching his ribs.

Matt saw Jesse and Scott standing over them. "Say 'enough,' Matt!" Jesse hollered, but Matt wouldn't, and Sam kept hitting him till he couldn't draw breath.

Finally Sam just stopped. "Oh, the hell with you. *I* say you've had enough." And he sat on the grass, breathing hard.

Matt lay still, his ribs and his pride hurting so much he didn't care to face anyone. When he did push against the ground to sit up, his left eye felt sore. Blood dripped onto the grass.

"Let's go, Sam." Scott held his hand to his nose.

Good. Jesse had made him bleed.

Sam got to his feet. "So long, Jess."

"See you, Jess," Scott grumbled.

"All right," Jesse said. He leaned in to look at Matt's eye, and made a face. "Might be a rock cut you. The way he had you down . . ."

Matt raised his sleeve to blot the blood, but blood stained clothing, and Ma would kill him for it. So he pulled up a bunch of prairie grass instead.

"Does it pain you much?"

"No. My ribs hurt prodigiously, though." They laughed, but Matt stopped short, grimacing. "Lucky I didn't get my throat cut with a Bowie knife."

"Oh, they ain't so tough. You saw they skedaddled pretty quick at the sight of blood. Doggone it, Matt, why didn't you say 'enough'? Scott said 'enough.' "

He didn't answer.

"You got to know when you're beat, boy."

Matt picked more grass and bunched it to his eye.

"Better come to my place. Let Pappy see to it."

"No," Matt said firmly. There was no chance he'd let Susie see him this way—bloodstained, beat to rags by Sam Wright.

"Then you ought to get home."

Jesse started to stand, but Matt said quietly, "Hey, Jess."

In reply, Jesse sat down again, as though he knew what was coming. Matt took a slow, deep breath. "I'd rather not be stood up for that way again."

"You mean—" Jesse made his hand into a pistol and pointed it at Matt.

"Yeah. I mean that. You know better."

"Don't schoolteacher me, Matt," Jesse snapped, jumping up to retrieve the revolver.

Matt threw down the bloody clump of grass and pulled more.

Then Jesse said grudgingly, "Well, you're right. Let's go."

Riding home, Matt was furious he'd said nothing—not a word—to Scott and Sam. Not to get one punch in, that was the worst shame of all. Why had he even ridden over to them? He should have declined when Jesse said to get down. Then Jesse wouldn't have had to defend him again—and Matt wouldn't be troubled about that blasted revolver. It almost felt like his fault, Jesse's pointing that gun. And now here he was, coming back whipped and supperless.

He tied Salt and went right to the pump to scrub his face.

"What happened to *you*?" came Clayton's voice.

"I got myself on the wrong end of a fight. Don't tell Ma."

Clayton inspected his face. "Guess what? She'll see for herself."

"Is it bad?"

"Not too. It's not bleeding. Don't *touch* it."

Matt drew his hand back.

"So . . . You tangle with Jesse?"

"Jesse and me don't fight, Clay."

"Well, then? Betsy said you went to shoot fowl."

"I did. But Jess was out there with Scott Moore and Sam Wright, shooting at nothing. And those two started right in calling me names."

Clayton nodded. "Who'd you go with?"

"Sam, if you could call it a go. I think he broke every rib I own."

"I noticed."

"And neither you nor Ma can think I'm any more a fool than I think myself," he went on. "A fool for going down there instead of tending to my own business, a fool for fighting, and a fool for getting beat."

"Did *you* start the fight?"

"No. That would be Jesse. But he was just standing up for me because I'm too much a fool to stand up for myself."

"Matt," Clayton said mildly.

"Well, I am. And that's the way of it."

"What'd they call you, anyway?"

Matt hesitated, then mumbled, " 'Half-and-half.' " He tapped his chest. " 'Matt Coward.' That's what you get when you don't take a side."

Clayton frowned. "I don't see them going off to fight."

"They will, though, Clay." Matt turned away, kicking at the dirt. "They will."

16

"It's like Christmas!" Molly clutched a wrapped present to her chest.

"Let's see . . . This says 'for Betsy.' Here's one for Ben . . . Matt . . . Clayton." As Ma pulled parcels from the box, she tossed aside the newspaper packing.

Yankee newspapers! For the first time, Matt had a desire to

look at a paper, and at the same time, he dreaded it. His present was long and heavy and flat, tied with red ribbon.

"Wonder what's in there." He nodded at Clayton's thick rectangular package.

Clay grinned, shaking it next to his ear. "Hmmm. I can't imagine."

"Here, darling." Ma handed a package to Tyler, who tore at the colorful wrapping. A carved gray horse with a real mane and tail stood on four small wheels. Its saddle was tooled leather. Tyler began to chew a red wooden knob at the end of a long rope that hung from the bridle.

Matt's package held a leather case that snapped open. Inside was a hunting knife, the like of which he'd never seen. It had a gleaming blade, a carved-wood handle, and a leather sheath with an engraved brass tip. He turned it over and over, sliding it into the sheath and out again. He ran his thumb along the blade so carefully, but still a thin line marked his skin, and then a trace of blood. This was just the knife he needed for deer. But where would he be when the cold weather came?

"Oh, my," Ma said, standing over him. "Isn't *that* something."

"What is it?" Ben asked. "Whoa! Look at that!"

Matt put the knife away fast. "What'd you get, Ben?"

"A book," Ben said, making his eyes go wide, and Matt almost laughed. "And a ball. Here." He handed Matt a small, sewn-up, hide-bound ball. "What is it again, Ma?"

"Mother says it's for a game called baseball. Boys play it back East. Men, too."

"A game?" Matt tossed the ball up and caught it.

"You throw the ball toward a person holding a stick called a bat. The person with the bat tries to hit the ball."

"Kind of like how we do with rotten apples," Matt said to Ben, returning the ball.

"With a few more rules, it seems," Ma added.

Molly cradled a dressed-up china doll. "She's beautiful, Moll," Matt said.

"Yes. I'll call her Peggy," Molly said in a dreamy whisper.

"What's *that*, Betsy?" Ben asked, just as Matt smelled something strange.

"It's perfume," Betsy said importantly. She held a tiny blue bottle. "Patchouli."

"Smells like something under a heap of moss in the woods," Ben said.

Matt laughed with him. "You have to rub that stink *on* yourself?"

"Mama!" Betsy protested.

"Boys." Ma was wrapping a many-colored shawl around her shoulders.

"That's lovely, Ma," Betsy said.

"What do you call that?" Matt asked. "That . . . fabric?"
Betsy snorted at his ignorance.

"It's silk," Ma said, leaning toward him and Ben. "Here. Feel."

"That's the softest thing I ever touched," Ben said.

"Now I know why they say 'corn silk,'" Matt said, and Ma gave him a gentle smile.

Clayton had been silent. Matt turned to see him absorbed in a book, his brow knitted, his thumb rubbing and rubbing his chin.

"*Isn't* that darling!" Betsy said, as Molly showed Tyler how to pull the horse.

But the little toy made Matt so melancholy he had to look away, and he stretched out on the floor with his arm for a pillow.

"All right," Ma said brightly. "Now we'll all write letters to thank your grandparents. Young ones first, while I put Tyler to bed."

Ben and Molly went to the table. Matt took some balled-up newspapers and smoothed them out as quietly as he could. There were long lists, all starting with "Wanted." "Wanted: Apprentice machine hands." "Young man to fit glasses in spectacle frames." "Assistant for apothecary store." "Boy, to learn engraving." And on and on. There sure was plenty of work to be had in Philadelphia, but nothing Matt would ever care to do. Auctions, houses for sale, long columns of advertising: "Schenck's Seaweed Tonic." "Bonnets & Hats." "Fresh Minced Meats." "Jayne's Expectorant." "Ladies' and Children's Fancy Furs" . . . Children's fancy furs? *There* was a revolting notion.

Then he came to the front page of a paper called the *Philadelphia Inquirer*, dating back to the middle of May. The headlines read:

GEN'L "STONEWALL" JACKSON DIES OF CHANCELLORSVILLE WOUND

ARM AMPUTATED BELOW SHOULDER——DEVELOPS PNEUMONIA

MISTAKENLY SHOT BY HIS OWN TROOPS

HIS WIFE AND CHILD ARE AT HIS SIDE AS HE EXPIRES

Matt's heart pounded to read it told this way—noble North, treacherous South, and wasn't the Union fortunate to be rid of so formidable a foe as General Jackson. He resolved once again not to go up North, and yet . . . what would he be leaving Ben to face alone? Men who hit a ball with a stick. And Tyler, dragging a silly wooden horse around some grand house, would he ever ride a snorting, sweating one across a broad prairie?

"What're you reading, Clay?" he asked, talking in order to stop thinking.

"It's called *A Tale of Two Cities*. By an English writer, Charles Dickens."

"Oh. What's it about?"

Clayton looked up. "Well, it's about the French Revolution."

"When they were cutting everybody's heads off?"

"Right," Clayton said, chuckling. "I've been wanting to read this book."

"How do you suppose they knew to send it?"

"I imagine Ma told them what we like."

Matt handed his knife to Clayton, who examined it carefully.

"Yes, I'd say it's a fair bet Mama told them what we like," Clayton said, returning the knife as they laughed. "Here. Let me read you the beginning."

"All right." Matt shut his eyes, folding his hands behind his head.

Clay's voice was steady and soothing:

"It was the best of times, it was the worst of times, it was the age of wisdom, it was the age of foolishness, it was

the epoch of belief, it was the epoch of incredulity, it was the season of Light, it was the season of Darkness, it was the spring of hope, it was the winter of despair, we had everything before us, we had nothing before us, we were all going direct to Heaven, we were all going direct the other way."

Matt let the words rest awhile. "I like the sound of it. How it goes best and worst, hope and despair, everything and nothing . . . You sure that's not about our war, Clay?" he asked, and Clayton smiled a little sadly. Matt held out the front page. Clay took it, glanced at it, and looked at him with arched eyebrows. Then he started reading in earnest, and didn't see Matt anymore.

"Matt, Betsy, your turn to write."

Matt stood. Betsy was holding something called *Godey's Lady's Book*, with drawings of women in dresses. "You got that, too?" he asked. "*And* perfume? And to think all I got was one old knife."

"Now, Matthew, don't be envious," Ma scolded.

"He's taunting me, Ma," Betsy explained, and Ma laughed at her mistake.

Ben was hunched over the table, staring at his book. "See here, Matt," he whispered, looking stricken. Matt leaned close. The book was called *Helps Over Hard Places*. A colored picture showed groups of boys in two sailboats. The boys wore fancy suits, and curls stuck out from under foolish ribboned caps. They shook their fists in anger. One boat flew the Stars and Stripes, the other the Stars and Bars.

"What are you two looking so glum about?" Ma asked cheerily.

"Mama, just *look* at this!" Ben said, offended, sliding the book to her.

She examined the picture, then burst out giggling.

"What is it, Ma?" Betsy said.

Ma handed her the book. "I don't suppose I could get either of these two into an outfit like that!" she said, and Betsy joined her in laughter.

"But Ma," Ben persisted. "Give it here, Betsy." He tapped the picture. "Is that what the war is to boys up North, Ma? Is it?"

Matt saw that Clayton was paying attention now.

"Boys," Ma said firmly. "Children back East are having an entirely different war than you are. There's absolutely no question about it. However"—she rubbed Ben's hair—"I don't think the boys are all out on boats in suits, either."

"But, Ma, do you still want to go up North?" Ben asked.

"Ben," Matt scolded.

Pa, or even Ma not long ago, would have told him not to question his elders, and Matt couldn't believe it when Ma answered: "My folks are there if we need them. Whether we'll go remains to be seen." Ben breathed a dramatic sigh of relief. "Brush your teeth," Ma said. "Matt . . ." She tapped the paper before him; he was to write on the back of Ben's page. "Dear Grandmother and Grandfather," Ma prompted, then went upstairs with Molly.

Matt dipped his pen in the pokeberry ink, feeling sick to his stomach. He had been so glad to finish his final school composition last spring. Now not only did he have to write, but to these grandparents he didn't know. He tried to make his letters neat and clean, but he always *did* smudge the ink.

"Dang," he said, and Betsy slid a blotter across the table. "That's not going to help any, it's already messed up."

"Maybe it will help *next* time," she said in a humoring way.

Thunder rumbled in the distance. "Clay, what shall I write?"

"Whatever you like." Clayton had his face in the Philadelphia papers.

Matt wrote "Thank," but when he got to "you," Betsy called out, *"Matthew!"* It startled him so, he smeared the *y*. "Stop bouncing your knee!"

"How in the world is that bothering you?"

"You're shaking the table and I can't write!"

"Matthew, Elizabeth," Ma said, coming down the stairs.

"Is this good, Ma?" Betsy asked.

Ma read over her shoulder. "Very nice, dear."

"*Thank* you, Ma." Betsy gave Matt a simpering smile and left the table.

He looked out the window. It was too dark to see rain. Clayton sat beside him with a new sheet of paper and started at once. Matt wrote slowly until his note read:

July 2nd 1863
Dear Grandmother and Grandfather,
    Thank you for the knife. It is nice and I am glad to have it.

He glowered at the page, drumming his fingers.

"Maaatt," Clayton complained.

Ma stood behind Matt. "What have you so far?"

His face burned to have her see his words and his smeared writing, knowing this would be her parents' first glimpse of him. They'd think he was slow and stupid, uneducated, just as they'd thought Papa.

"Can't you think of any more to say?" Ma asked gently.

"Such as what, ma'am?" Now the rain beat the roof hard.

"Oh, words such as 'I am sure to make good use of it.' "

"Can I write that?" The thunder was loud and close. Salt didn't like thunder, and Matt was anxious to get to him.

Ma made an amused sound. "All right, Matt. Then sign it 'Your grandson, Matthew.' Or Matt, if you prefer."

"Yes, ma'am." He wrote the words fast. "There!"

He ran for the barn, tilting his face to feel the warm rain. Lightning cracked the sky. If he was lucky it would rain all night, and all day tomorrow.

17

Jesse and Susie clanked into the lane, buckets hooked on their saddles. Ben rushed to greet them, but Matt hung back, peeking from the window.

"Hey, Jess! Howdy, Sue!" Ben called, swinging on the gate.

"Hello, Ben!" Susie sang out as she brought her horse up.

She rode like a boy, her stockings showing right up her legs.

Matt couldn't help but smile. Did her ma know she was still riding that way? He thought he'd like to just stand here and watch her, in secret, for hours. She looked so nice, wearing no bonnet, her hair shining in the sun.

"Where's Matt?" Jesse said. His voice—surly, almost—turned Matt's head. Jesse wore no trace of a smile.

Ben waved a hand. "Oh, he's indoors . . . Susie, I haven't seen you since school finished."

"Will you ride with us?" she asked. "We'll pick some berries, too."

"You bet! I'll just ask Ma." He darted past Matt in the lean-to.

Matt went out slowly, hands in his pockets, sure he looked awkward and stupid, sure he'd stumble over his words. "Hello, Susie. Hey, Jess."

"Hello, Matt." She tucked some hair behind her ear.

"I wanted to ride with you," Jesse said. "But Ma said I had to take *her* along."

"Why?" Matt said, and then he wanted to kill himself.

"Huh!" Susie pretended to take offense, tossing her head dramatically.

"I only meant—"

"Protection," Jesse said, dropping his voice. "Ma says it ain't safe for boys alone in the woods now."

"What?" Matt asked, puzzled.

"Matt, you want to go or not? Let Ben come. They can play and we can ride."

"Play," Susie said scornfully. "You're not to ride away from me, Jess. Ma said."

Ben flew past, heading for the barn. "Ma says all right!"

Riding down the lane at a walk, Susie and Ben fell behind, chattering away. Matt wondered if he'd get to talk to Susie alone. Would he act normal, or just make a fool of himself? What would they have to say to each other? Why had she come, anyway? What was this about needing a girl along?

"I didn't get your meaning," he said to Jesse. "About protection."

"Matt. Why is it the wife who goes to the door at night?" Jesse asked with forced patience.

"Because they won't shoot her."

"So if a boy's got his sister along . . ."

"Oh."

"You know, sometimes you're slow as a pollen-packed bumblebee."

Matt didn't reply. What was this dark mood? Would Jesse feel better if he could talk about the war? "Jess? What do you know about Jim Vaughn?"

Jesse gave a short, sharp laugh. "What do *you* know about Jim Vaughn?"

"Only what my ma told me, which ain't much."

"Matt, it's a mighty sad state of affairs when a fifteen-year-old boy knows less about this doggone war than his mama."

"I intend to follow the proceedings from here on."

"Right," Jesse said sarcastically. "So, what'd your ma say about Jim Vaughn?"

Matt told how Ma had found out about Buck, and how she'd slapped him, and about the Bible, and finished with her story of Jim Vaughn.

"Your mama left off the tag end!" Jesse's voice was false-cheerful, with a hard edge. "And the tag end of this *particular* story happens to be the best part. Right before they hung him, Jim Vaughn swore vengeance on Blunt and all his men. He said, 'For every guerrilla you kill, my friends will kill ten Federals.' A couple weeks later, the guerrillas raided Westport. The Feds had forty killed, no wounded. After the fight, they found one of their dead with a note between his teeth. It said: 'Remember the dying words of Jim Vaughn.'"

A shiver crawled right down Matt's back. He said nothing.

"They give no quarter?" Jesse continued. "We give it back tenfold."

"What happened to Quantrill's prisoners?" Matt asked as they left the road.

"He let them go. Because they were honorable men, he said."

Matt just gave him a skeptical look.

Jesse shrugged. "Follow the proceedings, like you said. You'll find that's the truth."

They splashed across the stream. "That disturbs me," Jesse said, "your ma knowing about Buck and them. How *did* she?"

"Uh . . . I didn't think it judicious to ask, Jess."

"There was nobody in the woods," Jesse said, more to himself than to Matt. "So somebody saw us leave my place. Then saw me come back with Buck." He paused, eyes fixed on the distance. "Dan Askew?"

"Slowpokes." Susie and Ben rode around them. To Ben, she said in a deep voice, "They're having a serious parley," and the two laughed and trotted ahead.

"Stay near, Ben," Matt called, and Ben waved back.

"And another thing." Jesse nudged Salt with July. "Why is it when people cite the Bible on war, they always quote Isaiah? Do you know the Book of Joel, Matt?"

"No, but I daresay I'm about to."

"The Book of Joel says it just the opposite: Turn your plow-shares into swords and your pruninghooks into spears. Just like in Ecclesiastes: To everything there is a season. And one season is for war. A time for war and a time for peace, that's what it says. And there's a verse in Joel I want to show you, Matt. I won't try to recite it because I won't do it just right. But when we go home, let's stop by my place so I can show you."

"Lord," Matt mumbled, "isn't it enough I got preaching this morning?"

Jesse laughed and dug his heels into July. "Let's catch those scalawags."

The blackberry brambles brimmed ripe fruit. The boys beat at the shrubs with sticks to scare off snakes; then they all fell to picking along the edges. Berries never tasted so good as they did right off the vine, sun-warmed: It meant one in the bucket, two in the mouth.

"You folks celebrate yesterday?" Ben asked.

"Sure," Jesse said. "I rode down to Liberty with my Seces-sion flag, shouting huzzahs for General Price and President Jeff Davis."

"Really, Jess?" Ben said eagerly.

"Yep. Then six men carried me home . . . in a pine box," Jesse answered, and Matt had to laugh along.

Ben should have known better than to ask. No sane person celebrated the Fourth these last two summers. Best to keep your mouth shut and your head down.

"My head is frying like sausage," Susie announced.

"Here, Sue," Ben said, putting his hat on her.

She pressed her hands to her heart. "Why, Ben, what chivalry!"

"Ben, you shouldn't give yours up. It's her own fault," Jesse said. "Who ever heard of a girl going out without a bonnet?"

"I hate bonnets," Susie said. "I like feeling the wind in my hair when I ride."

"You are just a tomboy," Jesse teased.

"I am not!" She shot a glance at Matt and threw a berry at her brother. Jesse whipped one back, and they all started firing berries. Ben pelted only Susie, until she dropped her bucket and pinned him down, tickling him till he howled.

"Susie, you're too big for that," Jesse said with solemn disapproval. "Get off him now or I'll tell Ma."

"Oh, Jess, you stick-in-the-mud," she complained, sitting up. "What's your view, Matt? Do you think it's all right?"

They were her first words to him since "hello." He stammered, "Well—no. *I* don't know."

She flung a berry at him, and he caught it. "Anyone'd think I'd know better than ask you to side against *him*."

Matt tossed the berry back. Their eyes met, and he felt a sudden jolt that spread down right through him. He smiled a little, and she smiled back, then both turned away. Something had happened.

"I'm all thorn-scratched," Ben said. "Let's go to the creek."

"We can't *swim*." Jesse nodded at his sister.

"We can wade," Ben said.

"Yes, let's." Susie smoothed her skirt as she stood. "Do *you* want to, Matt?"

"Sure," he said, and watched her mount her horse.

Now she fell back to ride beside him, and Ben started talking guerrillas with Jesse. Matt knew he shouldn't allow it, but right at this very moment he just didn't care.

"Buck told what he did to you and Jesse," Susie said. "Jess said he wasn't much scared, which I don't believe. Of course he *will* say that in front of Buck's friends."

"Well, *I* sure was scared."

"Will you go to Quantrill, too, Matt?"

With Ben, it was all laughing and joking. To Matt, she talked bushwhacking. Did that family think of nothing else?

"Don't know," he mumbled. Maybe he didn't want to be with her, after all.

"Your corn tassel yet?" she asked brightly, and he nearly laughed: That was a quick change of subject, and a strange choice for a girl.

"Not just yet, miss, but I thank you for asking."

"You raising it on your own?"

"Ben helps."

"I'll bet," she said, giggling. "He's so *sweet*, though. But I suppose that runs in your family."

Their eyes met, and this time neither looked away.

"Susie!" Jesse called back. "Ben wants to hear that song of Buck's, the one they sing like 'Roving Gambler.' "

"All right, you start."

Jesse sang:

"Oh I'm a roving guerrilla, I ride from town to town,
And when I spy a pretty girl, so willingly I get down."

Susie said, "Then the girl sings:

"I'll bundle up my clothing, with my true love by my
side,
And I'll rove this wide world over and be a guerrilla's
bride."

"Susie wants a guerrilla husband, don't you, Sue?" Jesse taunted. "Maybe that yellow-haired boy."

"Shut up, Jess!" she snapped. "I do not."

"You sure were making eyes at him!"

"I sure *wasn't!*" Her cheeks were crimson. "It was him doing the flirting!"

"He was, at that," Jesse admitted, turning to Ben. "You should've seen Aunt Lotty shoo that fellow away from her! Ma and Pappy were killing themselves laughing!"

"At least I wasn't strutting to show them how tough I was," Susie said, glaring at her brother.

"When we had Quantrill men to breakfast, I got whipped just for talking to one," Ben piped up.

"You *did*, Ben?" Susie said. "Matt didn't whip you, did you, Matt?"

"Nope."

"It was Clay," Ben said. "And it was ferocious, wasn't it, Matt?"

"Yep."

"Matt's getting irate," Jesse announced. They rode in silence the rest of the way.

Susie pushed up her sleeves, tore off her shoes and stockings, and dashed into the creek. Ben was right behind. Matt and Jesse skipped stones.

"Ben tells me you got something from your grandpappy the other day," Jesse said.

"I did." Why couldn't Ben let him tell his own news in his own time? "You want to see?" He opened his saddlebag and handed Jesse the knife.

Susie and Ben splashed each other merrily. She took his hat from her head and put it on his. She leaped from rock to rock on tiptoe, holding up her skirts. She didn't much look like a tomboy at all.

"You got all *kinds* of Yankees trying to buy you for the Union."

Matt snapped his head around. Jesse held out the knife.

"It ain't like that," Matt said, taking the knife.

"No?"

"He's my grandfather." Matt shut the knife up in its case. "He's just being kind."

"I wonder how kind he'll be when he finds he's got a Secesh grandson." Jesse sat to pull off his boots. "When are you going?"

"I never said I *was*."

"Well, I asked Ma if you could stay at our place, and she said yes."

"Dang, Jesse! I said not to tell your ma!"

"Ma can keep a confidence," he said sullenly, rolling his pants.

"And I wish you'd quit talking to Ben about Quantrill."

"Where's the harm in it?"

"The harm is to my individual self if my ma finds out, that's where."

Jesse laughed and went sloshing into the water.

An old willow tree stretched thick branches over the creek. Matt took a notion to get up into it. He couldn't reach the lowest limb, so he got a rope from his saddlebag. Jesse and Ben were going on about guns, ambushes, and skirmishes. Matt tossed the rope, pulled it down and made a slip knot, then yanked it tight. He rubbed his palms on his pants, grabbed hold of the rope, climbed the tree trunk, and slid onto the branch. His blood was racing, since he knew Susie might be watching. He worried he'd mess up and look like a fool. Now he saw she *was* watching, her face turned up, eyes sparkling. She returned to gathering watercress.

"And I already told Ma I won't go," Ben was saying. "I won't live in no Northern state."

"Oh, yeah? What'll you do, Ben?" Jesse teased.

"I'll go and join Quantrill!"

"If you go to Quantrill, you got to take his oath. You ready for that?"

"You know the oath?" Ben's glee spilled into his words. "What is it?"

"Well, he brings you apart from everybody else. And then he asks you only this question: 'Will you follow orders, be true to your fellows, and kill those who serve and support the Union?' And if you say 'I will,' then you're a Quantrill man."

"Whoa! I'll say it, Jess! *You* will, won't you?"

"Quantrill takes no crybabies," Matt called down. "I can just hear you, Ben: 'Oh, Captain, I'm too tired for picket duty tonight,' " he said in a high voice.

Susie tipped her head back, frowning at him.

"Shut up, Matt," Ben barked, then stomped up the creek.

"Well, you shut up about Quantrill!" Matt shot back. "I'm dog-tired of hearing it!"

Susie went after Ben, and Jesse squinted up at Matt. "You're a ray of sunshine today, boy," he said with half a grin, and started downstream alone.

Catching Ben's hand, Susie pulled him to her. They swung arms as they waded. She tickled his face with her watercress. He laughed, and she popped some into his mouth.

Jealousy and anger flooded through Matt. Never again would he let Ben come along. Then he could just about hear Papa saying it: *Oh, quit feeling sorry for yourself.*

Susie and Ben sat on rocks, his outstretched palm resting in hers. *Now* what were they doing? A purposeful splashing caught Matt's ear, and Jesse stopped abruptly.

"Matt, one question."

"What?" Matt said wearily.

"That grandpappy of yours. What's he do up North?"

"You mean his business?"

"Yes. Does he make anything to try and help them whip us?"

"I don't—I don't know what he does," Matt stammered. How had he not thought to ask? A rich Northerner, a big city—how *did* he get his money?

"Well, that just beats all." Jesse started splashing away again.

"Hey!" Matt shouted. Jesse stopped. "You've been picking a fight every inch of this afternoon. Calling me dumb, at me about Ma's father, like he's some kind of my fault, at me about Yankees buying me. You tell your ma what I said not to, you keep talking to my brother about bushwhackers. *I'm* a ray of sunshine? What're *you* all stormed up about? That's what I want to know."

They just stared at each other, and Matt didn't know who was more astonished. He had never spoken to Jesse with such unbridled anger.

Jesse blinked a few times, then disappeared downstream.

18

Matt lay along the branch, watching the water. It struck him that the creek flowed this way all the time, whether he was in a tree or on the ground, whether he was here to watch or back at home. Whether he was three miles away at home or a hundred miles away in a guerrilla band or a thousand miles away in the North, the water would run like this. And when he next came back, it would be here still, running the same way.

He closed his eyes. Crows were haw-hawing, water gently rushing, cardinals singing *purty, purty, purty,* willow leaves swishing, and the air smelled hot and damp and sweet. These things would always be, and he could take them wherever he went . . . just as Betsy said she took Papa.

"Matt, you're right in everything you say." Jesse was on the bank, putting on his socks. "I've a lot on my mind, but it's no excuse. I haven't been much of a friend today."

"That's all right, Jess. Come on up. Tell what's on your mind."

"All right, let me get my boots on."

But just then, Susie and Ben raced downstream, breathless with laughter. Susie grabbed the rope and started scrambling up, shoeless and all.

"Susie, I'm going up to talk with Matt," Jesse said sternly.

"Not if I get there first!" She was out of his reach before he made it to the tree.

"You little squirrel," Jesse said, but with admiration.

Susie hopped to the next branch and lay facing Matt, so close he could see the berry stains on her lips. What was she thinking? What should he say?

"No more talk about you-know-who," came Jesse's voice.

"Aww, Matt's a pain," Ben replied.

"It ain't him, it's your ma," Jesse said firmly. "And I need to respect her wishes." Their voices faded downstream.

Now the day was as it should have been. He and Jesse were

all right, and it was him Susie had chosen to be with. But he dared not look at her. She peeled off a willow shoot and tickled his face with it. He felt himself blushing. How could she be so bold?

"Matt, recall how you and Jesse would talk about seeing the Rocky Mountains?"

"I do." It seemed an odd topic, but no more so than corn tassels.

"And recall you two telling me I couldn't go? Making me so mad? Hmm?" She tickled him again.

Embarrassed, he turned his face, laughing.

"Anyhow, do you still want to go there?"

"Well, there's a whole lot of Kansas between here and Colorado," he said, which made her laugh. "Still . . . one day, maybe. But once I saw the mountains, I guess I'd turn right around and come home."

"Would you? I'm not sure I *will* live here forever. I don't want to be cooking and cleaning and weeding the rest of my life, like Aunt Lotty and Ma. Aunt Lotty teases me, she says, 'Child, with such notions, best find yourself a *rich* man to marry!' So, often I wonder where my life will lead."

"You never know, I reckon. My pa said life's like the Mississippi, twisting and turning at will."

"That's nice." She gave a gentle smile. "I like that . . . Do you want to farm all your life, Matt?"

"I do." Perhaps it wasn't the right answer, but he wouldn't say different just to please her.

"Buck's friends, they taught me a song girls in the Ozarks sing. It goes:

"I do not like the farmer who works in all that dirt,
I'd rather have the guerrilla man who wears a fancy shirt."

Now Matt forced himself to look at her: "Is that how you feel, Sue?"

"No," she said, slowly shaking her head. "You know the yellow-haired boy Jesse teased me about? He said something that chilled me to gooseflesh."

"What?"

She sighed a sorrowful breath. "Buck was telling about the day he met Quantrill. Said he expected such a mean, awful man, but Quantrill's really so pleasant and kind, no wonder all the boys love him at once. Then the yellow-haired boy said, 'Yes, but isn't it peculiar how he gets you to do things you never dreamed you'd do?' "

The tree seemed to be trying to shake Matt loose. He held tight to the branch and swallowed hard and said, "Did Jesse hear that, too?"

She nodded. "Then it was deathly quiet and the other boys looked so uneasy. Finally Jesse said, 'What do you mean by that?' But no one answered."

Susie looked away, then sat up fast. "Here, I'll read your palm," she said breezily, swinging her legs. "Aunt Lotty taught me last week."

As Matt sat to face her, their knees brushed. If he moved his away, she would know he noticed. She might think he didn't like it. He held out his hand, hesitantly, afraid it might tremble. She took it, lightly tracing his palm: "Your life line is good and long. You'll live to old age in good health . . . This is your heart line. See how deep it is?" She fit her fingernail into it. "It means you feel everything powerfully, both good and bad. Is that so, Matt?"

Her touch was so pleasurable, he could barely breathe. He thought somehow she oughtn't to be doing this, but he sure didn't want her to stop.

"And this shows you'll have one, two, three, four, five, six, seven children. How does that sound, Matthew? Seven children?"

He couldn't trust his voice. She slowly closed her eyes and slowly opened them again, as if she might be feeling sleepy. He leaned closer, and she bent toward him . . .

Then she pushed him off the branch.

She screamed as he was falling, backward, twisting like a cat. The heel of his left hand hit the creek bed, and his left knee struck a rock.

He looked up in shock and she looked down in horror, hands clapped over her mouth. "What'd you do *that* for?" he yelled as Jesse and Ben rushed toward him.

"I didn't mean to!" she called.

"Yeah, you just reached over and shoved me!"

She began to cry. Pain shot up his arm; his wrist was already swelling. When he stood, his knee ached something fierce.

"You all right, Matt?" Ben said. "Why'd she do that?"

"I don't know, ask her," he shouted up the tree. "She's *your* friend."

"Susie!" Jesse scolded. "Get down from there!"

"No!"

"You best come right now, girl!"

She came down by the rope, weeping piteously. If Matt hadn't felt so pained, so furious and humiliated, he would have wanted to comfort her.

"I'm taking you to Pappy," Jesse told him. "Can you walk?"

"Yes."

"What'd you *do* that for?" Ben confronted Susie, now struggling with her stockings and shoes.

"I don't know" was all she would say, crying and crying.

"Bring Salt over, Ben," Jesse said. "You'll have to mount on the off side, Matt, won't you?"

He would, because he couldn't bend his left knee and then bear all his weight on it.

Salt backed up in confused protest. "Whoa, boy, whoa," Jesse said, patting him. "You be good to Matt, now."

They started at a trot, Susie bringing up the rear.

"How're you doing?" Jesse asked.

"Fine," Matt answered, but in truth he felt dizzy and sick.

"He doesn't *look* so fine, Jess," Ben warned.

"No, he doesn't, does he?"

Matt struggled to keep his head up. The voices seemed far away.

Ben yelled, "Jess!"

Then Jesse was right up alongside, swinging into the saddle behind Matt.

"I'm all right, I'm all right," Matt said, but the prairie grass swirled.

"I didn't mean to." Susie was sobbing. "I'm sorry."

"Okay, Matt? Okay?" Jesse was holding him around the middle.

"Wounded Man," Matt mumbled.

"*You're* okay." Jesse's voice raced from relief to anger: "Susie! Take July's reins!"

Matt slumped down over Salt's neck. "Hee-yah!" Jesse said, and they rode at a clip. "Pappy! Ma!" he hollered from the road.

"Quit it, Jess, they'll think somebody's dead," Matt said. Sure enough, here came Dr. and Mrs. Samuel, thudding across the porch. "Get down, Jess." He was powerfully embarrassed—nearly fainting like a frail girl just because of a bruise or two. "I can do it myself. Get down."

"What is it?" Mrs. Samuel cried out. "Oh, Lord, where's Susie?"

"She's the cause of it, Ma! She's coming with July!"

"She pushed Matt out of the tree!" Ben added.

"Pushed him?" Dr. Samuel said.

"Oh, Matt!" Mrs. Samuel rushed toward Salt.

"I'm all right, ma'am." Matt dismounted gingerly. "Jess, can I get some water?"

"He is *not* all right!" Jesse called as he went.

"Come on, son." Dr. Samuel put a hand on Matt's shoulder. "Let's get you on the porch and take a look. Your leg?"

"My wrist, mostly, sir."

Ben hung back, picking at the bark of the coffee bean tree.

"You needn't fret, Ben," Matt told him. "You know how it hurts when you bang your knee hard? But I'm okay now."

Ben didn't look any too convinced.

Susie rode up to the house, dismounted, and quickly tied the horses.

Mrs. Samuel hollered, "What's this, daughter? What have you done?"

"I pushed him," she admitted tearfully.

But at the very same time, Matt said, "I fell."

Mrs. Samuel looked from one to the other. " 'I pushed him,' 'I fell,' which is it?"

"I pushed him," Susie said, "but I didn't mean to!" Then she ran indoors without waiting to be told.

"Zerelda, can you mix some molasses and salt?" Dr. Samuel said calmly as Jesse handed Matt a cup of water.

Mrs. Samuel rushed inside, muttering about pushing boys from trees.

"Jess, fetch my doctoring bag." Dr. Samuel pressed here and there on Matt's wrist. "It's just a sprain, thank goodness." His gentle voice and kind face gave Matt a keen longing for his own pa. "We'll take down the swelling, then wrap it good and tight—and hope your ma doesn't swear out a warrant for my girl."

"She wouldn't do that, sir."

"Oh, she might!" Ben put in, sidling up to the porch rail.

Jesse returned with the black leather bag. "His knee, too, Pap—did you look at his knee?"

"I think it's all right, sir."

"We'd best take a look." Dr. Samuel rolled up the pants leg. He poked at the knee and rocked it back and forth. "How's that, son?"

"Not too bad, sir."

"It's well bruised. I imagine it'll pain you for a few days. But all in all, Matt, I'd say you were mighty lucky. And Susie, too," he added with a smile.

Mrs. Samuel came out with an earthenware bowl. She put it on the floor and propped her hands on her hips. "Now, suppose you boys tell me what-all occurred?"

Dr. Samuel began to apply the warm, sticky mixture to Matt's wrist.

"I don't know, Ma," Jesse said. "Ask your daughter."

"I'm asking you!"

"I only saw him coming down!"

Mrs. Samuel stared at Matt. He looked up to reply—and suddenly saw she was expecting another baby. "I'm—I'm not quite sure, ma'am. She just . . ." He shrugged.

"Well, were you fussing at each other?"

"No, ma'am," he mumbled, his face flaming up.

"I see." Mrs. Samuel turned from him. "Jesse, put up the horses."

"Why can't she put up her own horse!"

"Because I won't let her out of her room till the Second Coming!"

Jesse stomped off the porch, then right back up with the berry buckets and off again, banging the gate.

"Never *can* tell how Jesse's feeling," Dr. Samuel said quietly, and they all laughed—even Mrs. Samuel, as she went indoors. Dr. Samuel patted Matt's shoulder. "Have a seat, Ben," he said, and went inside, too.

Ben sat on the porch step and whispered, "When can we go?"

"Soon." Matt looked off toward the barn, but a flash of color caught his eye. A red shirt on a porch chair, a sewing basket on the floor. Bright embroidery, big pockets. Matt felt sick all over again. Mrs. Samuel was sewing a guerrilla shirt, and it was surely meant for Jesse.

"Here, boys. Cherry cobbler."

Matt jumped at the sharp sound of her voice.

"Thank *you*, Mrs. Samuel," Ben said, accepting a bowl.

"No, thank you, ma'am," Matt said. "I'm not hungry."

"That's a first." As Jesse walked up, he lifted the other bowl from his ma's hand.

"You scamp." She slapped his head, but looked at him warmly.

"If you *do* get hungry, Matt, just lick your arm," Jesse suggested, and Ben howled as though he'd never heard anything so humorous.

Dr. Samuel returned and wound a long strip of white cloth around Matt's wrist. "Now, I'm sure that aches," he said, and he wasn't jesting. "But it's necessary. After supper, remove it, wash off the molasses, then have your ma wrap it tight again."

"Much obliged, Dr. Samuel. We ought to be getting on. Ma'll be starting to worry." He tried not to wince as he got to his feet. "Thank you, Mrs. Samuel."

"For what? For a girl who commits mayhem?" Mrs. Samuel said.

"Tell your ma how sorry we are," Dr. Samuel added. "Try to take your ease."

There was no chance he would—or could. But Matt said, "Yes, sir."

"I've a mind to send Susie over to do your plowing," Mrs. Samuel said.

"I'm all right, ma'am."

"Can you manage the ride?" Jesse asked, walking them to the hitching rack.

Matt fought a grimace as he mounted. "I'm fine."

"Right," Jesse said to Ben, who nodded knowingly.

Matt kicked out at Jesse with his stirrup.

Jesse laughed. "Joel, chapter 2, verse 20," he reminded Matt, walking alongside him for a few steps.

"All right, Jess." He tugged the reins as Ben went on. "I never heard what was on your mind."

"It'll keep," Jesse said.

Matt cautioned Ben not to make this a big thing, but no sooner were the horses put up than Ben dashed to the house. Ma met Matt in the lean-to, wiping her hands on her apron and looking baffled.

"Matt? Is this true? Oh dear. Come in here." He let her lead him to a chair.

Betsy was fixing supper. Clayton, coming in from the porch, asked, "Who pushed whom? From a tree?"

"Susie pushed Matt! It was the doggonedest thing, Clay. You should've seen him coming down! It was like watching a shot duck tumble out of the sky!"

Clayton sat. "Are you hurt bad?"

"I believe I'll survive."

"Why would she do such a thing?" Ma asked.

"You should have heard the hollering at Jesse's place! They sure holler a lot over there, Matt, don't they?"

"Jesse's folks were awfully rattled," Matt told Ma. "They said tell you sorry."

"Lord." Ma shook her head. "Every time you go with those children of late, you come home damaged." She examined his arm. "What did they do for it?"

"Molasses and salt."

Ma looked doubtful. "Hot water for a sprain, Papa always said."

It didn't seem wise to point out that Papa was not a doctor.

"Oh, guess what else, Ma?" Ben chirped. "Mrs. Samuel's having another baby!"

"*Is* she, Matt?" Ma asked.

He was mortified. "Ben, don't talk about such things," he mumbled.

Ma laughed right at him.

"Back to the incident," Clayton said. "We haven't heard what precipitated it."

"Clay, Matt almost pitched right off Salt. Jesse had to jump in the saddle and grab him!"

"Is that so." Clayton didn't sound overly impressed.

"Ben, please stop talking for just a moment," Ma said pleasantly. "Go outside and bring the little ones in. They were behind the house."

Matt was uncomfortable in the silence.

Ma said, "Matthew?"

He shrugged at the floor. "We were up in a tree and she pushed me out."

Betsy turned, one hand on her hip. "And *why* were you two up in a tree?"

"We were just talking, Betsy!" he said, shooting her a look.

"Just talking," Betsy said to Clayton. They snickered.

"Well, we were!"

"I believe she's sweet on you, Matt."

"Not likely," he muttered.

"Goodness, is that how a girl shows it nowadays? Ho! I'm glad I did my courting twenty years ago!" Ma said, and all three laughed.

Clayton sang quietly:

"All I need to make me happy is two little boys to call me pappy,
Hey, pretty little black-eyed Susie . . ."

"Oh, leave it, Clay, would you?" Matt scowled.

Ben ran in, trailed by Molly and Tyler. "And Susie cried the whole way home!" he said. "I never in my life heard a girl take on so!"

Betsy and Clayton were near hysterics now.

"What're you laughing about?" Ben asked.

"About Susie being his sweetheart," Betsy said.

"His *sweet*heart!" Ben hooted. "You wouldn't say that if you heard him hollering at her!"

That put Betsy and Clayton into an uproar. Ma turned away, but her whole body was shaking.

"Fine." Matt pulled Tyler onto his good leg. "Fine, have a good laugh at my expense, I don't mind."

"All right, children," Ma finally said, and there was quiet as she and Betsy finished getting supper.

"Another baby," Ma murmured. "At a time like this." She sighed deeply, stroking Tyler's flaxen hair. "Well, the good Lord never gives us more than we can bear."

For the first time, Matt really thought about that expression. He decided it made no kind of sense.

As Matt lay in bed, his knee ached and his arm burned and his mind would not keep still. What was weighing on Jesse? That guerrilla shirt? Why did Susie push him? Why hadn't Jesse said his ma was having a baby? What was so all-fired important in the Book of Joel?

"*Maaaaaatt*," Clayton complained. "Lie still."

"I'm *trying*, Clay."

"Try better. Count sheep or something."

"Count sheep. That don't work, and anyhow, ours are so dumb they'd never jump the fence to be counted."

Clayton chuckled quietly. "Your arm hurting you?"

"Not too much."

"Go to sleep," Clay said, and pulled his pillow over his head.

Matt tried to rest his brain, to think of something pleasant . . . Pretty little black-eyed Susie.

Something had been said, and he'd put it away in his head to take out and think about when he was alone. What was it? . . . *I've a mind to send Susie over* . . . Now he imagined her in his fields, pushing the plow, her bare arms looking to have the feel of Ma's silk shawl. When she got to where he was, she would come to him in the tall corn . . . So close up in that tree, her knees touching his, her finger on his palm. *How does that sound, Matthew? Seven children* . . . Now the throbbing in his arm and leg was a kind of pleasure, a reminder of how she was looking at him just before he fell.

Part Two

SEASON OF DARKNESS
JULY–AUGUST 1863

★ ★ ★

19

In his sleep, Matt heard a wildcat screech, then a shotgun blast. Before he was even awake, he had his pants on.

"Matt! Matt!" Ma pounded up the steps, Tyler crying in her arms.

"I'm up, Ma, I'm up." His voice sounded calm, even dull, but his heart was banging inside his chest.

"What was it?" Ben asked in sleepy panic. "What was it?"

Clayton was on his crutches. The yell came again. It was no wildcat, but a woman. Ma clutched at Matt's arm as he passed: "I'm going with you."

"No." He jumped down the stairs, grabbed Pa's rifle, and unbolted the door.

"Matt!" Ma cried, then: "Betsy! Take the baby! Betsy!"

In the lane, he smelled smoke. He stopped running when he reached the road. His eyes closed tight, then opened wide: The Stones' house and barns were bright with flames that clambered up the walls and whipped the darkness. Mrs. Stone flew down the hill, ghostlike, nightgown billowing, gray hair streaming. The wildcat shriek was coming from her.

"Oh! Matthew!" She threw herself against him.

Uneasy, he draped an arm around her shivering shoulders.

Ma rushed up the lane and took Mrs. Stone in her arms. "Oh, Mrs. Stone! Where's your husband? Oh!"

Mrs. Stone didn't answer, didn't need to.

Matt found himself walking toward the fire.

"Matt!" Ma said sharply.

He turned. Ma shook her head. Mrs. Stone wept with her eyes squeezed shut.

They started home. Ben and Clayton stood where their lane met the road, watching the fire. Matt stopped with them, avoiding Clay's eyes. Ma led Mrs. Stone toward the house.

"Can't we do anything?" Ben said.

"No," Clayton replied.

"What do you suppose happened to the animals?"

"Stolen. Burned."

"You think Mr. Stone's dead, Clay?"

"Yes, I do."

"Well, *where* do you think he's dead?"

Clayton shook his head. "No telling. Ten feet from here. Ten miles away."

"But I heard shots. Didn't you, Clay?"

"Shots?" Matt couldn't tear his eyes from the flames. "There was only one."

"Two," Clay said.

"Woke me straight up. Me!" Ben said.

Clayton turned away. "Let's go."

Mrs. Stone was in Ma's chair by the hearth, with Ma right beside her. She'd put a shawl around Mrs. Stone's shoulders, and a glass of Pa's Kentucky bourbon in her hands. Mrs. Stone's voice was trembling as she told Ma: ". . . and Bill said, 'Well, at least let me get my boots on,' and they said, 'You'll need no boots, old man.' " She broke into tears again.

Ma's eyes went from Clayton to Ben.

Clayton said, "Come on, you two." He climbed the stairs with Ben. Matt put up the rifle and bolted the door, moving slowly, hoping to hear more. Had Mr. Stone recognized the men? Had Mrs. Stone? Was Buck there? But Mrs. Stone just cried and cried.

"Matt," Ma said, and when he turned she nodded toward the stairs.

The others were in the girls' room. Tyler sucked his thumb, half-asleep on the bed, and Molly huddled in Betsy's arms. Ben, sitting on the bed's edge with his head in his hands, shook with sobs.

"Ben's just realized it was guerrillas," Clayton explained.

Matt leaned down to touch Ben's shoulder. "Ben? Who'd you think did it? He's a Union man, you know that."

"I won't take that oath," Ben choked out, pushing him away. "I don't want to be a bushwhacker."

Matt straightened up fast. The way Clayton's and Betsy's eyes were locked on him, anybody'd think *he* killed Mr. Stone. "What're you two looking at *me* for?" he said fiercely, and turned away.

In his room he paced, arms folded tight on his chest . . . *I've a lot on my mind*, Jesse had said just a week ago. Then Clayton's words came to him: *Truth is, you have no idea what Jesse knows and doesn't know* . . . Matt punched the wall hard. Then he turned and there was Ma, like a spirit at the door.

"I have Mrs. Stone in my room," she said quietly, "and I need to get back to her. But you must stop walking. The floor-boards creak so."

"Yes, Ma."

Matt sat in the window, pressing his forehead to the glass. Ma said a few words to the others. Clayton came in. "The girls aren't keen to be alone. Are you willing to take the tick in there and lie with Tyler?"

Without a word, Matt dragged the tick into the girls' room. When he reached for Tyler, Betsy held up her hands to stop him. "Clay, tell *him* what you just said."

"I said we all need to stick together now. There'll be hard times from here on out. But if we stick together, it might be a little easier."

Matt nodded and picked up the baby. When Ben and Clayton had gone, he laid Tyler on the tick, stroking his back when he fussed. Betsy put out the candle.

" 'Night, Matty."

" 'Night, Moll." He hesitated. " 'Night, Betsy."

"Good night, Matt," she said softly.

I never heard what was on your mind, he'd said, and Jesse had said, *It'll keep.* It had seemed a bit peculiar, Jesse's not coming by this weekend. And Matt had kept away from the Samuel place, not wanting to chance facing Susie this soon . . . *Jesse's on the grapevine*, Clayton had said. *Don't fool yourself about that* . . . Matt hadn't been much inclined to look up that Bible verse. But now he stared hard into the darkness and wondered about the Book of Joel.

20

"Damnedest war," Matt grumbled, driving from the yard with Betsy next morning. "A boy needs girls around for protection."

Betsy paid him no mind.

In truth, he wasn't unhappy to have her along. Ma told him to go for the provost marshal, and he'd rather meet the devil himself than loathsome Mr. Ford. Betsy was not to go into the office—Ma had other errands for her—but at least Matt had company on the way.

Right when a person died, it seemed you barely had time to notice he was gone. The arrangements, the chores, the people coming to call. Matt dreaded that most, after the provost marshal. Word would spread, and likely he'd come home to a full house.

Then he felt ashamed, thinking about himself. How about Mrs. Stone, her whole life taken in minutes? Her husband of how many years? Forty? Everything gone, not a piece of clothing or a stick of furniture. And Mr. Stone. Dragged from his house in the dark of night, not allowed to put on his boots before they killed him.

"Oh, Matt," Betsy said as they drew closer to the Stones' property. "Look."

Nothing stood but two chimneys. Acrid gray smoke hung in the humid air.

"Lord, this is an awful place. I just wish we could leave right now. If——"

And then she was screaming, so sudden and shrill it spooked the horses. She clutched Matt's arm and crumpled against him.

"Where?" he whispered, putting his arms around her.

"Back there . . . in the ditch."

"Stay here," he said, handing her the lines.

"Don't go, don't go." Her voice was a high-pitched wail.

"I've got to." He thought to take an oilcloth from the wagon box before leaping into the ditch.

As he drew near, his steps faltered. "Go on," he told himself angrily, and then he was at the dead man's side.

A cloud of flies rose up, but most continued about their business. Clay was right: two shots. The shotgun had torn Mr. Stone's chest to a gory, gaping pit. And in his forehead was that neat, round hole made by a Navy revolver. Shot twice, when just one of those guns was enough to kill him. Shot a second time when he was already dead—or mighty close. Blood caked the skin, soaked the ground, glared against the remaining white parts of his nightshirt. His lips were stretched back from his teeth, so he looked to be grinning. The hair on his legs was surprisingly black; his feet were bare and bluish white. Matt pulled the oilcloth over the body and became aware of his own voice: "Oh, God, oh, God, oh, God."

Then the skin around the pistol shot moved. He couldn't possibly be— Leaning in, Matt smelled decaying flesh, hot stale blood, and he saw why the skin was twitching: maggots. He dropped the oilcloth over Mr. Stone's head and began to run, but had to stop and double over, hands on knees, vomiting into the ditch.

"Matt!" Betsy was shrieking. "Matt!" But he couldn't answer, and after a long time he wiped his sweating face on his shirtsleeve and trudged up the bank.

Betsy huddled against him on the wagon seat, sometimes weeping, sometimes quiet. Neither spoke. Back in the yard, he helped her down. "Call Ma," he told Molly, who was tending Tyler. "Right away." Molly ran off. "You all right, Bet?" How strange—he had all but forgotten what he'd called her when they were little.

Clayton and Ma rushed out. "We found him," Matt said. "Betsy did—"

"Dear Lord," Ma said, and Betsy clung to her.

Clayton followed Matt to the pump. "Where is he?"

"About a hundred yards beyond our fence, in the ditch." He took a drink.

"Could you see much from the wagon?"

"The wagon? Hell, Clay, I got right down and tucked him up in oilcloth."

"You did, Matt?" Clayton sounded awestruck.

"What was I to do, Clayton? Not even cover the man, just leave him there for buzzard food?" Matt took off his hat and soaked his burning head. "He was crawling with maggots. Didn't think maggots came so fast."

Clayton was studying him.

"I won't say it didn't trouble me, Clay. I threw up in the ditch about ten times," he admitted, and Clayton laid a hand on his shoulder. "Well, I'm fine now. And I'd best unhitch the wagon so I can go to town with Salt."

"Hold up," Clay said. "I'll tell Ma I want to go along."

"All right." Matt walked to the herb garden for some mint to chew, to take the vile taste from his mouth.

"Ma says I've got to stay and make the coffin," Clay announced, returning.

Matt nodded. "No matter."

"You'll do fine. Just answer each question as it's put to you. Say no more and no less."

"I'm not worried, Clay."

"And I'm sure you'd tell me if you were," Clayton said, trying for a smile.

As Matt rode toward town, thoughts of coffins and provost marshals put him in mind of Palmyra. The provost marshal there, a man called "Beast," had made ten Southern men sit in their own coffins. His firing squad did its work, and there was a neat end to it.

What if Ford asked about Jesse, or Buck? Would Matt find himself sitting in a coffin before long? How should he start when he walked into the office? *My mother sent me* . . . No, too childish. *I came to tell you my neighbor's killed.*

When Matt got to town, he felt as though he'd swallowed rocks. At the provost marshal's ramshackle building, he tied Salt and approached the door. Inside there was raucous laughter. On impulse, he backed away. But someone called out, "Come in, boy, come in! You here to see me?"

Matt stepped inside, taking off his hat, and turned in the direction of the voice. He could see only an outline as his eyes tried to adjust from the harsh sun to the dim office. Haltingly, he said, "I need to see Mr. Ford."

"Well, you *found* him!" the man behind the desk said jovially, raising both arms. "Now what do you *want* from him?"

Matt glanced at another man leaning against the wall. He wore a natty blue uniform, shiny black cavalry boots, and a saber on his belt. Matt tallied the stars on his shoulders. Colonel? General? Jesse would know.

"Um, I need to report a death," Matt said. "Last night. My neighbor. He was killed and his wife burned out."

Turning solemn, Ford took up his pen. "What's the man's name, boy?"

"Bill Stone."

Ford's eyes darted to the officer, who stepped away from the wall and asked, "Bill Stone, the hog farmer?"

"Yes, sir."

"How do you know he's dead?"

"Well, sir, I just covered up his body."

"God damn," the officer said to Ford, who flung down his pen. Then the officer directed his voice to the back of the room: "Ride to camp. Tell them the bastards got Stone."

Now Matt saw a younger man, also in uniform.

"Yes, sir," the soldier said, saluting, and walked out briskly.

The officer turned to Matt. "Who are *you*, boy?"

Matt looked to Ford.

"Go on, tell him. He's the deputy district commander."

Still, Matt was reluctant, and only said, "I—we live across the way."

"Well, then"—Ford gave a wicked smile—"you must be the Howard boy."

It made Matt's skin crawl, Ford knowing who he was. Pa used to say that the people you trust least are the ones you ought to look right in the eye. And Matt did now. "Yes, sir."

"And what's your given name?"

"Matt, sir."

"Perhaps you can tell us about your part in this," the commander said.

One piece of his mind was on Ma, sending him here like a hog to slaughter. But he had to think now, concentrate, make sure he said everything just right. "We woke up in the night—"

Ford interrupted him. "We?"

"My whole family. There were shots. I went out—"

"*You* went out?" the commander said.

"His father's dead," Ford explained, his words chilling Matt again.

"So you went out—"

"And Mrs. Stone was in the road and their place was fired."

"You heard nothing beforehand?"

"No, sir."

"You're sure about that?"

"Yes, sir. I was asleep."

The district commander narrowed his gaze. "How old are you, boy?"

"Fifteen."

"Old enough to fight, in some quarters."

Matt pulled in a careful breath. "Sir, I don't fight. I farm. My whole family's depending on my crop."

The silence was fearful as they stared at each other. Then Ford said, "Tell Mrs. Stone I'll be out to see her this afternoon. And you, Matt Howard, you can show me your crop. And the corpse."

"Yes, sir."

Ford eyed him up and down. "You can go."

"Sir?"

"What is it?"

"My ma said to ask if a telegraph message could be sent to one of the daughters. I have their names and where they live." He slid the paper from his pocket.

The commander reached toward him. "I'll take that."

"Thank you, sir," Matt said, handing it over. He left slowly, so as not to appear anxious. He unlooped Salt's reins, mounted, and rode at a walk to Mr. Mead's store.

His thoughts leaped like a grasshopper, helter-skelter, barely alighting. So Jesse had been right: Mr. Stone was spying for the Federals. If he'd been just a loyal Union man, his death wouldn't have caused such a stir. If he was a spy, no wonder the guerrillas killed him: he was surely getting plenty of them killed. The day Matt brought the duck, how skittish Mrs. Stone had acted. The coverlets on the line, some sort of signal. *Well, then, you must be the Howard boy.* Had Mr. Stone been telling the Feds about him? Because of Jesse and Buck and their folks? Did Mr. Stone think he was involved? Was Mr. Stone the one who told Ma about Buck? When Mr. Stone came to check on his crop, was he really checking on Matt? It seemed sinful to have such thoughts about a dead man, especially one who had been a good family friend. The fat little piglets, Jesse's mean grin: *Maybe he's trying to buy you for the Union.*

In the store, Mr. Mead rushed to him. "Matt, I just heard."

"Yes, sir. News does travel fast. Uh, here's what Ma needs."

Mr. Mead took the list. "Oh, Matt," he said, shaking his head, "I'm glad your pa's not here to see these times."

Matt was so angry his eyes hurt, but he calmly said, "Well, sir, that's odd. Because here's me all the time wishing he was."

Mr. Mead's face turned pink, and he walked away fast.

Matt wandered the store, picking up and putting down things he didn't want and couldn't afford: a box of ink, a tobacco pouch, a can of gooseberries, a parasol. He looked at all the candies in the jars. And then he saw the *Liberty Tribune*:

CONFEDERATE LOSS AT GETTYSBURG
LEE'S INVASION OF PENNSYLVANIA
THOUSANDS KILLED IN THREE-DAY BATTLE
WAR'S MOST TERRIFIC FIGHT
THE BLOODY AFTERMATH

Matt picked up the paper. The battle had ended on July third, more than a week ago. Glorious Union victory. Confederate dead buried in trenches. General Lee's army in retreat. A perfect and total rout.

"I've got Clayton's papers," Mr. Mead said, returning to the counter.

"I'll take this one, too, sir. And three of those peppermint sticks."

Mr. Mead looked doubtful. "You're sure, Matt."

"Yes, sir." If they had to have another funeral out of their house, his little brothers and sister would have a stick of candy. If the war's worst battle had been fought, Clayton would read about it firsthand. And if Ma didn't like it, she'd know better than to send him to town next time.

Mr. Mead wrapped up the things on Ma's list, but Matt kept the paper and candy separate. When he had been given his two cents' change, he said, "I'm sorry for what I said, Mr. Mead. I meant no disrespect."

"I understand, Matt."

" 'Morning, sir."

" 'Morning, son."

Matt put the newspaper and package in his saddlebag, and pocketed the candy. Now there was only the post office. He looked at the envelope:

Mr. and Mrs. Wm. Bennett
Germantown, Pennsylvania

Was Germantown anywhere near Gettysburg? Ma thought it was so safe up North. It gave him a vengeful satisfaction to know the war's biggest battle had just been fought there. Still, it wasn't like Missouri. At Gettysburg two armies, each in its own uniform, knowing the enemy, had come face-to-face on a battlefield. Nothing like Missouri . . .

In the post office, Matt handed over the letter. "Three cents," the clerk said.

"Uh—I—" He looked at the pennies in his hand. "I'll have to come back," he stammered, turning away.

Now he was done for. What in the world would he tell Ma? Maybe he could get another penny? Should he ask Mr. Mead to take back the candy? He flinched against the very thought.

What was in this envelope, anyway, and how important was it? Maybe it was just those foolish thank-you letters. Or perhaps she'd written during the night, scared by the murder, making arrangements to leave right away. Standing by Salt, Matt held the envelope up to the light, but he couldn't see anything. He pushed the letter into his pocket. "I messed up good, boy," he said, scratching Salt's neck, and Salt gave him a nuzzle.

He would have to put the matter out of his head for a day or two. There was nothing for it, and if the letter was delayed a bit, no one need know. He'd find a way to get the extra penny, hold on to the two he had, and get back into town. Ma counted every cent, and kept the money in her room, so it would not be easy. But something would come up, and then he'd make it right.

Ben and Molly were moping around, minding Tyler. Matt let Salt go in the pasture, then called to them, "Come down to the barn! I got something for you."

Clayton stopped work on the coffin when Matt came in. "How'd it go?"

"I don't really care to tell it." Matt put away Salt's tack and blanket.

"Ma said to see her soon as you got back."

"In a minute."

Molly skipped in. "What do you have for us?"

"Wait for me up in the loft. And look after Tyler. You carry him, Ben."

"All right."

Matt and Clayton watched them go.

"What's that about?" Clayton said.

"I bought them a bit of candy."

"Candy! We can't afford that."

"I don't care, Clay. And I got you something, too." He gave Clay the paper and pointed to the headlines. "You know this?"

"Noooo." Squinting at the print, Clayton seemed to forget all about him.

Matt scrambled up into the loft and presented the candies.

Ben reached for one, and Molly squealed. "Shhh," Matt warned. "You mustn't tell Ma, all right? You both understand? It's a secret."

"Is it a bad secret?" Molly asked.

"No! It's a—a good secret," he said, and Ben snorted in disbelief.

Molly licked slowly; Ben crunched loud. Matt longed for a taste, but these were for the young ones. He handed the third stick to Tyler, who took a bite, shuddered, and spit it out.

"Fool baby!" Ben tried to grab the piece, but Matt was faster and popped it into his mouth.

Tyler tossed the stick aside. Ben snapped it up, but then offered it to Matt. "No, you two split it," Matt said, savoring the one sweet, spicy bit.

"You have it, Matt," Ben said.

"No, let's give some to Clay and some to Betsy. How is she, anyway?"

"Ma put her to bed," Ben said. "Her head was aching something fierce."

"Anybody else in the house?"

"A few folks. The Askews. The Daytons."

Matt kept Tyler from pitching over the side of the loft. How long before the provost marshal turned up? He didn't want to see the man again. He didn't want to see anybody.

"Matt, come down from there," Clayton said sternly.

"Remember," Matt said to Ben and Molly, then carried Tyler down. "He didn't care for it," he told Clayton, holding out the candy. "You want some?"

"Are you telling those children to lie?"

"It's not a lie, Clay!" came Molly's voice. "It's a good secret!"

Clayton glared at him. "It isn't right."

"Well, I see you read that paper, Clay."

"You should not have bought those things. Now go up and tell Ma what you've done."

"I will not. *You* tell her, if you're so keen on it. You two talk about every damn other thing."

He started to walk by, but Clay stopped him with a crutch. "That's twice today I've heard you curse."

Matt put the baby down and turned to face Clayton. "Don't I have the right? I had to go up there and get grilled by the provost marshal and some *damn* district commander in cavalry boots, with a saber hanging off his belt: *Who are you, what's*

188

your part in all this, how old are you? Next thing I figured they'd be giving me the oath. Hey, guess what, Clay? Ford knew my name. What do you think about that?" But Clayton gave no answer. "Says he'll be by this afternoon to see Mrs. Stone. And me. He wants to see my crop."

"Your crop?" Clay said quietly.

"Yeah, he said I was old enough to fight, in some quarters, so I told him I farm. Let's see . . ." He frowned and rubbed his chin as if puzzling something out. " 'In some quarters.' What do you suppose he meant by *that?*"

He brushed past Clayton and went to the house.

Visitors were sitting with Mrs. Stone on the porch, so he went in through the lean-to. "Ma'am." He placed Ma's package on the table. "Mr. Ford said he'd come by later, to speak to Mrs. Stone."

She nodded, looking beyond him. "What a day, Matt, what a day. The poor thing. She wants to know . . . the condition of the body."

"Oh, Ma," he protested, tipping his head back.

"It'll be a comfort to her, in some odd way. We'll do it later, just the two of us and her."

Matt rubbed his forehead ferociously. Ma touched his arm. "I'm sorry you had to see it. Betsy told me everything."

"Is she awake? I thought I'd go up and see her."

"That's considerate, Matt. But peek in—don't disturb her if she's sleeping."

Betsy opened her eyes when he cracked the door. "Come in." A wet cloth was plastered across her forehead.

"You all right?"

"Oh, Matt, I keep seeing it, over and over. I see it with my eyes open, and when I shut my eyes I see it again, and again. And it was worse for you."

He took the peppermint from his pocket and frowned at it, picking off some lint. "I got these for the little ones, but Tyler, he didn't like it. You should have seen the face. He spit it right out. This ain't the part he spit. Want some?"

She managed a smile. "No . . . but thank you."

"All right. I just thought I'd see how you were." He went to the door.

"Matt—don't *you* keep seeing it?"

"Oh, don't tell Ma about the candy" was all he answered.

She nodded and closed her eyes. He shut the door and stood on the landing a minute, leaning back against the wall, eyes shut tight.

Downstairs, he was alone. The sideboard was loaded with food folks had brought: boiled ham and light bread and plates of pickles and potatoes. He put a slab of ham between two slices of bread. As he headed for the door, the Bible caught his eye, lying open on the table. He flipped it shut and tucked it under his arm. Looking neither right nor left, he went through the corn, over the fence, and into the woods.

21

But I will remove far off from you the northern army, and will drive him into a land barren and desolate, with his face toward the east sea, and his hinder part toward the utmost sea, and his stink shall come up, and his ill savour shall come up . . .

In the calm solitude of the duck blind, Matt wasn't sure whether to be disturbed or amused by the notion of Jesse deciding the Book of Joel was talking to him personally about the war, Jesse imagining bushwhackers driving the Northern army all the way through Kansas.

His stink shall come up . . . Matt shrank from the memory of Mr. Stone's body. He wished Jesse were here. When Papa died, Matt had wandered in a daze, hardly believing that what he'd so long dreaded had finally come to pass. His jaws ached, his eyes burned, everyone who talked to him said nothing—and then Jesse was there. All he said was "Come on," and they walked to the farthest fence on the farm without a word. Matt hung on that fence and wept till he thought his heart would break while Jesse stood by saying, "That's all right, Matt. That's all right."

Surely Jesse knew by now that Mr. Stone was dead. Matt didn't want to wonder whether he knew beforehand. Matt thought of the letter, getting wrinkled in his pocket. Jesse's ma said Matt could stay there, and it might yet come to that. Living in the same house with Susie, there was a thought. Then he could watch her when guerrillas came to stay. But with everything so different there, he'd never be at his ease. Jesse would drag him to Baptist church every Sunday. And how long before he and Jesse would be packed off with guerrilla shirts to drive the Northern army into a barren and desolate land?

Matt took one last bite of peppermint, then flung the rest of the stick far into the pond. He made his way home at a possum's pace, thinking to replace the Bible first thing.

Ma was lying in wait. "*Where* have you been?"

"In the woods."

"In the woods? With what purpose?"

"Reading the Bible."

She grabbed it as if his hand were on fire. "How *could* you? Papa's family Bible! If anything had happened to it—"

"Sorry, Ma. I wasn't thinking." He turned away. "I have chores . . ."

Catching him roughly by the arm, she said, "Don't you dare dismiss me, young man. I'll dismiss *you* when I see fit. The provost marshal was here. He expected you to take him to Mr. Stone."

"Clayton knew where to find him," Matt told the floor.

"He said you were to show him your crop. What was the meaning of that?"

He gave a slow shrug.

"How do you suppose it appeared when I couldn't tell him where you were?"

"Sorry, ma'am."

"Go," she said in her sick-of-you voice.

In the barn, Clayton was nearly finished.

"Where'd you get the boards, anyhow?" Matt asked, running his hand along the lid.

"Folks brought some. I had some. It isn't pretty, but I suppose it'll do the job."

Matt stretched out beside the coffin and closed his eyes.

"They took the body to church," Clay said. "Mr. Askew and some others will come out later for the coffin. Funeral in the morning, did you know? Afterwards, Mrs. Stone will go over to the Askews'; they have more space. She'll stay with them till one of her daughters comes for her."

Matt was glad his family's part would end tomorrow. Then he could get back in the fields, plowing the tall corn, alone.

"I think I managed to smooth it over with the provost marshal, your not being here." Clayton banged in a nail. "He seemed a reasonable man."

Matt took a measured breath. Clayton just could not, would not, understand how you got treated, by both sides, if they thought you might fight.

"And he said Mr. Stone thought highly of you."

"High enough to be telling the provost marshal about me."

"Did you ever think maybe Mr. Stone was standing up for you?"

Matt frowned. "How do you mean?"

"Ford knows about everybody, Matt. That's his job. So maybe he said to Mr. Stone, 'I hear your young neighbor spends an awful lot of time at that Secesh house.' "

Matt opened his mouth to protest, but stopped.

Clayton shrugged. "And maybe Mr. Stone defended you. Seems you ought to look at all sides before you rush to judgment."

"Clayton?" Folding his hands on his chest, Matt shut his eyes again. "How does Ma's pa make his living? Does his business help the North somehow?"

There was a long wait, then a cold reply. "Those are Jesse's words coming out of your mouth. I can just *hear* him saying those words."

Matt didn't answer.

"It's time for you to do your own thinking, Matthew, and ask your own questions. Get up from there now. I'm finding that morbid."

"I'm so tired, Clay."

"Well, you'd best get to bed good and early," Clayton said. "It's been a long day." He resumed hammering.

After supper, Matt joined Ma and Mrs. Stone on the porch.

"Oh, Matt," Mrs. Stone said, "my husband was *so* fond of you."

"Yes, ma'am," he replied, gripping the porch rail.

"Was he shot much, Matt?" Her voice trembled, and she clutched Ma's hand. "Did he look awfully bad?"

"No, ma'am, it wasn't too bad. Just . . ." Slowly he brought his finger to his forehead. "Just one."

Mrs. Stone burst into tears. "Oh, Matt, I'm sorry you had to see it." She brought a handkerchief to her eyes. "And I thank you, I *thank* you for covering him as you did."

"That's all right, ma'am. I'm only sorry for you."

When Mrs. Stone had composed herself, she turned to Ma.

"Well, perhaps—as Matt said it isn't so bad—in the morning I could have one last look."

Ma read the panic in his face. "Oh, Mrs. Stone, I think it would upset you terribly. Remember him as he was."

"Perhaps you're right, Carolyn." She patted Ma's hand and smiled weakly at Matt. "Your mama has been such a comfort to me, Matt. *Such* a comfort."

"Yes, ma'am."

Ma nodded to him. "Go along now, Matt."

Inside, Betsy was ironing funeral clothes.

"You feel better?" he asked.

"Yes, thank you."

"Reckon I'll just lock the barn. Then go up to bed."

"Good night, then."

But he sat by the hearth instead. With the fire going for the irons, the heat was enough to steal your very breath. Betsy kept stopping to wipe her face or gather her light brown hair off her neck.

"Don't put a whole lot of starch in my collar, would you?"

"I never do, Matt. I know how you hate it."

When one iron grew cold, she put it back in the fire and took out another. She had to press down hard on the clothing to get the wrinkles out. The whole process looked like no kind of fun.

"I thought you were going to bed?"

"I am," he said, but still he watched.

"What did you tell Mrs. Stone?"

"I told her he was only shot once, and it wasn't too bad." They looked at each other. "In other words, I lied through my teeth."

Betsy gave him a sad smile. "That wasn't a lie, Matt," she

said. "That's what you call a good secret." And she bent to her ironing once more.

22

The pastor stood at the pulpit with Mr. Stone beside him, shut tight in Clayton's coffin. Matt and his family were up front with Mrs. Stone and the Askews. At church he always sat on the end with Tyler, so he could take the baby out if he fussed. And though he was hoping Tyler would, so far the baby had been better-behaved than Matt.

He tried to sit straight, listen, be still. All he could think about was getting the tie away from his neck and tearing off the tight collar. But when the pastor began to preach, it caught his attention fast.

> *"Deliver me from mine enemies, O my God: defend me from them that rise up against me.*
>
> *Deliver me from the workers of iniquity, and save me from bloody men . . .*
>
> *The mighty are gathered against me; not for my transgression, nor for my sin, O Lord.*
>
> *They run and prepare themselves without my fault: awake to help me, and behold . . .*
>
> *Be not merciful to any wicked transgressors.*

"The Fifty-ninth Psalm is clear in its meaning: The wicked shall be judged. Just as Saul sent men to David's house to kill him, so the murderous guerrillas appeared two nights ago at Bill Stone's house. These bloodthirsty men lay in wait for Mr. Stone's life the way Saul's men waited for David. And what was Mr. Stone's sin? The sin of loyalty to his country, my friends, no greater wrong than that. Bill Stone was a man who loved this land and could not bear to see it ripped asunder by Secessionists and bushwhackers. He stood up to these workers of iniquity and said: No. For that was he murdered in cold blood on the night of the Lord's day, and left in a ditch to be found by his neighbors, young Betsy and Matt Howard."

It was intolerable to hear his name in the same breath with such venom against the South. At that very moment, Matt knew he would never enter this church again.

"For that was his farm torched and his wife bereft of her partner of forty-three years," the pastor boomed. "As the Fifty-ninth Psalm continues, it speaks of the evil men returning every evening, in search of food, and howling like dogs if they are not satisfied. How appropriate these words are to what we all suffer now! Do not the wicked transgressors sniff around like dogs at our very doors, wandering for food? And if they are not satisfied, do they not howl—and far worse? But we shall triumph over these evil men, because the Bible tells us in these words:

"*. . .God shall let me see my desire upon mine enemies. Slay them not, lest my people forget: scatter them by thy power; and bring them down . . .*

And let them know that God ruleth in Jacob unto the ends of the earth."

"Yes, the Lord will mete out His own justice to these bloodthirsty men, whom we have known, so recently, as the young sons of our own neighbors."

Matt stared straight ahead, squeezing his hands into fists.

"Pray today, dear ones, for the Lord our shield to scatter Quantrill's workers of iniquity, for the sake of dear Bill Stone's soul. Pray that the Lord may make them know that it is *He* who ruleth to the ends of the earth. And take comfort, dear Mrs. Stone and dear friends gathered today, in the final words of the Fifty-ninth Psalm:

"But I will sing of thy power; yea, I will sing aloud of thy mercy in the morning: for thou hast been my defense and refuge in the day of my trouble."

"Let us pray here today that our dear friend Mary will feel God's refuge in the day of her trouble, and know His mercy in the morning."

The organ began to play, and Matt took a deep breath, as if he'd been underwater too long. Any minute, he'd be outdoors, home, free. Everyone stood; he held Tyler. But now horror overwhelmed him: the recessional was "The Battle Hymn of the Republic." He didn't know all the words, and surely didn't care to, but he couldn't pretend he didn't know any.

*"Mine eyes have seen the glory of the coming of the
    Lord,
He is trampling out the vintage where the grapes of
    wrath are stored . . ."*

Even if you weren't familiar with a hymn, you had to try to sing it, especially at a funeral. It would be disrespectful not to, and Ma would be beside herself with fury. But it was impossible for him to sing this song, written first for that self-righteous murderer John Brown, its words changed to become the Union's anthem.

*"He hath loosed the fateful lightning of His terrible swift
    sword . . ."*

Matt could think of only one thing to do: reach under Tyler's dress and pinch his leg until he howled like a dog in the Fifty-ninth Psalm.

At the sound, Ma leaned over, frowning, and gave a quick shake of her head. Matt started down the aisle with Tyler bawling and the congregation singing:

"Glory! Glory! Hallelujah! Glory! Glory! Hallelujah!"

Everyone watched as he passed row after row, and then, at the back of the church, his eyes met the provost marshal's. The man gave a slimy smile.

"Glory! Glory! Hallelujah!
  His truth is marching on!"

"I'm sorry, baby, I'm sorry," Matt told his brother in the churchyard. Tyler was so trusting, he clung to Matt instead of hating him, and Matt felt himself near tears.

"What seems to be your brother's problem?" Ford asked, striding toward them.

"I can't tell, sir."

"Perhaps he didn't care for the hymn."

"You're all right, aren't you, Ty?" Matt held the baby away, but he reached for Matt.

"I missed you yesterday, young man," Ford said sternly.

"Sorry for that, sir." He patted Tyler's back, jiggling him up and down.

Now the music stopped, and the church doors opened.

"Just you mind how you go, Matt Howard." The provost marshal looked him up and down. "Mind how you go," he repeated, and walked away.

23

"Lord, I'm hot." Matt set the plow down as Ben approached with a jug. "I'm all chigger-bit. Are you?" He scratched his neck and took a drink.

"A little," Ben said. "Still, I'd rather do this than wash clothes."

Matt coughed out the water. The letter! "Wash clothes? It ain't washday."

"Well, they missed it Monday because of Mr. Stone, so they're—"

Matt ran for the house.

"What's wrong?" Ben yelled.

"Keep plowing!" Matt called back.

But Ma was already at the root garden, charging forward, waving her letter.

He held up his hands in surrender: "Mama . . . Mama . . ."

"What am I to think?" she asked desperately. "What am I to think?"

"I didn't mean it, Ma, I messed up, I—"

"Did you think if you didn't mail it, that would change anything?"

"No ma'am, I was—"

"Because we *must* leave here, I know that now! And we'll go with or without you!"

When she followed those words by turning from him, he didn't feel sorry anymore. "That's all right, Ma," he said calmly. "I can stay at Jesse's."

She whirled around with a strange, almost nasty smile. "Say that again, Matt."

"I don't know if I will, ma'am. You fixing to hit me again?"

"No." She shook her head. "Say it."

"I can stay at Jesse's. He asked his ma."

"Well, you tell Mrs. Samuel I'll thank her to look after her own boys, and I'll look after mine." Ma's voice started low, but rose higher with each word. "No, on second thought, I'll tell her myself! . . . No, I take that back, I won't tell her at all! If you'll be happier at the Samuel place, you go right ahead, Matthew! I'll not stop you!"

He found himself following her toward the house. "Ma, let me explain. About the letter, it's not how you think. I meant to go back, I swear. I only needed a penny."

"Whatever do you mean? You had plenty of money."

"I bought the children candy. So I didn't have enough for the stamp."

"What?" She stopped short, perplexed. "Why did I not see this candy?"

"I—I told them it was a secret."

"You told them to *lie* to me."

"Yes, ma'am."

"What am I to do, Matt? What am I to do?"

He didn't answer.

"I can't bear to look at you right now. Get on your horse and mail this letter." She thrust it at him.

"Yes, ma'am."

"No, wait! Hitch the wagon and take Clayton. I'll give *him* the money, since you clearly cannot be trusted."

"Yes, I can, Ma." He walked alongside her. "Please let me go on my own."

"No," she snapped. "Hitch the wagon."

"Don't say a word, all right?" Matt said when they were in the road.

"All right."

"You know what I hate? Papa did it, too. When a person's at his lowest, they just love to twist the knife."

Clayton said nothing.

"I've a strong notion she doesn't much care where I go, Clay, to Pennsylvania or to the devil."

Silence.

"I told her Jesse's ma said I can stay with them. She said, 'Go right ahead.' Dang it, Clayton, are you listening?"

Clayton shook his head. "You climbed up and told me not to say a word. But you haven't shut your mouth once. So do you want to talk, or don't you?"

"I don't," he said, and urged the horses on. But Salt wouldn't run right, and when Matt checked, he saw that Salt had thrown a shoe. "No foot, no horse," he mumbled by way of telling Clayton they had to go to the blacksmith's.

When they got to Mr. Mead's store, Clay handed over the money. "I'll meet you at Mr. Franklin's."

"I don't know, Clay. You'd best go with me to the post office. There's no telling *what* I might do on my own."

"Just go," Clayton called over his shoulder.

At the blacksmith's, Matt had to ask for credit before un-hitching Salt. Mr. Franklin agreed, as Matt knew he would—but it wasn't right to presume. After bringing Salt in, he went and mailed the letter. At least Clayton still trusted him. For now.

Matt walked back to Mr. Franklin's, head down, hoping not to run into Ford. Town seemed much hotter than the farm, and plenty more dusty. His corn had tasseled and silked, but the last few weeks had been plenty dry. They needed about two straight days of a steady, gentle rain. But did it matter? Even if he'd be here to see the crop in, nobody else would.

He scratched Sugar between her ears the way she liked, recalling other years at harvest, the whole family in the fields, cutting, piling, shocking the corn. Even the little ones had a task. Last year was both sad and joyful—taking in the last crop planned by Pa, with Tyler playing on a blanket while they worked. And in the orchard Matt and Ben climbed a tree, carefully dropping some apples for Ma and Betsy and Molly to catch in their aprons, and they sat together in the shade to taste the fruit . . .

"Hey."

Matt jumped.

"Settle down," Jesse said.

"I was a year away."

"Past or future?"

"I ain't quite ready for the future."

Jesse looked at him close. "You all right, Matt?"

"I been better."

"I heard . . . about things."

"I figured."

"We oughtn't to be seen together."

"I guess that's the way of it."

Jesse hesitated, glancing all around. "Come on, though." He walked around to the back of Mr. Franklin's shop. Matt followed after a minute, and sat with Jesse on a woodpile behind the shed.

"I heard it was you who found him."

"Betsy and me."

"I'm sorry for that."

Matt said nothing.

"But he knew what he was putting himself in for. And he took that risk. 'Therefore be ready, for in such an hour as ye think not, the Son of Man cometh.'" He hit Matt's shoulder with his own. "That's the Book of Matthew. And what it means—"

"I reckon I can work out the meaning."

"—is you should always be prepared to meet your Maker, because you never know when you're about to."

Matt pressed his finger to his forehead. "Neat little hole, just like you said." Jesse blinked a few times. "And then his whole chest blasted away. Laying in the ditch with his feet bare, covered in his own guts and blood."

Jesse dug a crater with his boot heel. "Your folks leaving?"

"Ma says yes."

"Well, you're a grown boy. You don't have to do what your ma says."

"What about you, Jess?" Matt tried to keep his words even and calm. "You have to do what your ma says? Or your brother? Your ma sewing you that shirt, whose idea was that? Yours, or hers, or Buck's, or whose?"

When Matt mentioned the shirt, Jesse set his jaw, blinking furiously.

"You're not the only one who notices things," Matt said quietly.

Jesse flipped his hair out of his eyes. "Well, my way's clear. What'll yours be?"

"I ain't sure. I got to think on it some more."

"What've you got to think on, Matt? Whether you'll fight for Missouri?"

"Whether I want to do it the way I saw done to Mr. Stone."

Jesse leaned so close their heads were nearly touching. "It's the only way there is. And the Feds are the ones who made it that way. And you *know* it."

"Yeah, I know well enough. At church I could hardly bear it, listening to that pastor talk so, laying the whole blame on the guerrillas, the bloodthirsty men."

"I heard about it all," Jesse said slowly. "And I know you walked out during that vile hymn."

Matt stared at him. "How do you know?"

"I just do."

"Well, you know about my new friend, the provost marshal?"

Jesse raised his eyebrows.

"He's got his eye on me now. After Ma sent me to report Mr. Stone."

"Sent *you*? What's she thinking, Matt, that ma of yours?"

"I don't believe she *was* thinking too clear. She had Mrs. Stone to worry over, and arrangements to make."

"She had to've known, though, Matt. Why didn't she send Clayton, with Ben along?"

"Clayton had a coffin to make," Matt said steadily, and Jesse looked away again.

"Anyhow, what all'd that devil say to you?" he muttered.

Matt recounted the conversation in Ford's office, and the one in the churchyard.

"Well, I just can't see your ma putting that attention on you," Jesse said, and Matt decided to say nothing about the attention Mrs. Samuel had been putting on Jesse for more than a year.

"Clayton says Ford knows everybody, anyway. Clay believes maybe Mr. Stone was looking out for me against the Feds. What do you think of that?"

"Matt, I don't think that old spy was looking out for anybody but himself and his blasted Union."

Matt made no reply.

"You asked me, so don't hold it against me."

"I'm all mixed up," Matt mumbled. "Sometimes I feel like I want to be out of it altogether. Just be under the ground with Papa."

"That's *sinful* talk, Matthew," Jesse said, frowning. "When you have evil thoughts like that, you ought to pray them *right* out of your head."

Matt stopped a bitter laugh.

" 'This is the day which the Lord hath made,' " Jesse went on. " 'Let us rejoice and be glad in it.' "

Matt shook his head. "*Damn*, Jesse! I *won't* rejoice in any days such as these, and don't tell me I ought to!"

"Shhh," Jesse whispered fiercely, looking left and right over his shoulders.

"Lord, you—" Matt flung his hat down and rubbed his hair hard.

"As for your preacher's remark about neighbor boys, what'd you think of that?"

"I don't know. Maybe you ought to tell me what to think."

"My brother wasn't there, that much I'm sure. If Buck had known about this trouble, he'd've come for me. I don't know who killed Stone, but I do know he deserved what he got."

"*Listen* to you! One breath you quote the Bible, and the next you say a man deserved to die like an animal! What's that about?"

Jesse grabbed Matt's shirtfront and held tight. "What's it about? It's about your neighbor would've got my brother, or my pappy, or me killed on the double-quick the second he could've managed it, and my ma thrown in jail. So don't expect me to feel sorry my side got to him first."

"Let—go—my—shirt," Matt said, biting off each word.

Jesse released him. They sat fuming.

Finally Jesse said scornfully, "Tell you what, *Matt*. Why don't you just go on ahead to your Union folks, and we'll take care of Missouri for you. When it's all over, you can come back nice and peaceful and make believe nothing ever happened."

Matt got to his feet. "Just so I'm clear, what is it you're calling me?"

Jesse showed him a wicked grin. "If the boots fit, boy, you got to wear them."

"Get up," Matt demanded, and Jesse tackled him.

Matt found himself on top, but he was so surprised that he lost concentration, and Jesse flipped him like a flapjack. His head bounced off the packed dirt. Before he could gain any ground, Jesse pinned him by the throat. He raised his fist high above Matt's face—and stopped.

Matt looked into those freezing eyes, waiting for the blow.

But Jesse just glowered back at him, and then came Clayton's level voice: "Hey, Jess. Get off him."

Matt heard Clayton coming closer until he was a shadow over them. Jesse put his fist down but kept hold of Matt, with his hand and with his gaze.

"I don't need you to defend me, Clay!" Matt choked out.

"All right then, Jess," Clay said. "Go ahead and hit him."

"I don't want to hit him." Jesse gave Matt a vicious shove before he stood. Then he picked up his hat and walked away.

Matt felt sure he was trembling, and sure Clayton could see. He knew how stupid it had been, to fight right here in town, but Clay didn't lecture as Matt sat up, then stood, then put on his hat.

"Salt's done," was all Clayton said.

Matt took time to rub Salt under his bridle before hitching him up. On the wagon seat, he held the lines out to Clayton, who took them in silence. Matt rubbed the bump on his head and scratched his chigger bites and ground his teeth. He kept imagining himself jumping from the moving wagon, and finally he said, "Clay, stop. I got to walk."

"That's three miles in powerful heat," Clayton said, slowing the horses.

"I don't care." He stood up. "Stop."

"Would telling it help?" Clayton asked.

"There's no help for this. Let me down."

"Whoa," Clayton called.

Matt jumped. Clayton made a clicking sound, and the horses set off at a walk.

"And don't tell Ma," Matt said.

"All right. You're sure about this?"

"Please, Clay. Leave me."

"Get up," Clayton told the horses, and soon the wagon was out of sight.

When Matt had been walking a few minutes, hoofbeats came up hard behind him. He stepped aside. Jesse flew by at breakneck speed, leaving Matt to choke on his dust.

It took him about a mile and a half to walk off a good part of his hurt and fury. By then his head was aching, his throat parched, his shirt soaked—and his brother up the road, waiting. When Matt got to the wagon, he climbed up without a word, and without a word they drove home.

24

Matt had been putting off what he needed to say to Ma—in fact, they'd both done a good job of avoiding each other the last few days, since the argument over the letter. But now it was Saturday night, and he could delay no longer. He walked from the barn with purpose and stopped by Ma's chair on the porch. "Ma'am?"

She looked up.

"I'd like a word, if I could."

Clayton and Betsy traded glances.

"Of course," Ma said politely, rising. "We'll go inside."

He held the door. She seated herself by the hearth, and he took a chair opposite.

"Mama . . ." He frowned at the floor, then at her. "I won't go back to church."

Ma said nothing.

"I mean no disrespect to you, ma'am, but I can't. I won't."

"I see. And this is due to what was said at the funeral, I suppose."

"Yes, ma'am."

"You do not agree with any of it."

"No, ma'am. I don't."

She leaned close and said with great urgency, "They are murderers, Matthew! They do evil with both hands! How can you not see that? You, who found our friend in that ditch, who saw his house on fire, who met his widow screaming in the road? *How* can you defend their actions?"

Matt thought hard before he made his reply. "It's always your side that's right and my side that's wrong, isn't it, Ma?"

"Oh." She was nodding slow, but smoldering fast. "Now it's your side and my side, is it?"

"I reckon so, ma'am."

She walked to the wall, then back. He thought he should stand to face her. She folded her arms, paced again, stopped before him. "For a solid year you've been deceiving me at every turn. Agreeing to everything, the soul of courtesy. Yes, ma'am; no, ma'am; three bags full, ma'am. It's all been lies, hasn't it, Matthew? All lies."

He was so stunned, he couldn't even imagine a response.

"Then you go down that road and you take their views. I asked you straight out if you and Jesse talked about going to the brush, and what did you say? Tell me!" She jerked him by his arm. "I mean to have an answer, Matthew. *What did you say?*"

"I said no."

"And that was a lie, just as you lied about the letter, and the candy, and Lord only knows what else!" Her eyes were desperate and wild. "And I knew! I knew it was all lies, but I told myself I was wrong because I couldn't bear to face the truth. And I asked you what you'd do if we left. And you said, 'Whatever you say, Ma,' and that was another lie. Wasn't it?"

"Yes," he said, and she slapped his face.

Betsy came into the house, followed by Clayton. Tyler's wails seemed to echo miles away. Then Betsy rushed him up the stairs.

"Leave us, Clayton, please!" Ma shouted, and Matt heard him go up, too.

He could not move, could not think what might come next.

"You take such offense when Ben speaks his mind to me and maybe sasses me a bit," Ma went on. "Well, I'll tell you true, Matthew—I'd rather have ten boys like Ben than one like you. At least I know what's in his head. I know what's in his heart." She lowered her tone. " 'The words of his mouth were smoother than butter, but war was in his heart. His words were softer than oil, and yet they were drawn swords.' And that verse is you, Matthew. I've prayed away the thought, I've begged myself not to believe it of you. But there is war in your heart, isn't there?"

Steadily he replied, "Whatever you say, ma'am."

She tossed her head with angry pride, pointing to the door. "Go. Go to Jesse's if that's where you wish to be. Get your things, take your horse, and go."

He would obey, as always, and Jesse would forget their fight soon enough when he said he'd go to Quantrill. And yet . . . was this the way to make up his mind? To spite Ma? No. He would go to the woods. Sleep out and study on it alone.

At the stairs, Ben was hunched on a low step, Clayton a bit higher, staring down. "Don't go," Ben whispered fearfully, grabbing Matt's ankle.

Matt pulled away and began to climb—but then stopped.

It was time.

He turned down the stairs, walked straight to Ma, and said, "You go on about Quantrill . . . Tell me, is he the one who started all this?"

"I don't—"

"Jim Lane, Doc Jennison, jayhawkers—those names mean anything to you, Ma?"

"If you think—"

"Killing Missouri folks *long* before Quantrill started up, and you *know* that, so why do you act like it's just the partisans who do bad?"

"I only—"

"And they all make a hero out of Old Brown, singing hymns about a man who would murder that way, a man hanged for treason!"

"I never—"

"And your Federal militia—"

"Stop interrupting me!" Ma shouted, stamping her foot.

"I will not!" His voice topped hers, and she drew back. "You want me to be like Ben? I can backtalk like you never heard before!"

Ma just glared at him.

"You want to know if Jesse and me talk about going to Quantrill? *Yes*, ma'am, we talk about it plenty. At least Quantrill's making it an even fight instead of letting Missouri get kicked down again and again by everybody from Kansas to Washington! And I can't run away, like you will. Because I loved Papa too much—"

"Don't bring Papa into it!"

"—to forget all about him and what he made for this family and go to your folks, who hated him—"

And then she pitched into him. "How dare you question my love for your father? How dare you!" She hit him in the face, in the head; hit his shoulders, his neck. He had crossed the line.

"He was my husband! He was my life! Do you think you are the only one who misses him?"

Her punches and tears pursued him to the lean-to door. But he couldn't see the latch, or find it with his fingers. And what was that peculiar noise? A whimpering animal? No, it was Ma. No . . . it was him.

At last the door was open, but Ma slammed it shut and backed him halfway to the hearth. He raised his arms fast to shake her off and huddled against the wall, hating her for making him cry, ashamed that his brothers and sisters could hear but unable to stop, and he held his fist to his teeth and shut his eyes tight.

Ma touched his shoulder. "Don't you know how desperate I am—" A great, wracking sob stole her words. "How desperate I am not to lose you?"

Then his sorrow was so deep, he nearly collapsed. He groped for the table and slid into a chair, holding his head, overcome, weeping like a child.

"If any harm should come to you, I don't know how I'd bear it, Matt. I couldn't bear it." She was beside him, her arms around him, her tears wetting his face as she kissed him. "You're so wrong about what I believe," she said. "How can you think I applaud the jayhawkers? But they're not who I fear. It's Quantrill I fear because it's Quantrill who will take you from me." She combed his hair with her fingers. "And who are you to Quantrill? One more farm boy to get shot off his horse and die, not in glory, not quickly or easily, but writhing in agony in someone's field. Or captured and hanged. Or put before a firing squad. And before you die, you'll do fiendish things to other human beings. That isn't what you want for your life, is it? It isn't what your papa and I raised you for."

She kissed him some more. He didn't think he'd been kissed as many times in his whole life as in these last two minutes. "I want you with me, and the children need you. They don't need candy. They need their brother. Think of Ben on his own, without you to help him through. And Molly, she worships you. And Tyler, he'd miss you so, and never even understand what he was hurting for."

"Ma, don't," he managed to say.

"And me, who would I have to look at . . . who reminds me

so much of Papa?" She started weeping again, clutching his hand in both of hers.

"Don't, Ma, please," he begged, and there were more tears, then more silence.

"I'd have been at the Samuels' door by breakfast," she told him at last.

"But you wouldn't've found me there, Ma," he said slowly. "See, Jesse and I, we're not on speaking terms right now."

Ma's eyebrows rose.

"I don't just blindly take their views, Ma. Jesse and I had a bad fight about Mr. Stone—about everything. I don't believe we'll ever be friends again." To say it was to finally admit it to himself. He shut his eyes tight, rubbing his forehead.

"Oh, Matt," Ma whispered. "I'm sorry."

"You think there's war in my heart, Ma?" he said after a time. "Well, that ain't so, but it's in my head. It's in my head all the time, and not by my own choosing. All I want to do is farm my land, but nobody'll let me do that, will they?"

She shook her head, lips pressed tight.

"Nobody," he said again.

"That's why we must go from here. All of us. Especially you."

"But the way of it is, if I go, I don't know if I'll ever be able to come back. And show my face. To everybody who fought. Don't you see that, Ma?"

She stared into his eyes and made no reply.

"He should've told me, Ma. He should've told me what to do."

"Oh, Matt. When Papa was sick, we only whispered the

name Quantrill around here. And Order 19, how could he have known? He thought it would all be over last fall. It comforted him to believe that."

Matt sighed. "I'm sorry, Ma. For all I said. And backtalking you that way. Papa would've knocked me cold."

She hugged him. "I want only one like Ben, and you just exactly like you. And you needn't be sorry for telling me the truth. We got into this fix because of your trying to save me from it. And my not truly wanting to know it. Let's not do that again."

"Yes, ma'am."

"We'll deal with things as they come up, and not both be so mulish."

"All right, then."

"Go ahead to the barn."

It was clear and hot, the kind of July night when Papa would say you could hear the corn growing. Matt's face was tight with bruises, and there was far too much to worry over. But he felt better than he had since long before Papa died.

He found himself sitting on the pasture fence, right where Papa spent months calling out lessons as Matt tried to break Salt.

"That's all right, Papa," he said to the stars. "I guess you didn't want to know."

He spoke to Salt and locked the barn, then went in to face his brothers.

25

"Papa always said, When it's wet I plow it till it's dry, and when it's dry I plow it till it's wet." Kneeling in the corn row, Matt scooped up a handful of earth. "But look here, Ben. We've been plowing for nearly two weeks. It troubles me to see it this dry so late in July, when the corn's trying to make its ears."

Ben's reply was an odd whine. Matt looked up and followed his brother's frightened gaze: a militia man had his carbine trained on Matt.

"Are you armed?" the man asked.

"No, sir."

The soldier slung the carbine over his shoulder. "Get up slow. Keep your hands where I can see." The man advanced and felt for a weapon. "Let's go."

"Matt?" Ben trotted nervously alongside.

"It's all right, Ben. Go on up to the house. Go ahead."

"You're being taken for a work detail," the soldier explained. "Provost marshal's orders. Get yourself a rope and an ax and a sledge and a wedge."

The soldier followed him to the barn. Matt collected the things, his mind racing. What did this mean? Was he officially under arrest? If so, would they bother to tell him? As they headed toward the yard, he saw Ma arguing with another soldier. His brothers and Molly watched. Betsy came from the house and handed Matt two blankets and a sack of corn-meal.

"Don't worry, ma'am, we'll not harm your boy," said the soldier with Ma. "Get some good hard work out of him, for certain, but we'll bring him back in one piece, I give you the word of the Federal government."

The word of the Federal government—was that a comfort to Ma?

"Can I speak to my brother alone?" Clayton asked.

"If you make it right quick."

At the pump, Clayton told him, "They say the bushwhackers are tearing up track and burning ties on the Hannibal & St. Joe. You're to fell trees and make new ties."

"All right."

"Do whatever they say, Matt." Clayton's eyes were search-ing, insistent. "Obey them to the letter. To the letter. Give them no excuse."

Matt tried to quench his fear with gulps of water. Southern men in Federal hands sometimes ended up dead, shot in the back—while trying to escape, the Federals claimed. "Don't worry, Clay," he said.

"I will, though," Clayton answered.

Walking to the road, flanked by soldiers, Matt's heart welled up in his throat. He'd never been away from home before, and now he was to go work and eat and sleep with strangers, under the Federals' thumb. Where, and for how long? Was he old enough to be taken for the Paw-Paw regiment, Southerners conscripted into the Union militia?

Two mounted soldiers guarded a wagon full of grim men

and boys. All had blankets, ropes, and grain sacks. Matt's stomach knotted when he saw Sam Wright.

The wagon jolted ahead. Sam slouched over to wedge himself in next to Matt. "What'd *you* do to get on this detail?"

"Nothing."

"You must've done something. That bastard Ford sent my pa to jail, claims he's been a lookout for the partisans. Said he'd have me on the detail for good measure."

Matt didn't answer.

"Maybe you just hang around too much at Jesse's."

Matt picked up his rope and coiled it.

Sam shut up for a minute, then asked, "You seen him much lately?"

"Nope."

"Feds did stop by his place," Sam said, and now Matt looked at him. "Went shouting hither and yonder." Sam shrugged. "Nobody around. He say anything to you about going away?"

"I ain't seen him for a couple weeks," Matt said, and Sam let him be.

Jesse gone? Matt studied on it as the wagon bumped along. The whole family, gone? Unlikely, even if a neighbor was feeding the hogs and milking the cows—and that was even more unlikely, considering their only near neighbor was Dan Askew. No, at least one person had to be left on the place. But Jesse—off to the brush? Did Buck come for him? Or this squad leader, Taylor? And what about Susie, where was she?

They rode for hours under a sun no hat could hide. One old man coughed and wheezed endlessly. Matt bent double, hands over his face, imagining he was in the tree and Susie scrambling up the rope. He dozed off for a while, and woke feeling sick.

At a stream along a dense wood, they were told to clear out their things, then get a drink. Matt and Sam went to the water together. When the Federals said to pair off for work, they agreed to without speaking.

Their first task was hauling rocks to build fences, to replace wooden ones guerrillas had burned. As they carried the rocks to waiting wagons, the Feds pestered them continually to pick up the pace. "Never thought Quantrill would be causing *me* personal hardship," Sam grumbled.

They were allowed to stop at dusk, and then they learned what the blankets were for: setting up dog tents like enlisted men. You tied a rope between two trees and hung a blanket over it, then anchored the blanket's corners with stones. Matt wanted to get in that tent and sleep till September, but a man on the detail told him and Sam to gather wood.

Sam muttered, "Bad enough the damn Feds are giving us orders. We got to take it from the Seceshers, too?" But they fetched the wood and built a fire, and the Feds gave them a bit of salt pork, a skillet—and some hard, flat squares.

Sam tapped one on a rock. "What in hell is this?"

"Boy, that's what they call hardtack," someone answered.

"And what in the devil are you meant to do with it?" Sam asked, and the others laughed. "Break your damn *teeth*—"

Matt gnawed on a square, but then laid it aside. An older man noticed. "You'd better pocket a few of those crackers, young fellow. You mightn't find them so distasteful in a couple hours."

He said nothing, but did as he was told. Some men mixed cornmeal with water and fried it with salt pork. It wasn't exactly Ma's cooking, but it was far more palatable than hardtack.

"How long you reckon we'll be at this?" Sam asked after they crawled into their tents, which they had hung from the same rope.

"Long as they've a mind to keep us, I suppose," Matt said. It seemed he had only just shut his eyes when the Federals were rousting them out again.

Breakfast was more hardtack, and chicory coffee. Matt had no intention of swallowing that foul-smelling liquid. The men were grateful to get it, though, and so was Sam. He said he drank it at home, and he encouraged Matt to try: "It gets you going."

"Soak the hardtack in it," someone suggested. "Let it sit good."

When Matt tried it, his face was a source of great amusement, and he couldn't help but laugh at himself.

"Choke down all you can, son," one man said. "That's all there is."

Matt drained the cup.

"Think of it as learning a valuable skill, boys," a cheerful young Federal told Matt and Sam, teaching them how to hew railroad ties. "Men get cash money for railroad ties, and if you've got timber woods on your place, you can make them at home."

"Yeah, all *my* cut timber goes to mending fences pulled down by you Feds," Matt said under his breath, and Sam snickered.

As Matt worked, he thought of Ma, looking so careworn and defeated when telling him good-bye. *This is all my doing*, she kept saying, as if finally figuring it out. He wished he had a way to let her know he was okay. When Betsy hurried out with the blankets, concern clouded her face. And Molly, serious and forlorn, watching with those big brown eyes. He'd only given the baby a quick kiss good-bye, embarrassed because the Federals were watching. Now he longed to take Tyler in his arms.

How would Ben do on his own with all the heavy chores? Ever since Mr. Stone was killed, Ben had been sticking close, seeming worried and scared. For so long Matt had been telling him to be quiet, to obey. Now Ben *was* that good boy, but with fear his reason. Matt found himself wishing for the old Ben back.

Then he wondered what was in Clayton's head, watching the Feds take him—unable to stop it, unable to go along. He pictured Clay brooding on the porch, rubbing his rough chin—and suddenly he knew that once Clayton went North, he would never live on the farm again. The notion hit Matt so hard he stopped swinging his sledge and stared over the landscape. Why hadn't he thought of this before? Clayton said that he wanted to go to college, that there was nothing for him on the farm. Yet Matt had still imagined him coming back—imagined them all coming back and taking up life as before.

"Boy!" one of the Feds called, and Matt lifted the sledge again.

They were allowed to fish and forage, but the pickings were slim, the creek too low. It was corn pone and corn mush, hardtack, coffee, and occasionally some salt pork, day after day. In the sun, the chiggers bit, and in the dark, mosquitoes. Matt was covered with welts and raked at them fiercely with a stick. The longer he was away, the harder it was to sleep. Each night seemed stickier and hotter. If he slept outside, it was a bit cooler. But if he slept in the tent, the mosquitoes didn't find him quite so readily.

Every morning they all dragged more, every day they talked less, every breakfast the coffee tasted better to Matt. He took to chewing whatever hardtack he could get. They moved camp twice; he was certain they were no longer in Clay County.

It had to be August by now, but he'd lost track of the days. Still no rain—that much he knew. How was the corn doing? Even if he might not be there for harvest, it was still his first crop. He wanted to remember it as a good one.

One afternoon the cheerful Federal, who turned out to be a sergeant, took Matt and Sam on the seat of a rock-filled wagon. They rode through a small town, and the sergeant stopped near a burned-out house and told them to build a fence from here to there. Matt and Sam tossed down rocks and set to work. The sergeant lay in the shade and had himself a festive time watching.

The wall was about knee-high when Matt heard wheels and hooves. Sam jogged him with an elbow: "Matt, look." The wagon was crowded with Negro women and children, and behind it rode four well-armed cavalrymen. The driver, some sort of Federal, stopped and hailed the sergeant.

"Keep working," Matt said, but Sam paid him no mind and gaped at the folks in the wagon. When Matt gave in to his own curiosity, he saw that a boy about their age was staring hard at him and Sam.

Matt gathered that the boy could hear the sergeant telling the driver who they were and why they were here. He tried to figure out what was in that boy's eyes. Not hate. Not anger. But what? Suspicion? Distrust? Then a woman beside the boy noticed him looking at them. Matt knew she was his mother when she gently gripped his chin and turned his face away.

"What's he gawking at us for?" Sam said angrily.

"Shut up, Sam," Matt said. "Keep working."

Sam did. But when the wagon left, he asked the sergeant, "Who were they?"

"They're contrabands," the sergeant said, "on their way to Kansas. Their fathers and husbands are in a Kansas regiment, and the commander promised those men he would get their families to freedom. And that's just what he's done."

"How many folks did he have killed to *get* that done?" Sam said, defiant.

"Shut up, Sam," Matt told him.

The sergeant didn't say a word.

"So what is it, boys?" the sergeant asked on the way back. "How'd you two get yourselves into this fix, anyhow?"

"Provost Marshal Ford took my pa to jail, but wouldn't tell why," Sam mumbled.

"Hmm. What about you, Matt?"

"I'm not sure, sir. Suppose I got myself on the wrong side of Mr. Ford, somehow."

"Really? Nice fellow like that?" the sergeant said, then roared with laughter.

Matt thought he could start to like this Federal.

"Anyhow, boys, I thought I'd tell you. Before this crew's released, you'll all be required to take the oath."

Matt said nothing. To his great surprise, neither did Sam.

"And you'd best go along with it if you know what's good for you. Hear?"

"Yes, sir," Matt said.

"Sam?"

"I hear."

They crossed paths with a woman carrying a crying baby, followed by a solemn girl Molly's size and a boy about Ben's age leading a tired-looking, loaded-down mule. The woman's eyes were empty, unblinking. Matt turned to watch her pass.

"Refugees," the sergeant said. "Burned out, I expect. Husband's dead, I imagine. Or a bushwhacker. Or a Federal." The family dragged on. He shrugged. "If it matters."

Matt stared till they were out of sight.

Matt had thought his hands were toughened to any work, so he was surprised to feel the blisters. At the water's edge, he sat on his heels and picked up handfuls of soothing mud, thinking of Susie's finger in his palm.

"My damn hands are so bad blistered I don't see how I'll swing that blasted ax tomorrow," Sam said, coming up beside him.

"Do like this," Matt suggested. "It helps."

Sam squatted down and sank his hands into the mud. "Matt?"

"Yeah?"

"You fixing to take their damn oath?"

"You reckon there's a choice?"

"We could refuse."

"Speak for yourself, Sam. You refuse, you'll end up in jail by your pa."

"Jesse says—"

"Jesse says what? Huh?" Matt snapped. "He ain't here, is he? The oath means nothing. You take it if they make you, or you're a fool."

"All right, I hear you," Sam shot back. "Jeez." He flung a handful of mud and stalked away.

"I know why it's called a dog tent," Sam said, adjusting his a couple of nights later. "Because you're so dog-tired, you'll actually *sleep* in the doggone thing."

"I could sleep on a picket fence."

"How long we been gone, anyway?"

Matt pulled off his boots. "Seven days."

"Eight."

"If you knew, why'd you ask?"

Sam sighed. "I'm worried over my pa. What do you reckon they'll do?"

Matt pictured Sam's pinch-faced pa sitting in a coffin. "Like as not, he'll just have to pay a fine."

"Well, that'd be some trick. We got no money."

"I know *that* feeling." If Ma had to pay a fine, he'd rot in jail till one side surrendered. And Sam's family was even poorer— white trash, some folks called them.

"What do you miss most, Matt?"

Matt shrugged. "Oh, I don't know." He liked Sam well enough now. Still, he wasn't about to tell Sam what he missed, which was every single person in his family—and so powerfully that, alone at night, fearing he'd never get home, he lost the need to sleep for a while.

"I miss my ma," Sam admitted. "I never thought I'd miss my ma so."

Matt stared at the starless sky, then cleared his throat. "Not so tough without Scott around, are you?"

"And you're not so quiet without Jesse."

Finally Matt got his rain. It poured down for two days. Still they worked. By day, not a needless word was said; by night, Matt was able to sleep only because he was more tired than wet.

At last word spread that they'd be released in the morning. Could it be? Tomorrow at this time, his family and his house and Salt and Ma's cooking and his soft featherbed? Matt wanted it so much he dared not dwell on it.

Daylight came, and they were told to gather their things. At the Federals' ragged outpost, they lined up by a dirty canvas tent. The cheerful sergeant stood just inside, raising the flap to admit them one by one. Each man came out angry or solemn or both. Finally it was Matt's turn.

An officer, sitting grandly at his desk of boards on boxes, didn't bother to look at him. "You know how to read?"

"Yes, sir."

"Read it." He thrust out a paper.

Matt stepped forward and squinted at the page. He had expected only a few lines, like Quantrill's oath, but this was long, peppered with words he'd never seen. His face felt hot and prickly, his voice sounded thick and dull: "I solemnly swear . . . that I will bear true allegiance to the United States . . . and support and sustain the Constitution and laws thereof." He swallowed. "That I will maintain the national . . . sovvvv . . ."

"Sovereignty," the officer said.

Matt took in his breath. "Sovereignty . . . paramount to that of all State, county or Confederate powers; that I will discourage, dis . . . dis . . ."

"Discountenance."

". . . discountenance, and forever oppose . . ." He paused. The next word swam before his eyes.

"Surely you know that damn word, boy!" the officer barked.

"Yes, sir." Matt stared at the paper.

"Then start from 'forever oppose,' and say it or don't say it!"

His blood was pounding so loud he could barely hear himself say, ". . . and forever oppose secession, rebellion, and the disintegration of the Federal Union." He bit his lip hard. "That I disclaim and denounce all faith and fellowship with the so-called Confederate armies, and pledge my honor, my property, and my life to the sacred performance of this my solemn oath of allegiance to the Government of the United States of America."

He was trembling so, the paper crackled. He kept his head down till the officer said: "Look at me, boy. You know what all those big words mean?"

"Not all, sir."

"There's only six I ask a boy your age to remember." He

counted them off on his fingers: "Forever. Oppose. Secession. Pledge. My. Life. You understand me?"

"Yes, sir."

He beckoned Matt toward the desk, holding out a pen. "Sign it."

Matt laid the paper down and bent over it. Sweltering with anger and shame, he signed the oath in a smeary, shaky hand.

"Go home," the officer grunted.

Outside, Sam ran to meet him. "That wasn't so bad, huh?"

Matt kept walking.

"That rattle you, Matt?"

"It did."

"Huh." Sam shrugged. "I didn't think it was so bad."

Later, in the wagon, someone asked, "What was the word he was hollering at you about?"

"Secession," Matt said.

"You couldn't read *that* word, boy?" The man laughed, along with a few others.

"I could read it fine," Matt said evenly. "I just didn't want to."

The mirth died down. "Ah, it don't mean anything," another man said. "It's just a bunch of damn words on a paper. Don't take it so hard, son."

Matt directed all his attention to rubbing mud off his boots, and huddled shivering in his wet clothes as they began the journey home.

26

Ben dashed up the lane and jumped right at him.

"Hey, boy." Matt roughed his hair. "You been taking care of things?"

"How was it, Matt? You all right? Did they beat you?"

"Do I look beat?" He scooped up Molly and Tyler, telling them, "I have never been so glad to see a batch of children in all my life!" He even kissed Betsy, and Ma held him to her, crying. "I'm all right, Mama. Played out. Starved. Filthy. Bit to pieces. But otherwise . . ."

She laughed through her tears.

When he saw Clayton making his way, Matt went to meet him. Clay moved both crutches to one hand, then reached around Matt's neck and pulled him close. "Hello, Haytop," he said.

"Hey, Strawtop." Matt laid his head on Clay's shoulder, shutting his eyes tight.

"All right?" Clay said.

Matt nodded, and when he stepped away Ben leaped onto his back.

"Get off him, Ben. He's worn out."

"I don't mind, Clay." Matt flipped Ben over his shoulders.

"What would you like most, Matthew?" Ma asked as they walked to the house.

"Food," he said, causing general mirth. "And a bath. With plenty of soap."

"Did they return me the right boy?" Ma teased, hugging him again.

They sat him on the porch and crowded around, bringing milk and ham and light bread with butter and apple jelly. Bread meant flour, flour meant money, and money could only have come from one direction: north. But it wouldn't do to kick up trouble over it, and besides, he was hungry. The milk was a little tart, just as he liked it, and he drank three cups. "Mama, guess what I've been drinking every morning—*coffee*."

"Coffee! Goodness!"

"I might even get to missing it. But now, *this* . . ." He fished hardtack from his pocket. "*This* I will not miss." He handed bits to Ben and Molly. "What do you suppose that might be, you two?" Ben shrugged. Molly wrinkled her nose. "Hardtack. What Union soldiers eat."

Clayton leaned forward. "So that's what hardtack looks like."

"Here. What do you think?" He gave them each a piece. "Taste it, Ben. Could you eat that morning, noon, and night? Go on, Moll."

All three took a bite and shuddered.

"Here, Betsy, give it a try," Matt urged.

"No, *thank* you!" she said, laughing.

"Give Tyler a bit," Ben said, and they howled as the baby gnawed eagerly. "That's the darnedest baby I ever saw! He likes hardtack, but he won't eat candy!"

At that, things got quiet. Matt cleared his throat. "Ben, I was meaning to tell you. And you, too, Molly. That day I brought the candy? It wasn't like I said, a good secret. Not telling was like lying, and I was wrong."

"It's over and done, Matt," Ma said briskly. "Let me try that hardtack."

Matt expected he would want to ride, but instead he only brushed and talked to Salt. Ben was anxious to show the corn. The ears were coming along fine, he said, with all the rain. But Matt didn't even feel up to walking to the fields. He put it down to being tired, and to the chill still upon him, probably from sleeping in wet clothes.

"I never thought I'd miss soap so much," he told Clayton, who sat in the yard while he bathed.

"Mama's relieved to find you so cheerful. She worried you'd take to the brush soon as you got home."

Matt began to wash. "Well, I'm not about to sit on that porch and cry to Ma about the bad of it," he said at last. "But nobody need think I'm not mad, being taken off that way." He splashed his face. "Still, Clay, I don't know but that I'm seeing things a bit different now."

"Oh?"

"The sergeant took Sam and me to build a rock fence, and we saw a lady come along with nothing but a mule and three children. He called her a refugee." Matt leaned back and shut his eyes. "The look about her, Clay, it was frightful. Like she wasn't even there. And the sergeant said, 'Does it matter if she's Union or Secesh?' And he's right. Either way, she's alone with small children."

Clayton said nothing.

Matt rubbed a handful of soap hard into his hair, and Clay poured a bucket of water over his head. It felt way too cold.

"Seen Jesse?" Matt asked, trying to sound as though it didn't matter.

"No."

There was a long silence.

"Clay, you never tell what you think about folks having servants."

A slow smile spread across Clay's lips. "Back when the statehood trouble with Kansas heated up, there was a lot of talk, all the time, about abolitionists and border ruffians. One day, when I was about Ben's age, I told Papa I didn't see *what* the fuss was all about. I'd been around Aunt Lotty and Aza and other folks' servants plenty of times. They all seemed content to me. Now, you know Papa had no use for abolitionists, nor border ruffians, either. But I never forgot his reply. He said, 'Might be, treating slaves kind is an unintended sort of cruelty, because then they could grow up thinking bondage ain't so bad.' "

Matt stared at the glittering water. "He never said anything like that to me."

"I suppose I only got that much because I made the comment. You know Papa wasn't one for speechifying. Or passing judgment. 'A man's got to . . .' "

" '. . . live amongst his neighbors,' " Matt finished with him, and together they quietly laughed.

After a time, Matt said, "We saw a wagon full of none but colored women and children, guarded by soldiers. Their men were Union soldiers in a Kansas regiment. The commander sent his soldiers to take those folks from their masters."

"And what did you think about *that*?" Clayton asked.

"I think no Kansan *ever* helped a slave from the goodness of his heart. The only reason they do anything is to punish Missourians."

"That may be so, but there might be one or two who aren't quite so bad as the rest."

Matt said nothing.

"Either way, I imagine those folks are glad to have their freedom."

"It ain't about the slaves," Matt mumbled.

"No, it's about a lot of things, Matt. But slavery's one of them."

"Clay, you know and I know that every slave in this whole damn state could be free tomorrow and it would all still go on!"

"Like I say," Clayton said patiently, "it's about a lot of things, things you and I don't even understand because we don't know enough."

"Well, I told you it all made me think." Matt almost grudged the words. "But I'm still a Southerner. And I always will be."

"And just why *are* you a Southerner?" Clayton challenged.

"Because I am. Because Papa was, and I am, and that's just the way of it."

"But what does it mean to *you*, Matt? In this war?"

"It means . . . well, it means . . ." He slapped the water. "Dang it, Clay, do you suppose I could have a little time to ponder? At this very minute I'm too tired to work my brain much."

"I'm sorry," Clayton said with an embarrassed grin. "I told you before, I've got too much time to think. Recall my telling you how I put myself in somebody else's place?"

"Yes."

"The day I watched those militia walk you up the lane, it came to me hard: I have no idea what it's like to be you, Matt. I never did. I remember the first time Papa put you up on Sugar on your own. You were about four, I suppose. You recall?"

Matt shook his head. He did not remember a time before he could sit a horse.

"Hoo, was I mad! There you were, this little rag of a boy, practically still wetting yourself at night, trotting in the pasture. And there I was, watching. Papa always tried to encourage me about riding, taking me with him. But you know I never wanted to do what I couldn't do on my own, and to watch *you* . . ." He whistled long and low, laughing at the memory. "Yes, I felt sorry for myself, but I got over it. Like I got over every other thing you did before me or better than me. I reflected on it once you were gone. How I never *could* put myself in your place, but only watch you, just as I watched you on Sugar that day: jealous, furious, worried—and proud."

Matt stayed very still, playing his hand across the water. At last he said, "Clay, of all the things that rattle me about you ones leaving—and believe me, there's plenty—the worst is knowing *you'll* never be back."

"Thank you, Matt."

Matt dried off and dressed in the clean clothes waiting for him.

"I'll always visit, though," Clayton said. "You know that, don't you?"

"I guess."

"Railroads'll be better. Faster."

"We might be living in different countries."

"People visit other countries."

Matt pulled on his boots. "Clay, you gave me an idea. Where's the baby? Molly!" he called.

Molly and Ben ran from the porch. "Good!" Ben said. "You're done."

"Is Tyler up? Go and see, Moll. If he is, bring him out."

"What're you up to?" Clayton asked.

"You'll see." He felt peculiar—still cold, and rubbery in his legs—but he went and tacked Sugar up and rode to the house. Everyone was in the dooryard.

"Give that baby here, Ma," Matt said, reaching down.

"Oh, I don't know, Matt . . ."

"You can trust me and Sugar, ma'am. Come on." Ma handed the baby over. He began to cry right away. "Oh, pipe down." Matt settled Tyler before him in the saddle, holding him tight with his left arm.

"Matt," Ma said again, and he trotted off to take the baby away from her worried voice.

"It's all right." At the road he rubbed Tyler's back till he stopped crying. "Isn't this fun?" he asked, walking Sugar back down the lane. "You're riding your papa's mare, Ty. You're a farm boy, don't ever forget that." He trotted gently to the barn lot.

Heading back to the house, he called out, "Is he smiling?" The answer was on their faces.

But Matt felt remarkably hot, and light-headed. He handed the baby down. "Here's your boy, Ma."

"*Mahhh!*" Tyler protested, reaching toward Matt.

Matt put Sugar to pasture. On his way to the house, his teeth started chattering. He could only see straight ahead, with everything around the edges black. Indoors, Betsy and Ma looked to be miles away.

"Matt?" Ma's voice echoed.

"Reckon I'll—" He headed for the stairs, but the floor tipped him sideways. "Whoa," he said, reaching for the table.

"Clayton!" Ma called.

The walls closed in as he started up the steps. His legs wouldn't hold him. He dropped to his knees and crawled, desperate for bed.

"Something's wrong," Ma whispered, and then Matt found himself on his bed, staring at the roof beams.

"I'm real cold. Cover me up, Mama. How can I be this cold?"

"Lord, he's burning up." Ma's hands were on his face.

"Cover me up, please."

"Yes," she said. "Yes, darling, it's all right."

27

It could have been two days, it could have been ten. He didn't rest when he slept, nor did he wake. He ached so, he imagined his bones had snapped. He had a powerful, constant thirst that would not be slaked. He sensed people, but did not quite see them. Someone fed him a bitter-tasting drink; it must be Ma. Someone read in the lamplight; that would be Clay. He was so hot he yanked off the bedsheet in a rage, struggling for breath. He was so cold his body shook, and he pulled Papa's buffalo robe tight around his neck. He spoke out loud in his dreams— the clearest dreams he'd ever had . . .

He was looking at his blistered palms and then Susie was there, touching each one, saying, "This one means you chop trees, this one means you haul rocks."

He heard his own laughter.

The provost marshal was in the lean-to, saying he wanted to see his crop, but the fields were empty as winter, and Matt said, "See what I grow?"

He was in a vast, crowded, noisy building, and the refugee woman went past with her children, and she became Ma, walking away from him, and from the sergeant's wagon he hollered, "Mama . . . don't leave me!"

She said, "I'll not leave you, darling," and he felt a soothing touch.

He was a small boy in the woods with Papa, asking, "Can I get him now?" and Papa said, "Now!" but when he looked up it wasn't a deer in his sights, it was Buck, and Buck stomped toward him, saying angrily, "Put the gun down, Matt! Put the gun down!"

Matt sat up with a start, heart pounding, breath coming fast, and he was gently pressed down.

"Shhh, it's a dream," came Betsy's voice.

"So thirsty."

His head was lifted, a cup held to his lips. He drank, then fell away.

He was streaking across the prairie, trying to pass Jesse, but when he finally caught up, it was Clayton, who turned with a grin, and then raced ahead.

In the duck blind with Ben, he was loading the dead Federal's Colt. But instead of a cartridge, he was pouring powder into the cylinders. It kept spilling over, and he said, "I can't measure up . . ."

He was on Papa's knee on the porch, rocking, his head tucked under Papa's chin, and he said, "Sing that song, Papa. About Kentucky."

He woke with the aching sense of loss a person feels when a good dream ends. Ma sat on the bed, wringing out a cloth in a basin on the nightstand. She smiled sadly and bathed his face.

"Did I say what I think?" he asked.

She nodded, pressing the back of her hand to her eyes. The dream slipped farther away as his mind reached out, trying to pull it back.

"How do you feel?"

"Tired." He closed his eyes.

She bathed his arms, his neck, and his chest, singing about the Southern boys and the Battle of New Orleans, slowly, as though it were a lullaby:

"I suppose you've read it in the prints,
How Packenham attempted
To make old Hickory Jackson wince
But soon his scheme repented.
For we with rifles ready cocked
Thought such occasion lucky,
And soon around the general flocked
The hunters of Kentucky.
Oh, Kentucky! The hunters of Kentucky,
The hunters of Kentucky."

She stopped, but the next part was his favorite.

"Keep going, Mama," he said.

"Well, Jackson, he was wide awake
And was not scared of trifles,
For well he knew what aim we take
With our Kentucky rifles.
And if a daring foe annoys,
Whatever his strength and forces,
We'll show him that Kentucky boys
Are alligator horses.
Oh, Kentucky! The hunters of Kentucky,
The hunters of Kentucky."

"*That's* what it means." He felt himself sliding away. "Tell Clay."

"What, Matt?"

"We fight back. We fight for our home," he said, and slept again.

28

"How's the patient today?"

Half-awake, too weak to move, Matt mumbled, "Tired." He wondered how many times Dr. Samuel had come, and he wished Ma hadn't called for him. But she must have been awfully worried to send for a doctor, even if he *was* a neighbor.

"There's two young folks on our place who are quite troubled over you, Matt," Dr. Samuel said, checking him over.

Matt's eyes closed. Two. He was on Susie's mind. And Jesse wasn't gone.

"I'm better now."

"I can certainly see that." Dr. Samuel turned to Ma. "He'll be fine, Carolyn. Feed him if he's hungry . . . and plenty of water. And rest."

"Of course," Ma said, nodding solemnly.

"You hear, Matt? You're not to dash out to your fields or your horse."

"Yes, sir."

Dr. Samuel patted his shoulder. "I'll see myself out, Carolyn, but just a word first." They stepped out of the room, but Matt heard Dr. Samuel say, "The boy wants to see him, but I said I'd have to ask."

"Of course, Reuben," Ma said. "Only, please ask him to mind how he comes."

"I'll tell him, but I know I needn't."

"I'm so indebted to you. And be sure to give Zerelda my regards."

"I will indeed." They said good-bye. Matt heard Dr. Samuel walk down the stairs.

Ma came back in, looking pleased. She propped her fists on her hips. "Well, young man—"

"Ma? What do you hear from your folks?"

She smiled nervously. "Do you feel up to talking about this right now, dear?" She began adjusting the bedsheet, a tuck here, a tug there. "Perhaps you should rest."

At that very moment, Matt realized his mind was made up. "Ma," he said, and she turned to him. "I'm going with you."

She sank down on the bed, searching his face. "Truly?"

He nodded.

Joy was in her eyes, her smile, even the pulse of her throat. But she only squeezed his hand quickly and said, "Oh, Matt, I *am* glad."

And he was glad she knew not to make a fuss, or ask how he'd come to his decision. He wouldn't have been able to say how much he'd missed them all when he was away. Or tell how he'd felt their comfort and care seeing him through this sickness. Or talk about his dreams, every one seeming to point him away from the war and back to them.

"I'm still uneasy about it, though," he admitted. "Letting others fight for me, then coming back when it's all over."

"You're fifteen years old, Matthew," Ma said quietly. "This is not your fight."

He looked away. "Some would disagree. And then—well, folks up North won't much care for me, you know."

"And why not? You're about the finest boy I've ever known, you and Clayton, and it's your papa I credit, so I don't feel prideful saying it."

He pulled the buffalo robe to him and smoothed its fur. "You know what I mean, Ma."

Sighing deeply, she took a letter from her apron pocket. "I broached the subject with my father. Here is his reply." She ran her finger along the page.

> "*As for Matt's being a Southerner, as you put it, I see no reason that should cause a problem, unless he'll be shouting it from the rooftop. Your mother and I have talked it over and we have agreed to respect the boy's attachment to his father's heritage.*"

"Well, Mama, when have you ever known me to shout from a rooftop—except 'Throw me up those nails'?"

Ma laughed.

"But I'll make no secret of it, either," he added quickly.

"That's fair enough," she said, nodding. "There's something else in this letter that I think will interest you." She turned the page and read:

> *"I would like you to tell Matt two things from me: If he comes to us, I shall do everything in my power to see that he feels comfortable here. Also, I shall somehow arrange to transport that treasured horse of his."*

He looked at Ma fast. "Bring Salt?"

"Isn't that wonderful?"

"Yes, ma'am, it is. And very generous." But he was glad he'd told her his decision before hearing it. He'd never want her to think the offer changed his mind. "But . . . when'll we go, Ma?"

"After Mr. Stone, I wrote that we would definitely be leaving," she said solemnly. "And your grandfather wrote back:

> *'I have decided to make the trip to Missouri to accompany you. I cannot countenance the idea of your undertaking all the arrangements and the long journey on your own.' "*

"He's coming *here?*"

"I think he's expecting to find his helpless little girl, Matt," she said in a confiding way.

"I can't believe he ever had one of those, Ma," he said, and she tugged on his hair. "But when'll he be here?"

"He was to write me when he expected to leave. But I haven't had a letter since this one, last week. He may already be on his way, though I've no idea how long it will take, what with . . . the situation."

Matt had a thousand questions now, about her father and mother, the rest of her family, the people up North. What was Philadelphia like? Were there woods and rivers? Places you could ride a horse for miles? Would Ma make him go to school? He'd rather work, save some money in preparation for coming home. But what sort of work would there be? Recalling the newspaper advertisements, he pictured himself in some grim factory. Perhaps it was best not to ask, not to know. Just take these days one at a time. Besides, he was too worn out to talk any longer. He closed his eyes.

Ma smoothed his hair and stood. "Can I get you anything, dear?"

"No, thank you."

"Get some sleep, then." Before leaving, she turned to smile at him once more.

Jesse showed up the next afternoon, poking his head in, hanging on the door. "Hey."

"Hey." Matt nodded him into the room.

"You all right?" Jesse asked, shutting the door.

"I am."

"Folks were concerned."

"I reckon."

Jesse jammed his hands in his pockets and went to the window. When he leaned down to look out, his hair fell over his eyes. "I expect that horse of yours is lonesome."

"Maybe you'd ride him for me."

"If you want."

"Well, Ben can't handle him."

"All right, then, I will." Jesse walked to the bedside chair. "Mind if I sit?"

"Before you get too cozy, I better say something right off."

"Okay."

"I told Ma I'll go to Pennsylvania." He fixed his eyes on Jesse's; Jesse didn't blink but once. "I've been thinking and thinking on it. I'll stay with my family. It's what my pa would have wanted. It's what I want."

"All right." Jesse sat backward on the chair.

"And there's more about that."

"Go on."

"My grandfather says he'll fix it so I can bring Salt."

"All the way to Pennsylvania? How, by train?"

"I reckon."

Jesse nodded thoughtfully. "Well, I'm glad. He'll be a comfort to you up there."

"No remarks about Yankees buying me?"

"No remarks."

"Because a couple times, you said—"

"Never mind. There's some things a body knows, despite what he might say."

"All right. And my leaving, you fixing to hold that against me? Will I be hearing about it the rest of my life?"

"I won't hold it against you. Listen." Jesse rocked the chair forward on two legs, studying the floor. "When I heard you were so sick and I figured you might die with us still mad, I couldn't be lived with. Ask Susie. I kept recalling you telling that neighbor of yours no war would divide us." He set the chair down. "You go ahead up there, Matt. I'll count on you to set those doggone Yankees straight about Missouri."

They stayed silent for a while. Matt said, "I sure am ready to get out of this bed."

Jesse tapped his arm and whispered, "Pappy says your ma was madder than a trapped badger when he first came. She said, 'That boy never had more than a cold his whole life until those Federals got hold of him.' "

"*Ma* said that?"

"Pappy and Ma were joking she might just turn Secesher right then." They laughed quietly. Then Jesse grew serious. "I'm sorry you were on that detail alone, Matt. I should've been there, by rights."

"Where were you, anyhow?"

"Things got mighty hot, and—you know my Aunt Jane?"

"Let's see, which one of your thousand kin—"

"Ma's sister, down by Liberty."

"The one with all the bratty children?"

"Right, and she's got a brand-new one as well. She wrote Ma that her four servants ran off, and—"

"Really?"

"Yep, and her husband's in Arkansas with General Price, so she was all on her own. We went up to stay with her awhile; took Aunt Lotty and Aza, too. Ma said we could get along without them for a time, so they stayed to help out Aunt Jane."

"Bad move. I bet your bratty cousins'll run *them* off, too."

"Oh, they'd never leave us. They're like kin—better than

kin, compared to my bratty cousins," Jesse added, and Matt laughed along.

"Anyhow, I wasn't alone on that detail. Don't you know Sam was there, too?"

"Sam Wright?" Jesse was taken aback. "He give you a hard row?"

"Truth to tell, we got along fine."

"Oh, yeah?"

Matt told Jesse about the railroad ties and the rock fence, the hardtack and the coffee, the dog tents and the rain. He left out the contrabands and the refugees. No sense getting Jesse into a foul temper about Kansas or the Union. As Matt talked, he recognized his pride at going on his own, experiencing a part of this war Jesse could not know or share.

"You never could find a single good thing in Sam," Jesse said when he finished. "Right down to how he sits his horse. Now you two are friends?" His tone left no doubt that he didn't care for the idea.

"Well, you get to know a person, you're with him in a situation like that," Matt said. "Sam's not so bad."

Jesse shifted uncomfortably.

"There's one more part," Matt said.

"What's that?"

He looked into Jesse's eyes. "I took the oath."

"Yeah? Everybody takes the oath, it's no big thing."

"No, Jess, that's just it," Matt said, trying to sit up straighter. "I thought the same way before. Sam was bothered at first, but when we came out, he said, 'Oh, that wasn't so bad.' But I was sick about it. I *know* it's what made me sick."

Jesse was shaking his head, frowning. "Pappy says it was fever and ague."

"No, it was that oath. You know the expression, to choke on your words? That's how it was, Jess. I nearly couldn't force myself to speak. And there's no point to the damn thing. It's only done to shame us. It made me madder than ever."

Jesse turned his head, blinking. His thoughts couldn't have been clearer if he'd shouted them: *You're so mad, why don't you fight?*

So much for avoiding sore subjects.

"You're doing it," Matt said, sliding down on the pillows. "The eyes. And I know what you're thinking."

"Bet you don't."

"Bet I do, but just leave it."

Jesse got to his feet. "Well, Pappy said don't stay long. So I'll take Salt out."

"Thanks."

"And listen, Susie and I are having this . . . well, party."

"A what?" Matt said, sure he'd heard wrong.

Jesse shrugged. "Ma says it's too dismal around here, and by my birthday, who knows where I'll be. Susie pestered me all morning to remember to ask you."

Matt rubbed his face to hide it. "So your ma let her out of her room?" he said, and they laughed.

"Anyhow, it's Friday night."

"Uh, what's today?"

"Monday."

"I should be better."

"Pappy reckons you will."

"You ask Martha?"

"No." It was Jesse's turn to blush. "That's done with."

"Oh, yeah? How come?"

He twisted his mouth. "Too darn bashful, I guess."

"Boys!" Ma called. "Enough for today!"

"Just coming, ma'am! See you, Matt."

" 'Bye, Jess."

As Jesse clattered down the stairs, Matt lay back and shut his eyes. He felt he could sleep well now that he and Jesse were right-side-up. But as he drifted off, a troubling image took shape: Jesse in his guerrilla shirt, riding wild—off to Quantrill with a revolver in his belt, yet too shy to court a girl.

29

Punched-tin lanterns lit the dusk, casting stars around the Samuels' yard. Matt smoothed the brown-and-blue plaid shirt, his only one that wasn't a hand-me-down. He propped his gun against the house, singing under his breath with two fiddlers and a banjo player.

Boys and girls were dancing, shouting, laughing. Susie and Jesse stood with Sam, Scott, and a few others. Sam was doing the talking.

Susie was beyond pretty in a yellow dress, her hair caught up in a matching ribbon. But as Matt approached, he winced to see her staring—with what looked to be adoration—at Sam. Then he heard Sam say, "So Matt tells him, 'I could read it fine. I just didn't want to.' "

Matt jabbed a finger into his back. "*What* tall tales are you telling?"

"Hey!" Sam grinned, hitting his arm.

"Your pa back home?" Matt asked.

"For now. But he's got to haul fodder for the Feds twice a week. I heard you took sick."

"I did. You?"

"Nah."

Matt greeted Jesse and the rest, even Scott, and finally said, "Hello, Sue."

"Hello, Matthew." Her soft, warm voice wrapped itself around him. She smiled with her lips pressed tight. Surely everyone could see how they looked at each other.

"Hey, Matt, recall?" Sam deepened his voice: " 'There's only six words I ask . . .' "

" '. . . boys your age to remember,' " Matt joined in, and they both counted on their fingers: " 'Forever. Oppose. Secession. Pledge. My. Life.' "

Scott said, "You two sure did remember!" and they all laughed.

Jesse gave Matt a curious smile. "You didn't tell me that part."

"Do you have to tell him everything, Matt?" Sam asked.

Susie saved him from a reply, grabbing his hand. "Come dance with me."

"You know I'm Methodist," he said, following. "I'm not allowed to dance."

She stopped to face him, tipping her head. "Do they allow you to talk?"

"I'll have to check my Book of Discipline," he said piously, reaching for his pocket, and she giggled.

She held tight to his hand, and he felt stirred up as he squeezed hers and looked into her eyes. "It's a foolish rule," she said.

"I won't disagree. But because of it, I don't know how to dance, so I couldn't if I *did* want to."

"I'll teach you," she said, tugging him forward.

"No!" He stood fast. "If you think I'll try to learn dancing in front of everybody, you're mixing me up with some *crazy* boy you know."

She was laughing as he spoke, but all at once she dropped his hand, frowning. "There's Ma."

"Oh, you're not scared of your ma, now, are you, Miss Susie?"

She tossed her head. "Anyhow, I'll teach you to dance one day. When it's just us, all right?"

"All right," he said, nodding slowly.

"There, she's gone. Give me back that hand." She stretched hers out.

How could she be so brazen? "Whose hand is it, anyway?" he mumbled, but gladly obeyed.

"Jesse bet me you wouldn't be here tonight."

"Oh, *did* he?"

"He didn't believe your ma would allow it."

"Well, he got that part right. There *were* some words."

"How come she let you?"

What can *Mrs. Samuel be thinking?* Ma had said. *It's far too dangerous.* And he replied, *I'm going to Pennsylvania. Can you not let me have this one last time with my friends?* Ma said, *Yes, it isn't just Jesse anymore, is it? It's Susie, too.* He said, *Yes, ma'am,* and Ma threw up her hands. *Truly, Matt, how can I stop you?*

"Well," he said gravely, "I told her I just had to see that choir of angels."

Susie looked puzzled and shook her head.

"Your ma said she wouldn't let you out of your room till the Second Coming."

Her laugh came fast and full. "Oh, *wasn't* Mama mad! Matt"—she laced her fingers with his—"*you* know why I pushed you, don't you?"

"It sure is time you told me."

"Because what I *wanted* to do was this." On tiptoe, she quickly kissed his lips.

Shock and pleasure nearly knocked him backward. "You're a funny girl, Sue." At that, she darted off, and he ferociously regretted his words. He wanted another kiss so much, his lips burned.

Just then Jesse stalked toward him, glowering. "I'm getting mighty tired of Sam carrying on about that doggone detail, with you some kind of hero. Never thought I'd see him bragging on *you*."

"Don't worry, Jess. He'll hate me again when he hears I'm going up North."

Jesse didn't laugh. Matt watched him move from group to group, distracted and surly, never staying long, never dancing. Meanwhile, Susie kept to the girls, making it a point not to look at Matt, and he was wondering if he oughtn't just go home.

After the fried chicken and biscuits and coleslaw were served, Jesse took his plate indoors. "I'm not feeling very social," he muttered when Matt found him in the dining room.

"You want me to go?"

"No."

Matt sat across the table. "What's wrong?"

"What isn't?" Jesse sneered. Matt frowned in reply, and Jesse worked up a smile. "Still, it's good food, even if Ma and Susie *did* cook on their own. Get yourself some."

"All right." He grabbed a drumstick off Jesse's plate, and Jesse rapped his knuckles with a fork when he went for a biscuit. "I live hand-to-mouth these days," Matt explained, both of them laughing.

"Look at you." Jesse shook his head. "Not even out of the South yet, and already forgetting your manners."

Sitting in the grass eating watermelon, Jesse seemed cheered by a seed-spitting contest. But Matt was not cheered by watching Susie ignore him, and when she started flirting with another boy, he took action.

"Sue, I'd like to talk to you." A defiant look was her response. "Come on over here," he said firmly. She followed.

"First you . . . do what you did, then you don't so much as turn in my direction. What's that about?"

"You thought I was too bold. You called me a funny girl."

"But I didn't mean it bad," he said, softening at once. "And I *maybe* thought you were bold, but . . . not *too* bold." He took her hand, stroked her fingers gently. "I liked it, Sue. I liked it an awful lot."

"Oh, Matthew . . ." How could two quiet, warm words send such a thrill through him? "In a minute," she said with that sleepy look, "go where I go."

"Sue, I can't do that!"

She laughed right at him, not in a mean way, but merry and devilish, just as when she'd scrambled up the rope. Then she sauntered off.

Behind the smokehouse she stood, back to the wall. He felt a powerful need to take her in his arms the way he'd seen it done by Papa and Ma, when she pressed her face into his neck and murmured *David, the children.* If he pulled Susie to him like that now, would it be wrong? He dared to stroke her hair. It was just as he'd imagined, soft and silky. "You look prettier than ever tonight, Sue. Your hair's fine, this way."

"You scrub up pretty good, too," she said with a grin. "What's this shirt?" She rubbed the sleeve. "It suits you."

"This?" He pinched the cotton fabric. "This is the shirt you put on when you want your brothers and sisters to torment you about who you're going to see in it." As she laughed, he took her hands and drew her closer. "When your brother bet you I wouldn't come? He had no idea how bad I wanted to see you."

"Oh, me, too. Every *day* since the creek. I wish I hadn't pushed you, Matt. I'm awful sorry for it." She kissed him again, her lips watermelon-sweet.

Right out of breath, he touched his forehead to hers. "Push me every day, if that's how you put it right."

"Now you tell me what you're sorry for," she whispered.

He tipped his head to the stars, pretending to think. "Mmm . . . sorry about the milk snake," he said, and kissed her. "Sorry about the honeybees." He kissed her again. "Sorry about the mud bombs . . . the stinkbugs . . . the ice fight . . . the snapping turtle." They kissed with each apology, smiles leading to laughter. A person could surely die from such joy.

At last he held her face in his hands, searching her eyes. "Sorry for every sort of devilment I ever did you." And he kissed that unbearably soft mouth again and again until he knew he must stop. "Sue, we got to go back."

"No."

"I can't stay here with you alone."

"Jesse says you're going away."

"I am."

"But when will you come home?"

"I don't know."

"Then I won't go back." She clasped her hands behind his neck and pulled him in. They kissed long and slow.

He finally backed off, trembling. "We got to stop."

"Matt—" She reached for him. He shook his head, walking backward, heart pounding fit to burst. "You won't go without saying good-bye, will you?" she asked.

"No," he said, and turned. How could he feel so good, and yet so bad? He ached all over, it was true pain and astonishing bliss. Was it wrong, what he'd done? What he was thinking?

He had the sudden fear everyone was looking for them, Susie's ma in a fury. But things were as before, and when Matt fetched his gun, Scott said, "You seen Jess?"

"Nope," Matt said, then set out to find him. At the side of the house, he collected his breath. Maybe he'd go to the pump, douse his head. Maybe he'd go back to the smokehouse . . . He forced his feet around the coffee bean tree, toward the lamp-lit porch.

Mrs. Samuel sat alone. Could he sneak away before she saw him? Too late. Starting up the walk, he saw Jesse on the porch floor, his head against his ma's leg and her hand in his hair. When he spotted Matt, he jumped up. There, in Mrs. Samuel's lap, was the guerrilla shirt.

"I got to be going. Thank you, ma'am, for having me. This was real nice."

"You're welcome, Matt," Mrs. Samuel said. "Mind well, before and behind."

"I will, ma'am. Thank you."

"Come on," Jesse muttered, brushing past. At the hitching rack, he turned on Matt. "You dang fool. You know what would've happened if Ma'd seen you two?"

Matt was stunned silent.

"Don't give me that slow-wit look, boy. Did you reckon you'd get past me?"

He couldn't begin to respond.

"I figured I ought to keep Ma company or she'd go looking around for Susie—then take after you with a shotgun!"

"We—we—we weren't doing anything," Matt stammered.

"Well, just how much of nothing weren't you doing?"

Matt ducked his head, toeing the dirt.

"Matt, she's too darn young!"

"She'll be fourteen in November," he mumbled.

"I *know* her dod-dingus birthday, Matthew," Jesse said evenly.

Matt held his breath and bit his lip—but laughter pushed its way out in a burst.

"Oh, you think it's funny, do you?"

Matt shook his head, but couldn't speak.

Jesse began to laugh, too, then threw his arm across Matt's back and gave him a stomach-punch that was definitely on the serious side of playful. Matt groaned. "You deserve that much, anyway."

"It's a small price to pay," Matt said stoically, straightening up.

"Lord, you best watch your step, boy."

"Well, anyhow, I'll be away from her soon enough."

"Yeah, Matt, sure a fine time to start courting."

Matt led Salt into the road and mounted. "I'll see you before you leave?"

"You will," Jesse said.

"Reckon I'll go by the road," Matt said, looking down it.

"Mmm, the woods is better. But maybe not at night." Their eyes met. Jesse said, "I'll go with you partway."

"No," Matt said quickly. "I'll go by the road. See you, Jess."

"Watch your way, Matt."

"Giddup," he said, and started at a trot.

30

When the music mixed with crickets and the moon was the only light, Matt was about as scared as he had been in many a year. It wasn't like the scare of finding Mr. Stone, the shocked kind. This was the waiting kind of fear, when every shivering shadow rushed his blood and jerked his head. Of all the boys at the party, he'd been the only one to come alone. And he was regretting it mightily.

Still, home was only about a mile away. He'd traveled this road on his own plenty of nights. It was a shame to be going scared when he could be thinking about Susie, and he tried to fix his mind on her kisses.

At once there was a great rustling of brush, and the road was blocked with men and horses. Salt shied, snorted. Matt shortened his reins and reached for his gun.

"You mightn't want to do that, boy."

All hammers clicked into position, all Colts pointed his way. He raised his hands over his head.

"Get down on the double-quick."

When he complied, his knees buckled. He reached for Salt's bridle.

"Step away from your horse." The lead man dismounted and tossed his reins to another. A third took hold of Salt's.

Federals? Guerrillas? Armys? Navys? His mind was spinning like a revolver cylinder. They wore civilian clothes, but their hair was short—or else tucked under their hats. If they knew where he'd been, they couldn't be guerrillas. But maybe they didn't know. Were they just passing by, or had they been lying in wait for him, for anyone? He waited for the question: Union or Secesh? What was the answer? What should he say?

The leader shoved his gun in his belt and grabbed Matt's shirt. "What's your name, boy?"

"Matt Howard."

"You want to say 'sir' to a Federal officer, boy. Let's try that again. What's your name?"

"Matt Howard, sir."

"Where you off to?"

"Home, sir."

"Where you been?"

Matt hesitated.

The man took the scruff of his neck in a painful pinch. "I asked, where you been?"

"Liberty," Matt said, but before he got to "sir," the man backhanded him so hard he stumbled.

"I *know* where you been, boy," the man growled. Matt kept his eyes on the ground, trying to think, to breathe, to swallow his terror. "Your friend at that Secesh place, he's got a brother. I believe they call him Buck. Isn't that right?"

Matt nodded. Surely there was no harm in agreeing to what they already knew.

"Yes, sir," the man prompted.

"Yes, sir."

"Was he at that farm tonight?"

"No, sir."

"You sure about that? Because when we're done with our little talk, me and my men intend to escort you home. And I believe you have some young ones on your place. You don't want any harm to come to your kin, do you, boy?"

Matt folded his arms tight against his shaking. The man was bluffing, they never hurt women or little ones, and yet . . . Matt looked into those menacing eyes. "No, sir, I would not."

The man drew his revolver. Matt stepped back without wanting to, but the man locked an arm around his neck and lifted his chin with the gun's barrel.

"I'll ask you again." He cocked the hammer. "If I don't like your answer, I'll blow your head off. And then dump your dead carcass on your mama's doorstep. Did you see this Buck, or any other goddamn bushwhackers, at the Samuel place?"

"No!" His voice was strangled and wild. He covered his head with his arms and squeezed his eyes shut. If he died fast, he wouldn't hear the shot.

The man yanked his arms down. "Get on your horse. I'll have a word with your ma about the company you keep. Tom, take his gun."

Somehow, Matt walked to Salt and mounted. Sensation began to return: the smarting of his face from the blow; Salt's neck, warm and smooth.

"Move that horse from my side and I'll shoot you both. Hear?"

"Yes, sir."

It was clear the men feared ambush. They rode with guns drawn, eyes darting, reins tight, barely breaking out of a walk.

Their jaded horses didn't mind the pace, but Salt was fresh and he was scared. Keeping him alongside the lead man was no easy task.

Matt sighed with relief as they turned into his lane. When they reached the gate the door flew open, and Ma was outlined in lamplight. She rushed down the path, looking frantically from horseman to horseman, and then Clayton was behind her.

"We've got your boy, ma'am," the leader called, and she clutched at her throat. "Dismount."

Now he knew: they would take Salt. His panic outran his fear, and he said, "Can I put my horse up, sir?"

"Get down."

"Go indoors, Matt," Ma said, her tone low and even.

Matt dismounted, but held on to the reins. "Can I have my horse, sir?"

"You heard your mama."

"Can I please have—"

"Get in the house, Matt!" Clayton shouted, and Matt pressed his hand to Salt's flank, then dodged past Ma and Clayton.

Betsy gently pulled him inside and shut the door.

"They're not getting Salt," he told her.

"It can't be helped."

"Salt's going up North with me." He glanced at Papa's rifle.

"Matt!" Taking him hard by the shoulders, Betsy propelled him into a chair, then sat beside him. "What happened?"

"He took his gun . . ." Matt held his finger to his throat. "Said he'd throw my body on the doorstep. And what did I do, Betsy? I went to a party at my friends'. That's all I did."

Betsy got him a cup of water.

He drank it down. "Thank you," he said. His head felt so heavy he had to rest it on the table, and somehow it didn't surprise him when she laid her hand on his back.

After a while the door opened and Ma said in a starched voice, "The captain wants to speak to you. Come."

Back at the gate, Clayton wore a look of anguish.

"Take your horse," the so-called captain said. "I'll keep your gun. Consider yourself well and truly warned: You are not to go to that Secesh house again."

"Yes, sir." He caught the reins. "Thank you, sir."

"Be quick about it, Matt," Clayton said.

Salt was agitated as they rode to the barn. "It's all right," Matt said, removing the bit. "I got you now." As he curried and brushed him, Salt nickered and pawed at the ground. "You were scared, I know. You know I almost lost you."

"Matt!" Clayton hollered from the house.

Indoors, Ma, Clayton, and Betsy were at the table, all looking like death. This couldn't be about the party.

"Quantrill attacked Lawrence, Kansas." Ma sounded hollow. She stared at her hands, placed flat on the table. "This morning. They rode in at dawn. Went to every house and store and hotel. Brought out the men and boys . . . and murdered every one."

Matt sat next to Clayton.

"Every single man and boy, in front of their mothers and wives and little ones. One hundred and fifty boys and men, defenseless, killed in cold blood. They were after Jim Lane, but they didn't get *him*. They plundered the whole town. Then they burned each house and building. And they headed back to Missouri."

Matt reeled with dizziness and nausea: Did they know, over at Jesse's? Did it explain Jesse's melancholy? How could they have a party? How could Jesse's ma keep sewing that shirt? Did they know?

"I begged for that horse for you," Ma said tearfully.

"Thank you, Ma," he mumbled.

"Don't thank me. It was before he told me. I'd have been too ashamed to beg for a horse knowing so many mothers had lost their boys." She held a handkerchief to her eyes. "How long, oh Lord? How long will the wicked triumph?"

Matt slid his chair back and laid his face on the smooth, warm wood.

"All right?" Clayton asked, and Matt shut his eyes.

"Clay, that was no friendly escort," Betsy said bitterly. "They told him they'd kill him. They held a gun to his head."

"Oh, God, Matt." Clay gripped his shoulder.

"I *said* not to go there!" Ma's harsh voice was right by his ear. "Didn't I? You *must not* go there again. Do you understand me?" Matt was quiet. "Answer me!" she demanded, now in tears, but he could not lift his head.

"Ma," Clayton said.

"I thank God they showed mercy," she said. "They didn't harm *my* son."

Only the ticking clock broke the silence.

Finally Ma said calmly, "I wish we'd get word from my father. I don't see how we can wait any longer. But if he's on his way . . ." She sighed. "I hear the mail's been stopped. Bush-whackers. Tomorrow I'll go to Mr. Henderson, ask which animals he'll buy. Then I'll see the provost marshal about passes. Betsy, you'll come with me. Clay, you'll stay and watch Matt. Do you suppose they'll give me a pass for him?"

"He's been tagged Secesh, ma'am. They'll be glad to see the back of him."

"We must try to protect the children from frightening news. They needn't know what happened tonight. Or about Lawrence." She got to her feet, then began to wind the clock. "We'll take this, of course. But we'll have to leave so much."

Once he and Clayton were in bed, Matt said, "I'm wondering if any militia went down to Jesse's."

"Yes or no, there's nothing you can do about it."

Matt punched his pillow into shape, then fell back on it. "If nobody's been there yet, I could warn them."

"You kick that thought right out of your head, Matt."

Matt got up fast, stepping over Ben to the window seat.

"Didn't you get enough of a scare tonight?" Clayton said, sitting up.

"Clay, I was worse scared than I ever *have* been. He said if he didn't like my answer, he'd kill me. Put his Colt right in my face and cocked the hammer. I don't know what it was about my answer he *did* like. Ma calls it mercy. I call it luck."

"Well, what was the question?"

Matt polished a pane with his nightshirt sleeve. "Did I see Buck or other Quantrill men at Jesse's."

"And you told the truth?"

"Yes."

It hit him harder than the back of the captain's hand. With a gun to his head, he had told the truth. He thought about Jesse, half-drowned in the creek: *Don't know or ain't telling? Both!* Now he wondered about himself. If the truth hadn't been the safe answer, could he have lied?

31

A thunderous rumbling shook the earth, ever louder and deeper as Matt scaled the pasture fence. Ben rushed down the lane, yelling as the commotion moved on.

"Who was it?" Matt shouted.

"Militia! With extra horses, and I saw July!"

"Go to the house, Ben. Tell Clay I—"

"What's happening?" Clay called, making his way at his fastest.

"I saw militia with July!"

"I'm going," Matt said.

"What did that man say to you last night?" Clayton warned him.

"What man?" Ben asked.

"Clay, whatever hell they made, it's over now, and I've got to go!"

"Who knows but some aren't there still!"

Matt started up the lane. "I'm going!"

"Matt!"

He turned.

"Go by the woods."

Stumbling on rocks, tripping over brambles, Matt could hardly believe his own stupidity. Why hadn't he gone the second Ma left the yard for town? No, he should not have waited even that long. If he'd gone at daybreak, he'd have been there when Jesse came out to chore, and Jesse could have left right then— with July. And Ma need never have known. Instead, he let militia get to them. No, not stupid. Just a scared baby. Scared of the soldiers, scared of Ma.

He tried a shortcut through a scrub oak thicket, but the dense brush tangled his feet and it seemed like a dream in which you run and run and get nowhere. At last he was crossing the road, jumping the fence into the Samuels' tall corn.

The crop was damaged, he saw that right away. Hoofprints told that the stalks were broken by galloping horses. At the edge of the field, he stopped to look, to breathe, to listen. It was eerily peaceful, but when he held his breath, the high-pitched wailing of little ones pierced the silence, and he ran to the house.

Susie was furiously pumping water, with Sally and Johnny hanging on to her skirts. When Matt went to her, she screamed, throwing her hands up to protect her head—and when she saw it was Matt, she began to cry.

The glowing face he had held last night was twisted and anguished. The sparkling black eyes were red and puffy, and her mouth—that soft, sweet mouth—was swollen and bleeding. "They made me watch," she sobbed. "They made me watch."

"Watch what?" Matt asked.

"Mama wants the water. Oh, stop, Johnny, *please* stop!"

Matt lifted Johnny and the bucket. Susie hefted Sally onto her hip. "They hung Pappy in the coffee bean tree. They made me and Mama watch. Four times they did it: Tell what you know, tell what you know."

"Is he dead? Sue?"

She shook her head. "They left him up there and Mama cut him down and then they went for Jesse."

As they reached the kitchen door, so did Mrs. Samuel, calling, "Susie!" Her eyes went wide. "What are you doing here, Matt? What are you doing?"

Then he heard Jesse's shaky words: "Matt's here?"

"Come in, you foolish boy, hurry!" Mrs. Samuel took Johnny from him, slamming the door shut.

Jesse sat still as an Indian, the heels of his hands pushing the edge of the kitchen table, his back straight, shirt off. Across the kitchen, Dr. Samuel looked like a dead man who had forgotten to lie down. His face was pure white, and he rubbed at his neck and said in great gasping breaths, "The boy, Zerelda—the boy!"

"I'm all right, Pappy," Jesse said, but his voice said otherwise. "Ma, help him!"

"Reuben, you must stay in bed." As Mrs. Samuel led him from the room, Matt saw the bright red rope marks around his neck.

"What can I do, Jess?" Susie asked desperately. "What can I do?"

"Cold water." She rushed to give him a cup, but when he moved to pick it up, something stopped him. Susie lifted the cup to his lips.

Matt stepped closer, and saw: Jesse's back was raw and bloody, from his neck right down to his pants. "Look!" Susie held up his homespun work shirt. It was cut to shreds, stained red all over.

"Jess?" Matt said.

"Can't breathe."

"They were mounted," Susie said. "Three of them. They chased him down and lashed him with horsewhips. And stabbed him with bayonets. He had to crawl back."

Matt leaned against the fireplace wall, touching his head to the stone.

"I hate them." Susie broke into tears again. "I *hate* them."

"Pappy said . . . 'Lay low, Jess . . . I'll deal with this,' " Jesse struggled to say. "And I let him . . . I let him."

"You're not to blame!" Mrs. Samuel hollered, sweeping into the room. "Oh, the devils!" She stood behind Jesse and cried, "Merciful God, look at this child!" She bent over him, holding a bottle—some sort of medicine?

"Don't!" Jesse protested.

"I must."

Jesse yelped. Susie cried out. Matt jumped.

"Susie, make a fire in the stove," Mrs. Samuel snapped. "Matt, go home."

"Yes, ma'am. I only—"

"What *were* you thinking, coming here?"

"Ben, he—saw them with the horses. I only—"

"They got July," Jesse said.

Susie rushed outside.

"You must leave *now*!" Mrs. Samuel repeated.

"Don't holler at him, Ma."

"See you, Jess." Matt shut the door behind him.

Susie stood staring into the woodshed, seeming not to recall why she was there.

"It'll be all right, Sue," Matt said, taking her limp hand.

She shook her head fiercely, and he felt stupid for speaking such nonsense.

"What happened there?" He touched his own bottom lip.

"I bit it. When they were doing that to Pappy. You ought to have seen it, Matt. His face. Purple. They said, 'Tell what you know,' and they pulled him up, and then they said it to Mama. And she said, 'What I know I'll die knowing.' "

She squeezed her eyes shut, as though blocking the memory. "They said the bushwhackers slaughtered every boy and man in Lawrence. Did you hear that?"

"I did."

"I just know Buck wouldn't do such a thing. They're lying, I know it. Aren't they lying, Matt?"

Matt cupped his hand under her chin.

Susie broke down.

Matt took her in a hug, and he didn't care if her ma saw. She wrapped her arms around him and they rocked from side to side. "It isn't fair," she wept. "Oh, I hate them all."

"Susan!" Mrs. Samuel called.

"The wood." She pulled away. "Go, Matt. Ma says you must go."

He looked into her mournful eyes and brushed away her tears. "You take care." She nodded. He touched his lips to hers, and with the taste of tears and blood in his mouth, he headed for the corn.

Matt was spoiling for a fight, and if Ma said so much as a word, he would give her one. All the way home he tried to shake the sight of Jesse's back, the image of militia chasing him down. *Pappy said, "Lay low, Jess"* . . . So had Jesse been hiding? Did he know what was happening to his pap? Was he too scared to go up to the house when he heard Susie's screams? To think of Jesse that way made him sick, as it made him sick to recall Jesse in that chair, looking like a side of raw meat.

Now he hated Jesse's ma. Standing by the tree saying, *What I know I'll die knowing.* That was surely brave enough when you weren't the one hanging in the tree. And even if she didn't care so much about her husband, didn't it occur to her they'd go for Jesse next? She always acted so protective, wanting to know his whereabouts . . . her hand in his hair last night. She knew talking that way to militia only made them hurt you worse. But it wasn't her neck in the noose, or her back punched by bayonets. *That big loud-mouthed Rebel*, Mr. Stone had called her, and Matt heard her yelling at him to go home, shouting at Susie. He saw her on that porch sewing a guerrilla shirt when she should have been making baby clothes. It was like trading an old child for a new one—send one off to Quantrill with his red shirt, and then start to sew for the one still inside.

And there was his own ma, crying, *Don't you know how desperate I am?* By the time he walked past the barn, there was no fight left in him at all.

The wagon was in the yard, the horses still hitched. His whole family watched him come up to the house, and no one said a word.

"They hung Dr. Samuel in the coffee bean tree." He fixed his eyes on Ma's, appreciating her horror. "Susie had to watch, she can't hardly stop crying. Four times they put him up, and then they left him there. Mrs. Samuel cut him down, somehow."

"Alive?" Ma breathed.

"Barely. Thanks to your merciful militia." Ma looked away. "Then they went for Jesse. Chased him down and beat him with horsewhips and stuck him with bayonets. Three men, one boy." He turned to Clayton. "You just can't imagine how bad." He said to Betsy, "At least when we saw Mr. Stone that bloody, he wasn't still alive."

"Matt." Ma nodded at Molly and Ben, whose faces were pale with fear.

"I'll just take the wagon down," he said, turning away.

Ma followed him to it and took his arm. "Matt. There was a letter in town. My father should be here in a matter of days, God willing."

"All right, then." He started to the wagon seat, but she kept hold of him. He looked at her.

"There's more news. In Kansas City, there was a prison. All Southern women, mostly girls. One only seven years old. Sisters of guerrillas. Wives. The prison collapsed. Some were killed, others horribly injured . . . mangled. In town the talk is that the Union soldiers undermined the building. I just don't see how that could be . . ." She ran her hand nervously over her mouth. "The girls were trapped in the rubble. Folks say when the guerrillas got word, they raided Lawrence."

Matt nodded slowly. He climbed up and took the lines. "How long *will* the wicked triumph?" he said, and drove to the barn.

32

Two days they packed and planned. Two days Matt worried and wondered what was going on down the road. Two days the late-August heat was so brutal no one slept.

But then a storm blew through, and the weather turned.

Ma sat down to breakfast and said, "Matt, I've a notion to ride Papa's mare this lovely morning."

He choked down a mouthful of grits. "Yes, ma'am?"

"Will you accompany me?"

"You know how to ride, Ma?" He scanned the faces around the table. Surprise was on each.

"You needn't sound appalled!"

"I'm not appalled, ma'am. I'm just . . ." He shrugged.

"Matthew, I believe that is what Papa called your devilish grin," she said, and they all laughed.

Matt walked Salt and Sugar to the edge of the woods, and let the fence down. Ma rode sideways. Helping her up put Matt in mind of Susie, the way she rode like a boy, her happiness the day of the berrying. *When I pushed you, what I really wanted to do . . .*

"You're all right, Ma?"

"Yes."

He handed her the reins. "It's too bad we don't own a sidesaddle."

"This is how I learned."

"When, ma'am?" he asked, mounting.

"Oh, when I got here. Before I had Clay. Papa and I rode quite a bit, but after that, well, there was always a baby coming along. Or needing attention."

"Uh, you think you still remember how?"

"You'll help me," she said confidently.

In the woods, he stayed close. Occasionally Ma would say "Oh!" or "Goodness!" but as soon as Matt reached out, she'd say, "I'm fine." Riding that way looked much harder. How did she keep her balance, without a leg on each side?

"Ma," he said when they reached the prairie, "you look like you're about to fall off. I think you ought to ride like a man."

"Well, this does feel a bit precarious, but I couldn't!"

"It's just you and me, Mama." He swept out an arm. "If you even want to trot, I think you should ride like a man." Dismounting, he went to Sugar's side. "Come on, Ma. It'll only be hard getting on." She took his hand and hopped down. "Now hike up your skirt—"

"Matthew!" she laughed.

"I'll close my eyes. Go on. Left foot in the stirrup. Now take hold of the cantle with your right hand. Grab a piece of her mane with your left. And then you'll just swing your leg over . . . Jump!" He steadied Sugar and with a groan, Ma was on.

"Don't look," she said, arranging her skirts. "All right."

He opened his eyes.

"How did I allow you to talk me into this?"

"But isn't it more comfortable?" he asked, mounting again.

"Well, it is."

He shrugged. "Come on, then." He went into a gallop, and she trotted behind. He circled, letting her get ahead so he could watch her better, but her only blunder was bringing Sugar up a bit short. "Why'd you stop, Ma?"

"I want to take off this bonnet so I can feel the day." The words brought Susie back once more. Ma pushed the bonnet so that it was off her head, but still tied around her neck. "It's as beautiful as ever it was," she said as they looked over the prairie.

Flowers of all kinds and colors nestled in the tall, swaying grass that stretched and dipped for miles before meeting the cloudless sky. Meadowlarks flashed their golden bellies, flying from the ground as they sang for attention: *See here! Oh! See here!*

"Never think I'm not sorry to leave here, Matt," Ma said. "Never."

It wasn't the time to ask what he wanted to know: Would she ever come back?

"Let's ride," she said, and trotted on.

She never quite got up to a canter, but she did fine for someone Matt had never known to ride a horse. When she reined up again, he took Salt in another wide circle and stopped alongside her.

"You've had enough, Ma?"

"I think so. But let's sit a minute."

"You do all right, ma'am."

"*Thank* you, Matt. It's been a pleasure to amuse you."

He laughed, pushing his hat lower on his forehead, and they looked back the way they'd come. "Ma, I don't believe you know about Wounded Man."

"Wounded Man?"

"Jesse and I used to play it. One of us'd ride away, and the other'd lay down somewhere in the grass. When you saw the wounded man waving for help, you'd ride like mad back to rescue him. You'd lean out of the saddle and reach for him, and he'd reach for you, and without ever stopping your horse he'd swing up into your saddle."

Ma shuddered. "It sounds awfully dangerous."

"Thinking back, I suppose it was. You could never *see* the wounded man all that well till you got right up to him. More often I was the wounded man, Jesse being the better rider. And I recall rolling away from some big old hooves now and again."

"That is just the sort of thing a mother is better off not knowing!"

"Well, it's past history. I don't know why I thought of it."

"I imagine you've been thinking of Jesse a great deal. And Susie."

"Yes, ma'am."

"It's a shame, Matt. A terrible shame. When I came here, it

was so peaceful. Everybody got along. How we'd get together for music, and barbecue. We had our rough times, Papa and I. I'd never deny it. But he worked so hard. He had such plans."

"Yes, ma'am."

"The night he died, he said to me, 'Carrie, I wanted to give you everything.' And I said, 'You have, David. You have.'"

Matt pressed his hand to Salt's hot neck, then combed his mane with his fingers.

"Now," Ma said. "I'd like you to wait here while I ride down a ways. Then you two show Sugar and me how fast our boys can fly across this prairie."

He watched her go. She was more sure of herself now, more able. And when he raced past her, lying low with his chin on Salt's mane, he saw that she was laughing and crying at the same time.

Matt wouldn't have cared to admit it, but since his little parley with the Feds, he didn't like going down to the barn after dark. That night he approached the stalls carefully and hung the lantern.

"Matt."

Matt flinched, shielding his face. Then his eyes darted to the loft. "Jess. You trying to kill me?"

No answer.

"How long you been in here? How's your back?"

"Climb up. I've something to tell." Jesse's tone was flat and dull.

What now? What more? Matt slowly climbed the ladder. "Jess?"

"They took Ma and Susie."

"What?"

"You heard. Came this morning. Took them to jail."

"Why? Where were you? Where was your pap? How'd—"

"I was out. Pappy was there. Ma said she wouldn't go. They dragged Susie out. *Then* Ma would go. Little ones taking on. Nothing Pappy could do." His words were cold as January, and just as raw. "And Ma so near her time. Susie terror-struck, Pappy said, enough to tear his heart out."

"Where were *you* all this while?" Matt said, hearing accusation in his voice.

"Walking."

"*Walking?* Walking where?"

"Just walking. To see what I could see."

"Jesse, what in *hell* riddles are you talking?"

"Walking to see if I could find anybody. To take me where I need to go."

Matt considered, and said more kindly, "How could you even know who you found? What if you ran into Feds?"

"There are signals," Jesse said in a dead voice.

The words hung heavy between them.

"It's me they were after," Jesse explained. "They were mad I wasn't there, so they took Ma and Susie instead. Wouldn't tell Pappy where the jail is."

"Why didn't they kill your pap, when they found him still alive?"

"Who knows. Who knows their evil ways? Likely they saw he was ruined."

"What do you mean, Jess?"

Jesse covered his face with both hands, rubbing and rubbing at his forehead. Matt heard him fighting tears—and losing. Jesse had never once cried in front of him, through all the pains and sorrows they'd shared.

"I just want to kill those bastards," Jesse said at last.

The curse hit Matt even harder than the tears.

"When I get in it, I'll kill all I can and never tire of it. She cried, she wanted Buck so bad after they got to Pappy. Sue, I said, he *can't* come, they're all in hiding because of Lawrence, don't you see? But I couldn't protect her. They'd no cause to take her. And I'll kill every last one."

Vengeance is mine, saith the Lord. But Matt wasn't about to start quoting the Bible now. If Jesse ever had a choice, the Feds had stolen it for good, and there was nothing to do but help him escape.

"I can't leave the little ones alone with Pappy. Lord, I wish Aunt Lotty was here."

"Take them to her."

"No horses, remember?"

The words left Matt's mouth before he could stop them: "Take Salt."

Jesse stared at him.

"Get Sally and Johnny to your aunt's. Then go on to where you're going."

"No, Matt. It won't do."

Matt knew that dead-set tone, and he was shamed by his relief at hearing it. "Then borrow him. Later, I'll ask Ma to let you take Sugar."

"Your ma wouldn't send your papa's mare to a Quantrill camp."

"I believe I can persuade her."

"Pappy couldn't pay, Matt. They stole our money."

"Don't worry about that now. When can you take the little ones?"

"I don't know. Seems they'll catch me, day or night."

Matt swept bits of hay into a pile with his hand. "Jess, I've an idea."

"You plan to tell it?"

"I don't know if you'll like it."

"I won't know till you *tell* it."

"You know how they send us with girls for protection?"

"Yeah."

"Well, if you got yourself up to look like somebody you're not—"

"Matt . . ."

"You could go by day and be safe with those little ones."

Jesse's teeth flashed through the darkness. "Matt, I'm speechless."

"Will you do it?"

"I believe I *will*. And Pappy can help me."

"I wish I could be there to see it."

"Then I reckon I wouldn't do it!" Jesse said, and they laughed under their breath. "All right. I told Pappy I'd be back after I saw you. I'll sleep in the corn tonight."

Matt climbed down first, then watched Jesse make his slow way.

"What'd you mean about your pap, Jess?"

Jesse lifted a shoulder. "He ain't himself. Gets confused. Wanders off."

"He'll get better."

"Might could," Jesse said. But he didn't sound any too sure.

Clayton was sitting up in bed, reading. "You've been gone a long time. Everything all right?"

"Yes, Clay."

"You're sure?"

Matt pulled his shirt over his head. "I was just looking around. Recollecting."

When Matt lay on the tick, Clayton put out the light. The plan had to work. He would meet Jesse in the woods tomorrow, after chores. Nobody would see Salt was gone, and Jesse could get to his aunt's before dark. In the evening, Matt would speak to Ma. It would be sad, Sugar going to war instead of to Mr. Henderson's peaceful pasture. Of course, there was no guarantee she wouldn't get jayhawked or bushwhacked from him. Ma would understand. She would understand he needed to give Sugar to Jesse.

Susie in jail. Could he try to see her? She could be anywhere, and the Feds wouldn't tell. Even trying to find out might get you shut in the jail next door, worse off for being a man. Could she sleep? On a floor? On a blanket? Would they feed her enough? What if she got sick? Where was she? With her ma, or had the Feds separated them? Susie, alone, frightened. He dashed away tears. Susie in the tree, singing, *I'd rather have the guerrilla man who wears a fancy shirt* . . . What did she think of that now? What did she think of him, going North while she was locked in prison? Did she hate him? Did she regret those kisses behind the smokehouse? *Now you tell me what you're sorry for . . .*

"Matt," Clayton said, "you sure everything's all right?"

"Yes, Clay." He closed his eyes. Sorry for not coming to warn you. Sorry for you seeing your pappy hung up in the tree. Sorry they dragged you crying to a Federal jail.

33

"I'm still not sure about this." Approaching Matt in the woods, Jesse seemed himself again, confident and cool.

"You figure out the clothes?"

A grin took over Jesse's whole face. "I tell you, it ain't *natural*, how they dress! But it was worth it just watching Pappy. Did my heart good to see him laugh."

Matt handed him the reins. Jesse shook them, serious again. "It doesn't feel right, taking Salt. You talk to your ma?"

"Not yet."

"Well, that seems wrong, too."

"Salt's mine. I reckon I can do as I see fit. I'll tell her after supper."

Jesse sighed. "So, that grandpappy of yours turn up?"

"Not yet."

"I'll come back tomorrow late. Leave the cart at my aunt's and come back as myself. I reckon I'll be safer in the dark, on my own. Easier to hide."

"You have a gun, or did they get them all?"

"They took some. I have my Colt."

Matt nodded. "They took—" *my shotgun*, he nearly said.

"What?" Jesse asked.

"Your shotgun, I suppose," he said, feeling prickly all over.

"Everything they could find."

"I got to get back," Matt said abruptly. "I told Ma I'd only go for a quick ride." Salt pushed his nose into Matt's hair; Matt stroked his blaze.

Jesse said, "I appreciate this, Matt."

"I know," Matt said.

In the barn, Ben was leaning against the wall with his arms crossed. "Where's Salt?"

"What in the world are you doing here? It's suppertime!" Matt heard his own phony cheer, and knew Ben wouldn't be fooled.

"Where's Salt?" he repeated, squinting.

"That's my business," Matt said evenly.

"Then I'm telling."

Ben launched himself away from the wall. Matt caught his arm as he tried to pass. "Ben . . ." *Protect the children from frightening news,* Ma had said. "Don't."

"Well, where *is* he?" Ben asked.

"I don't think you ought to know."

Ben tried to squirm out of Matt's grip, but Matt held fast.

"Ben, look at me. *Look* at me."

Ben stopped struggling and obeyed.

"I'm begging you on Papa's grave," Matt said.

His brother's face crumpled into a troubled frown. "Just tell me, Matt. I won't tattle. Did you give him to Jesse? You did, didn't you?"

"I am not saying that to you."

Ben hugged himself tight and whispered, "I'm scared."

"I need you to trust me, Ben. All right?" Ben nodded, but trust was nowhere in his eyes. Matt clapped him on the shoulder. "Then let's eat supper. I believe Ma's planning to cook every chicken on the place before we leave. You ever think you'd get tired of eating chicken? Here, what's this?" He grabbed at the seat of Ben's pants. "Feathers growing out of your backside," he said, and Ben had to laugh.

Matt had every intention of speaking to Ma, but after supper, he changed his mind. When he went to lock up, he brushed Sugar for a long time. He felt bad, deceiving Ma again after they'd promised to be more honest with each other. But it couldn't be helped. If he told Ma, she'd tell Clay. And if the Feds came here looking for Jesse . . .

If the Feds came. What would they do? Whip him the way they did Jesse? He could take that. Burn his barn? That would be tougher to bear. Papa's barn. But surely Papa would understand that in such times, you had to sacrifice for a friend. After the war, Matt could rebuild. He picked up his deerhide shot bag and powder flask and slung Ben's gun over his shoulder. Then he went down to the woods and hid everything in the brush.

Staring into the night, he recalled his oath: Pledge my honor, my property, and my life . . . What if the Feds said they'd kill him unless he told? Briskly, he started back toward the house, jumping the fence. This was all just foolish thinking. The Feds wouldn't come. They'd taken Susie and Mrs. Samuel in revenge, because they believed Jesse had already escaped to Quantrill. That should put an end to it.

Tomorrow Matt would stop keeping secrets—for good. And explain everything to his family.

Clayton was downstairs, waiting. "How come Ben was so quiet tonight?"

"Can't say I know."

"You didn't talk much, either. Or eat much, for that matter."

"Just sorrowful, I guess. All this packing up and such."

"Nothing more?"

"No."

Clayton shook his head as Matt trailed him up the stairs.

"Ben, I was wanting to sleep there," Matt said, standing over the tick.

"I got here first."

"Come on." Matt nudged him with his toe. "Get in bed."

"No!"

"What's the difference, Matt?" Clayton asked.

"Do as I tell you," Matt said steadily, and Ben did.

Matt undressed and lay on the tick, facing the wall.

Clayton sat for the longest time before he put out the light.

When the clock struck eleven, Matt felt for his boots and placed them side by side. When it struck twelve, he crept down the stairs, avoiding the creakier floorboards, and took down Papa's rifle. Back on the tick, he sat, breathing slow and quiet. Then he unbuttoned the tick cover, and flinched against the crunching noises as he buried the gun in the straw.

Clayton stirred and said sleepily, "Matt?"

"Right here."

"All right?"

"Yes, Clay." He waited, slid his shirt and pants off the window seat, and got them on. He lay back and stared at the ceiling.

When the clock struck one, he began to settle down. They wouldn't be coming; Jesse was safe asleep at his aunt's. He'd been a fool to worry, and he was powerfully tired.

In the distance, a night bird was singing familiar, mournful tunes. Matt closed his eyes. The sooner he got to sleep, the sooner morning would come.

34

"Make a light!"

The thump of wood on wood, the clank of metal on metal, a sledge hitting a wedge. No, it was an ax on the barn-door lock, a gun butt on the front door. Matt sat straight up, struggling for breath, grasping blindly for his boots. Now Ma was in the room with crying Tyler, and as Matt jammed his foot into his boot, he saw Mr. Stone's bare blue feet in the ditch.

Then Ben was all but on top of him, and Clayton fumbling for his crutches, and Ma saying, "What have you done, Matt? What have you done?"

"Make a light!" The pounding commenced again.

"Tell, Matt," Ben whispered desperately. "Tell Mama!"

"Get my boot, Ben. Make a light, Ma. Clayton, make a light!"

A candle glowed through the darkness. Betsy and Molly were there, Molly whimpering, Betsy taking Tyler. Matt pulled his other boot on and drew Ben close, murmuring in the chaos, "Say nothing."

"Oh, Clay, where can we hide him?" Ma said frantically. "In the featherbed! Quick, Matt—"

"I'll hide from no man, Ma," Matt answered, and got to his feet.

"Matt Howard!" the voice bellowed.

"Coming to the door!" he called in the stairwell.

Behind him Ma was saying, "Be merciful unto me, O God, be merciful unto me."

"No! All of you stay here!" Clayton choked out.

"For my soul trusteth in thee, in the shadow of thy wings will I make my refuge, until these calamities be overpast . . ."

Matt unbolted the door and yanked it open.

Ma clutched his arm. "Oh, Matt!"

There was the captain, a carbine slung over his shoulder. Two other men stood behind, one holding a lantern, the other a revolver. At the barn were more men and horses and lanterns, and a wagon clattered down the lane.

"Captain!" Ma drew Matt closer.

"You have other children." The captain stepped between them, breaking her grip. "Get them out here."

If everyone must come out, it meant the house would burn.

"Clayton!" Ma called behind her. "Bring the others!"

The captain hauled Matt down the path, with Ma and the other soldiers at their heels. Outside the gate, he stopped: "Where's your Secesh friend?"

"I don't know."

The captain gave him the backhanded slap. Ma cried out and pressed against him.

"We'll see about that," the captain said, looking toward the barn. As Clayton came to Matt's side, men led Sugar and the mules toward them.

"Where's that handsome chestnut of yours, boy? Take your hands off him, ma'am, please," he said politely, yanking Matt away. "The one I so kindly relinquished, due to your mama's fervent pleas?"

He looks so much like Sugar, I think I got to call him Salt . . . Matt slowly raised his hand and pointed to Sugar, and the captain appeared confused. He looked her in the teeth, then showed his own in a nasty leer. "You're a goddamn liar, boy. Ma'am, your young Secesh vermin is a goddamn liar!" His shout reeked of liquor; Matt realized the danger was worse than he'd feared.

"Now, let's take stock for a moment." The captain tapped his cheek and tipped his head to the stars. "One missing Quantrill boy's brother, one missing chestnut horse. Do I flatter my own intelligence to make a connection?"

"They're just boys," Clayton said in a low growl.

"You. Shut up!" the captain shouted.

"Are you militia so cowed by Quantrill that you take your fury out on the boys still living at home?"

"Quantrill's killed younger. And he's got younger doing his killing, as well."

"But you Federals believe you're better than Quantrill, don't you?"

The captain put his face up to Clayton's. "If I would ever hit a cripple, boy, you'd be the one."

"You go right ahead and hit me," Clay answered.

But the captain turned back to Matt. "Boys still living at home, your brother says. Well, what if I was to tell your brother we caught your friend on the road tonight, on *your* horse, and it was perfectly clear where he was going?"

Matt smiled. Not with intent, not to be smart—that smile just had a mind all its own. Because when the captain lied, Matt knew Jesse was safe.

But the smile enraged the captain beyond all reason, and he howled, "Get him!" As the two men grabbed Matt's arms, the captain seethed. "What'll it be, boy? The gun or the rope?"

"Gun," Matt said.

"No!" Ma's scream was savage as she wrapped him in her arms.

"Get away from him, ma'am!" the captain hollered, prying her loose, and the men tugged at Matt.

Clayton, by his side, said, "You don't have to die for this, Matt!"

"What do you know?" the captain yelled.

You got to know when you're beat, boy, Jesse had said. And Matt said, "Nothing."

"Tell what you know, Matt!" Clayton shouted.

"I know nothing," he repeated, and the captain swung a fist against his head.

"Oh, dear Lord," Ma said, "do not take him away in the midst of his days."

"I won't do it near your ma," the captain grunted in his ear. "Go like a man!"

"I'm begging you, captain!" Ma cried out. "Don't take my boy!"

Matt was dragged a few steps, staggering, numb. And then Ma hurled herself against them, swinging at the soldiers, pulling at Matt. Finally turning all her attention on the captain, she gripped his coat, and her words tumbled out: "Think of your own mother, captain. I'm begging you, in the name of God. We're going North, I'm a Union lady. My father's coming from Pennsylvania any day. We have our passes, the provost marshal issued this boy a pass. He's going North with me. He's a fine son, captain, a good brother. Look at my little ones, they need him, they've already lost their papa, look at me, captain, I'm begging you, can you bear to do this?"

Then there was no sound but her desperate sobbing. And Matt, shivering in terror, whispered, "Therefore be ready, for in such an hour as you know not . . ."

"In the name of God!" Ma gasped. "He's my child!"

The captain shrugged her off and held Matt by his shirt. "You answer me two questions, boy, within your mama's hearing: Did you take an oath?"

Matt looked into the hard, glazed eyes. "I did."

"And did you break it?"

"I did."

The captain stepped back, taking his carbine in both hands. Ma gave a blood-chilling scream as the gun butt hit Matt in the stomach and pain folded him in half.

"Take him up North, then," the captain snarled. "See what they make of him there."

The carbine's stock crashed on the back of Matt's neck. Ma dropped to the ground with him.

The captain knelt, grabbed a handful of Matt's hair, and yanked his head back. "You'd best thank your Maker every day of your life for this mother of yours."

"Thank you, captain." Ma wept. "Thank you. Thank you."

"I'll be back here in three days. If you're not gone, you're mine." He shoved Matt away and shouted, "Fire his barn! Take what you can!" Then, quietly: "Leave her house."

Ma blanketed Matt's body with hers, weeping pitifully. "I'm sorry, Mama," he tried to say. "Papa, I'm sorry." He shut his eyes. His arms were numb, his head a boulder, and from his throat came strange grunting noises that somehow soothed him. Tyler was wailing. Matt felt all his brothers and sisters near. Mules braying, men hollering, wagons rattling, fire crackling . . . and then he heard no more.

35

"I think Jesse has Salt."

Matt heard Ben's quiet words through the open window.

"He wouldn't say for sure. And he said not to tell."

"Since when do you follow orders?" Clayton asked.

Matt pulled the door open and stepped gingerly onto the porch. His legs worked all right, but walking jostled every aching bone. He had awakened at dawn in Ma's bed, with no recollection of getting there. He fell asleep again and woke again and finally forced himself to his feet.

Now he looked into each face: Ma's was worried and sad, Betsy's tearful, Ben's hurt and scared. Clayton was just angry. When Matt's eyes met Molly's, she ran to Betsy. Tyler alone paid him no mind, as if this were any other day and the wheels of his toy horse the only thing worth his attention.

"Don't put it on Ben, Clay," Matt said. "It's none of his fault."

"I *know* whose fault it is," Clayton said bitterly. "I know *just* who to put it on."

"Clay," Ma said.

Matt nerved himself to look to the barn. Papa's barn, so carefully built, so quickly destroyed. All the animals led out and carried off. Sugar . . . What would Papa think of him now?

"Matthew," Ma said as he walked off the porch.

"Leave him, Ma," Clayton said.

In bare feet, Matt carefully circled the smoldering rubble. Every tool, plow, harness, hoe, cider press . . . charred metal. The wagon had been loaded up, his own mules pulling it for the Feds. The pelts—well, Molly would forget her cape with a trip to Philadelphia's fancy furs store. But his whole life was in that barn. Would he ever get it back?

He turned toward the fields. The corn was still standing, and the joke was on him. When they were gone and it was harvest time, his first crop would feed Federal horses and Federal soldiers.

The chicken coop had been burned, and the smokehouse, and the woodshed. They had left the privy. That was considerate. He used it, then went to the pump, where he soaked his head and took a drink. But when he walked back to tell his family everything and ask forgiveness, he could not speak a word, only sit and stare at this new view of the woods.

"Matt," Ma said at last, "are you hungry?"

He shook his head.

"Do you feel all right?"

He nodded, and folded his arms on his chest.

"Leave him be, Mama. He'll talk when he wants." Clayton's voice was thick with contempt. "Just like he does everything else."

Ma said sharply, "Clayton, I'll thank you to allow *me* to speak when *I* wish to."

Clayton leaned toward him. "How many chances did I give you to tell me what was wrong? You shut me out every time. Then you got Ben in it. You put us all in danger—"

"That ain't so!" Pain cut through him as he turned to Clayton. "It was only me they wanted!"

"Stop it, boys!" Ma said.

"You keep your own counsel!" Clayton shouted. "You and *Jesse*." He spat out the name. "And the devil take everybody else!"

"That is not true!"

"You could have talked to me!" Clayton yelled over him. "I could have helped! And now look!" He swept an arm toward the barn.

"What do you care, anyway?" Matt said, hearing his own venom. "I'm the one who'll come back and put it right. You'll be off at some damn college."

"Matt!" Ma said.

"You're right, Matt. I don't care about the barn, or the plows, or the animals, or *any* of it!" He slammed his fist on the chair's arm. "What I care about is not what *did* happen but what *almost* happened. Are you too big a fool to understand that?"

"Clayton!" Ma said. "That will do!"

"That's right, Clay, I'm a fool, and you just—"

"Stop fighting, you two." When Ben spoke with no expression in his voice, Matt cut himself off. He hunched up his shoulders to try to ease the pain, but it didn't help. He felt the same cold as when the oath sickness came on him. Shutting his eyes, he slid one hand over his face.

Clayton gave a disgusted "Ahh!" and hit the chair again, then pulled himself to his feet.

"Clay," Matt said. "Susie and Jesse's ma are in jail."

"No!" Ben cried, and Ma drew a sharp breath.

"Militia came for him, and took them instead. His pap's not right in his mind, Jesse says. After they put him up in the tree. Jess came to me for help. I loaned him Salt so he could get his little ones to Aunt Lotty. She's down near Liberty with Aze, helping out his ma's sister. Jesse's coming back before he goes away."

Nobody so much as moved.

"I thought if you ones knew, and the Feds came, you would tell. Because what's Jesse to you? If you thought it might save me, you'd give him up in a second, any of you, wouldn't you?"

Still silence.

"That night they got me on the road, I told the truth when there was a gun to my head. And last night I didn't know, not till the moment he said 'Gun or rope?' what I might do to save myself. So how could I put that choice on all of you? I knew you'd give up my friend to try to save me. Tell me, Clay. How could I?" He didn't expect an answer, and he didn't get one.

"I *am* sorry, don't think I'm not. For what all of you lost, and what you had to see. I brought this down on you, and now my own little sister won't even look at me."

Molly hid her face in Betsy's lap. Betsy petted her head and stared misery at Matt.

Slowly he got to his feet and walked to the door. "You've every right to hate me, Clay. I reckon right now I hate myself. But I didn't see what else I could do. Funny, Mama, isn't it? This time I spotted the trouble. I just couldn't get out of it."

It took him a while to get up the stairs. His head ached viciously, and he was dizzy and weary. But it felt so good to lie down on his soft bed. He closed his eyes and slept.

Wheels and hooves awakened him. Matt lay taut with fear. The captain had changed his mind and come to kill him or take him for a Paw-Paw. Perhaps it was the provost marshal, here to arrest him—or all of them.

"Oh, my Lord," Ma said.

Matt shut his eyes tight.

Then he heard a deep-voiced laugh, and Ma's running steps. He went to the window to see Ma in a man's arms, being kissed again and again.

"Carrie," the man said. "My girl."

"You found us." Ma was weeping. "Oh, Father, you found us."

He towered over her, much taller than Papa. He was all dressed up, in a gray frock coat and pants the same color, a white shirt and black tie, and a hat like Lincoln's. He had silver hair, a trim silver beard, and a walking stick.

"What's happened here, Carrie? What's happened?"

"Oh, Father, I'll explain. But everyone's all right, praise God for that."

Matt watched his brothers and sisters walk off the porch to meet their grandfather. Matt knew he must go, too, but he took his time. He inspected the purple bruise on his stomach, prodded the lump on his neck. He reached out with his left arm and stretched his fingers. The last two were numb. He made up the bed, carefully arranging Pa's mother's quilt. At last he went to

Ma's room, found his socks and boots, put them on, and stepped onto the porch.

Everyone was just coming back up the path.

"Matt," Ma's pa said, studying him with care.

"Yes, sir." Matt put out his hand. His grandfather shook it gently in both of his. Looking into those warm blue eyes, Matt felt safe—but downright disloyal to Papa for it.

"You've had a spot of trouble."

"Yes, sir."

"Nothing that can't be remedied."

"No, sir."

Ma's father chuckled, releasing his hand. "Why, among all you children, I've been sirred more in five minutes than I have in five years!"

"Don't children up North call folks sir?" Ben asked.

"Not nearly as much as they ought to, Ben." He ruffled Ben's hair and put his arm around Ma again. "What a fine crop of children, Carrie. And you—you're even more beautiful than I remember."

"Oh, Father," Ma said. She did look prettier and happier than she had in a long time, and Matt felt another pang of grief.

"What do you think of this mother of yours, children?"

"We like her tolerable well, sir," Ben said, and they all laughed.

They agreed to call him Grandfather, when they weren't calling him sir. And while they ate a dinner of corn bread and vegetables, he told them of the difficult journey from Philadelphia, filled with detours and delays. Once he got to St. Louis, he'd had to cross Missouri on a patchwork of stages and trains.

"So much track is torn up and bridges burned, at first I

thought we'd go back to St. Louis by steamer. But then I was told we're better off returning the way I came, because the guerrillas have been attacking the Missouri River steamers."

Matt squirmed, uneasy at the mention of guerrillas and uncomfortable in the chair.

"I heard something else," Grandfather continued. "And it is not pleasant. Perhaps you already know. It's called Order No. 11."

That sounded ominous. Orders generally were.

"No, we haven't." Ma began to rub her throat.

"It was issued on the twenty-fifth. Everyone in the four counties directly on the border . . . What are they?"

"Jackson, Vernon, Cass, and Bates," Clayton said.

"All must leave their homes by the ninth of September."

"Leave?" Betsy said.

"Yes," Grandfather said. "Everyone."

"All Southerners, you mean, sir." Matt crumbled a piece of corn bread onto his plate.

"No, Matt. Everyone." Their eyes met. "I'm quite sure of it. Everyone."

"Oh, Lord," Ma said. "That's less than two weeks from now. What will they do? Where will all those people go?"

"Why'd they make that order, Grandfather?" Ben asked.

"Well, Ben, apparently General Ewing feels he cannot control the border because people are aiding the guerrillas. And as they can't sort out who's loy—" He stopped himself, then went on. "Who's on which side, they'll move everyone. The roads are filled with soldiers heading for the border to carry out the order."

"Fools," Matt mumbled. "They'll just make it worse."

"Matt," Ma said in a quiet warning.

"Well," Grandfather said briskly, "we leave in the morning. We'll set out by stage from Liberty."

"How will we get to Liberty, sir?" Matt asked.

"Grandfather's arranged it with the man who drove him here," Ma told him. "Father, what about Salt? Matt, do you suppose—"

"Salt stays here," Matt said to his plate.

"What?" Ma said.

"When Jesse comes back, I'm giving him Salt."

"Oh, Matt—"

"I've made up my mind, ma'am. I've a way out of this, but Jesse hasn't. I was hoping you'd let him take Sugar, but—"

"Let him take Sugar to a Quantrill camp?" Ma bristled, getting to her feet.

"I believe Papa would have approved."

Ma opened her mouth, then shut it. She began to clear the table. Betsy and Molly joined her. Grandfather was rubbing his chin with his thumb, exactly the way Clayton always did, and frowning at Matt.

Matt didn't know whether to stay put or go outdoors or what, and then Ma stopped by the table and said, "You brought that horse up entirely on your own from a newborn foal."

"Yes, ma'am."

"He's everything to you."

"Not everything, Ma." He stood up, trying to keep them from seeing his pain. "Excuse me, ma'am, sir," he said, and went outdoors.

He walked to the empty pasture and sat on Papa's rail. How would he do it—part with this place, part with Salt? It was one thing to say it, to think about it, but now that the time was upon him . . . He stared at the grass. He was twelve years old, trying to teach Salt to walk on the lead line. But Salt was rearing up, landing on Matt's feet, trying to kick and bite him, and he finally did kick him hard enough to knock him over. He was mad and hot and fed up; Salt ran off, looking back as if to taunt him. Then Matt threw his hat and said, *I can't do it! It's too hard!* But Papa called out, *Aw, come on, boy! You fixing to give up so quick? Quit feeling sorry for yourself! Catch that colt and try again!*

The night he died, Pa's voice was raspy and urgent as he repeated what he'd told Matt a hundred times: Tend to your own business. Rely on yourself. Trust in your good judgment. Matt said through his tears, *Yes, Pa, I know, Pa, don't worry, Pa.* And Papa said, *Oh, Matt, to leave you this way, it's so much for a boy.*

Now Matt repeated his answer: "I can do it, Papa." He jumped from the rail. "I can."

36

Matt knelt beside Molly under the cherry tree. She busied herself with the tiny buttons on her doll's coat.

"Hey." He tickled her neck.

She frowned to show she was concentrating much too hard to pay him any mind. "Stupid buttons," she grumbled.

"Moll. Aren't you my sweetheart anymore?"

"Susie's your sweetheart," she said defiantly.

"Moll." Gently he took the doll. "Were you awful scared last night?"

She turned fierce new eyes on him. "I *hate* those Federals."

"You mustn't hate anybody," he said, and she threw her arms around his neck, crying a summer's worth of tears. It hurt to be hugged so tight, but he didn't care. He patted her back, stroked her hair. What business did a little child have with hate? The seven-year-old guerrilla sister, how hard did she hate? If it had been Molly crushed under bricks and rubble, he would have gone and attacked Lawrence, too. Wouldn't he?

When she got the hiccups, he knew she'd finished crying. He dried her eyes with his shirtsleeve. "Listen, what do you think of what Grandfather said, about the hotel in St. Louis and the dining room? Won't that be fun?"

She nodded, smiling a little. "In Pennsylvania, I'll have all the ice cream I want."

"Is that so?"

"Uh-huh. Grandfather's kind, isn't he, Matty?"

"He is."

Her face clouded over again. "What happened to the barn cats?"

"Oh, they all ran away. I saw one of them, out in the woods," he lied.

"The Federals took the lambs, and the little pigs," she told him solemnly. "I saw them. I saw them take Sugar and Tug and Tatters."

He kissed her forehead. "I'm sorry you had to see all that, Moll."

"And they burned my rabbit skins."

"Never mind. I'll bet there's plenty of rabbits to hunt in Pennsylvania."

"Is Susie really in jail, Matty?"

"She is. But they'll let her go soon. And this war'll be over before you know it, and by the time you're big like Betsy you won't even remember it happened."

"Oh yes, I will. I'll always remember."

"I hope not, anyway. Come on, let's go ask Grandfather about that hunting."

They found him on the porch with Clayton. "Molly was wondering if folks hunt rabbits in Pennsylvania," Matt said.

"She was, was she?" Grandfather took her onto his knee.

"Yes, Grandfather, because Matty was saving skins to make me a cape, and the Feds burned them up!"

"There's all kinds of hunting in Pennsylvania, Molly. We have a man named Remy who takes care of our grounds and stable. His wife is Lo. She keeps our house and cooks for us. They were slaves at one time, and now they're free. Remy knows a great deal about hunting. I'm sure he'd be pleased to tell Matt the best places."

Grandfather stared at Matt curiously, seeming to expect something. Did Grandfather think he would bear a person malice just because that person was a freed slave? Would these folks who worked in his house think so?

"I'd like it if he did," Matt said slowly, and Clayton smiled at him.

Matt dug his hands into his pockets. "Grandfather? Would you care to go with me, and take a look at what's left of this farm?"

Grandfather stood Molly on her feet and reached for his walking stick. "I can't think what I'd like more."

As they walked, Matt pointed out the burned outbuildings. "This was our smokehouse . . . That was the woodshed . . . the chicken coop."

"I'll help you with all of it afterward," Grandfather said.

"I appreciate you saying that, sir."

Grandfather stopped. "Matt, they told me about last night. You mustn't think all Union soldiers behave that way."

"Yes, sir," Matt mumbled.

"Your uncle Will is a Union major. He'd be appalled by such goings-on."

"Yes, sir."

"The situation here is beyond complex," Grandfather said, sounding bewildered. Matt didn't respond. They started walking again.

"That's the hay meadow yonder, and over there's the wheat field. And here, well, you can see what this is."

"My Lord." Grandfather planted his feet and looked around in wonder. "What do you do with all this corn?"

"I sell some and keep some. Some of it's for feed. Bring some to the mill, and there's meal for cooking. Sir, did you never live on a farm, then?"

He chuckled. "Never, Matt. I was born in Philadelphia in

1801. My father was a storekeeper. *His* father fought in General Washington's army. Told me stories, when I was small, about the summer the Declaration of Independence was written, and winter camp at Valley Forge. Our new nation united against foreign tyranny. Thinking of it makes this damned war seem all that much sadder."

Some would say *this* war is about a new nation united against foreign tyranny, Matt wanted to say. But it was too soon to chance getting on Grandfather's bad side, so he answered, "Yes, sir."

"Well!" Grandfather said cheerfully. "Tell me about your corn, Matt."

"It's pretty high for such a dry summer. Right about the time it tassels, it stops growing taller. Then it concentrates on making the ear. When the weather's right, it'll grow over an inch a day."

"No fooling!" Grandfather took corn silk between his fingers.

"Good hot sun, plenty of rain. In July my pa would say—" He stopped.

"What did your pa say, Matt?" Grandfather asked, looking into his eyes.

Matt shook his head, smiling to recall. "He'd do like this." He stood stock-still and held up his hands. "Shhh, children. What's that sound? Why, I *believe* you can hear the corn growing!"

Grandfather laughed.

"And you almost could, you know. We sleep in the corn sometimes, when it's real hot, or for fun I'd do it with my friend. Not so much since the war. Ma doesn't like us sleeping away from the house. But we'd lie here and it'd be so quiet. There'd be this almost crackling sound. I imagined it to be the corn growing. Probably the wind."

"Perhaps not."

"Anyhow, no better place in this world for hide-and-seek," Matt said, but it made him think of Dr. Samuel saying, *Lay low, Jess* . . . their trampled corn . . . Jesse's back. He winced, and saw his grandfather notice. "Hide-and-seek," he repeated, biting his lip, trying to untangle the line of his thought. But Susie crying at the woodshed; her bloody mouth; that final kiss, tasting of salt and metal. "I can't recall what I was saying."

"It looks like a fine crop," Grandfather said softly.

"Thank you, sir. It's a pretty fair crop." He snapped off an ear. "The Feds'll get it from me, when I've gone."

"There will be many more springs and summers and harvests," Grandfather said. "Many more growing seasons, much happier than this one."

"Yes, sir," Matt said.

Grandfather pointed to the north field. "And over there?"

Matt stared down at the weedy mess. "That . . ." He nodded slowly. "I'll cultivate that field when I come home." He led Grandfather through a maze of corn rows until they reached the orchard.

"Now *that* is a lovely sight," Grandfather said.

"Thank you, sir." Matt breathed the sweet smell of ripening fruit. "We get a good crop. Papa raised these up from saplings. He claimed he got some from Johnny Appleseed himself when he and Ma—" Again he brought his words up short.

"Were on their way from Pennsylvania," Grandfather finished.

"Yes, sir."

Grandfather waited before he replied. "Is that so?"

"We children have never really been sure. Ma always stuck to his story, but with a sort of laugh in her eyes. And I'm not sure I *do* want to know if it's true or not." He twisted off two apples, handing one to his grandfather, biting into the other. "Not ready."

"Not bad," Grandfather said at the same time, and they laughed a little.

"I wish you could taste them when they're a whole lot better than not bad. And Ma bakes the best apple pie you'll ever eat."

"Then I'll look forward to having one in Pennsylvania."

"But she won't do much cooking there, sounds like."

"Not unless she wants to."

Matt tossed the apple aside. "I'm a bit skittish about it, sir. Going where there's so much of things. Ice cream and schools and cooks. Seems like I'll never get anybody to come back here."

Grandfather studied him and said nothing.

"Sir, there's one more place I'd like to take you."

They walked up the hillside, to the spot beyond the highest trees.

"This is where we buried Papa."

Right away Grandfather knelt and bowed his head. As Matt dropped to his knees, he blinked back tears. Maybe Grandfather did hate Papa once. Or maybe it was something else. And maybe in twenty years, all sorts of things had changed.

Matt stood when Grandfather did. "I dug the grave myself, and Clayton made his coffin. Mama didn't think we ought to, but Clay and I talked it over and decided we didn't want anybody else doing those things for Pa. He picked the spot out himself. Well, he picked it out for the babies, so then he wanted to be here, too. Papa made their marker out of cherry wood, and Clay carved Pa's. Someday we'll get one made of stone."

"Perhaps while you're in Pennsylvania, you'll earn some money and have one made."

"I've no idea what I'll do there," Matt said quietly. "I won't know how to be, away from this place." He stared at the lush green grave. "Sometimes I've had this notion . . . that I wish I was right beside him."

Grandfather gently rested his hand on Matt's shoulder. For just a moment, Matt let it be. Then he walked away.

37

Matt's mood darkened with the evening. After Papa's clock struck nine, Ma stilled the pendulum, lifted the clock down, and wrapped it in a blanket. Matt turned from the sight, cooling his forehead on the window glass.

When the knock finally came, no one spoke. Matt followed Ma to the lean-to.

"Who is it?" she called.

"Mrs. Howard? Mrs. Howard?" came Jesse's panicked reply.

Ma let him in. When Jesse saw Matt, he leaned hard against the door, showing his relief.

"Matt . . . what?" He pointed toward the barn.

"You see what you see," Matt said, and Ma left them.

"Everybody all right?"

"Yes."

"Dang." Jesse tore off his hat. "Dang it all! Why'd they come here?"

"That's a long story."

"You plan to tell it?" Jesse asked, narrowing his eyes.

Matt glanced over his shoulder. "Come on." He lit a lantern and they backed down the root-cellar ladder. First thing, Jesse fished a carrot from the bin and crunched into it. "You're hungry?" Matt said.

"This'll do me. What happened?" Jesse sat on the bench.

Matt tossed him another carrot, then began lining up empty jelly jars.

"Matt?"

"I've something on my conscience." He looked at Jesse. "And it wants getting off."

Jesse shrugged.

"When I left your party, militia got me on the road. Asking if I'd seen Buck. They brought me home and took my gun. Said to keep away from your place. Ma begged them out of taking Salt."

"The night of the party," Jesse repeated, rising.

Matt adjusted the jars. "I wanted to come and warn you next morning. But Ma and Clayton said no. And I'm ashamed of it, listening to them. And that damn militia captain."

"So you could've kept it all from happening." Jesse's voice was so cold, Matt didn't care to see his eyes. "Pappy . . . July . . . Susie and Ma."

"And you," Matt added. "What they did to you." His blood seared his face. He was shaking in the endless wait for a response.

"And if they'd been there when you got to my place, then what?"

Matt lifted his shoulders.

"I suppose you'd've fought them all off, single-handed?"

Matt started to breathe again.

"With what, your Barlow knife?"

"You've made your point, Jess."

Jesse raked back his hair with his fingers. "So why'd they come back?"

"Because they figured out I gave you Salt."

For a long time Jesse stared past him, blinking. Then he said, "I'd never have taken him and put you in that danger had I known they'd already been here. Never."

"I know that."

"And what'd they do to you? Why're you moving so peculiar?"

"I had an unfortunate encounter with the butt of a carbine." He shrugged. "I'll live."

Jesse saw no humor. He crumpled back down on the bench, looking worried, defeated, and played out.

"Hey." Matt pushed Jesse's shoulder, nodding toward the ladder. " 'The North' has arrived."

Jesse's brows shot up.

"Got here this morning. He missed all the fun."

Now Jesse managed a grin. "What do you make of him?"

"I like him, Jess. He's a good man."

Jesse nodded.

"So . . . you get there all right? As Jessica?"

"No hitch. Little ones are fine. Coming *back* was lively. Seems like I signaled the wrong side, down by Liberty, and got myself chased for a while."

"Lord, Jess!"

"I ran like a scalded dog," Jesse admitted. "But Salt took fences their horses wouldn't, so I got away quick enough."

"Jess . . . I want you to take him."

"Where?" Jesse asked, puzzled.

"Where do you think?"

"No," Jesse snapped. "He goes with you."

"But I want you to have him."

"No, Matt. I say no." He set his mouth and gave his head one stubborn shake.

"Either you take him or I set him free in the woods."

"Well, aren't you a first-rate fool."

"Look, up there he'd just be in a stable all day, not even out in a pasture. Just standing in a stall till I'd come and ride him. That ain't Salt, you know that."

"At least he'd be alive. He could get shot out from under me at any time. They go for the horses first, then they can get you easier."

"I reckon I know the tactics. And besides——"

Jesse interrupted him. "Just sit tight a minute, would you?" He leaned his elbows on his knees and held his head, then bolted straight up. "You want me to take Salt because you reckon it's your fault I don't have July?"

"I want you to take Salt because I want you to take Salt," Matt said steadily. "Because with a horse like Salt, you'll have a better chance. All right? You need me to explain any of those big words?"

Jesse waited a bit before he said, "I won't miss that smart mouth of yours, Matt." Right away he added, "Or maybe I will."

"You'll take him?"

"Yes."

"All right, then," Matt said, but neither moved.

"When you leaving?" Jesse asked.

"In the morning."

"Halfway across the land on railroads. I'll probably never step foot on a train in my life."

"Railroads'll be around a mighty long while, Jess."

Jesse went to the ladder. "I'm thinking to sleep in the cave."

"The *cave*?" The notion caught Matt by surprise.

"I figured it's the safest place. I've seen no Feds nearby—they're all hell-bent for the border, just itching to terrorize folks with this Order 11. But why press my luck? I'll just tell Pappy good-bye and go out to the cave, then head off at first light."

"To where?"

"There's a rendezvous I reckon I can find. They call it the bull pen."

Nodding slowly, Matt said, "I'll go to the cave with you."

Jesse looked skeptical.

"You leave me at the prairie in the morning. I'll walk home."

"I sure wouldn't mind the company. But what about your ma and Clayton? And The North?"

"I'll manage it. Go on down to the woods. I'm behind you in five minutes. Come and say good-bye."

In the kitchen, Jesse backed up when he spotted Matt's grandfather.

"That's my grandfather, Jess," Matt said. "This is Jesse, Grandfather."

"Hello," Grandfather said solemnly, offering his hand.

"Say hello," Matt prompted, elbowing Jesse.

Jesse gave half a grin and shook hands. "Hello, sir." Then he went to Ma. "Mrs. Howard, he says I'm to keep Salt."

"Yes, I know," Ma said quietly.

"And I want you to know, ma'am, I'd never have taken his horse yesterday had I known militia'd been here already."

"Yes, Jesse."

"And when this all is over, I plan to help him build back the barn."

"All right," Ma said with a forlorn smile.

"And I apologize to you, too, Clay."

"You've done nothing wrong," Clayton said—and even seemed to mean it.

"Ben, you'll be here to help us, isn't that right?"

"That's right, Jess," Ben said bravely, shaking his hand. "And you tell Susie I said 'bye, too, when you see her," he added, and Matt had to turn his face. That was when he saw Grandfather watching him, stroking his whiskers and watching.

"I sure will, Ben. Betsy, good-bye."

"Good-bye, Jess," Betsy said tearfully.

"Sir," Jesse said, nodding to Grandfather.

"Best to you, young man."

"Clayton." Jesse reached out. They shook hands.

"My brother would have taken a bullet for you, Jess."

Jesse's eyes darted to Matt's.

"What, you didn't *tell* him?" Clay asked Matt. Then he said
to Jesse, "Would have, and nearly did."

"I'll tell you," Matt mumbled.

Jesse said, "Ma'am . . ."

Ma hugged him close. "Oh, Jesse." She gripped his shoulders and kissed his cheek. "God be with you."

"Thank you, ma'am." His voice was barely a whisper. He
turned away fast. "Good-bye."

When Matt returned from seeing Jesse out, Clayton stared at
him. "That was an awfully quick farewell. So, when *will* you
tell him? After the war?"

"Matthew?" Ma asked, confused.

"He's planning to sleep in this cave of ours, Ma. I want to go
with him."

"No!"

"We'll leave at first light."

"No!" She paced to the hearth.

He trailed after her. "That captain said three days. And you
heard your pa say they're all heading for the border anyhow.
And Jesse said it, too. There's nobody around anywhere."

"Matthew!"

"Nobody's ever tracked us to this cave, Ma."

"You can barely walk!"

"I do all right."

Ma folded her arms. "Haven't you had enough, Matt? Haven't you?"

"Yes, ma'am." He nodded slowly. "I have."

"Ma, don't let him go," Clayton said.

"Well, Clay, is he asking me or telling me?" Ma said.

"I'm asking, Mama." Matt held her eyes with his. "He's scared and worn out and I'm asking to do this one last thing before I leave."

Ma's shoulders dropped.

"Ma, tell him no."

"I agree with Clayton," Grandfather put in.

"I'm not asking them, Ma. I'm asking you."

"Carolyn, this is absurd—" her pa began.

Ma whirled on him. "What would you have me do, Father? Forbid him? Don't you and I know well enough what that'll bring?" She turned her back, pressing her fingers to her temples.

With no clock ticking, the silence was complete.

"This cave," Ma said, "you can find it in the dark?"

"I could find it in my sleep."

She just barely nodded. "Go."

Matt looked to his grandfather. "What time do we leave, sir?"

"Seven o'clock," said Grandfather evenly, piercing him with a stern gaze.

Ben caught up with him at the door, looking fearful. "Don't you know Jesse and I have nine lives?" Matt said. Ben rested his frown. "We're only on about our fifth, I reckon." He roughed up Ben's hair. "Don't look for me till you see me."

"All right."

Then Ma was there, cupping her hands under his chin. "You *will* be back," she said more than asked, desperately searching his face.

"I'll be back, Ma." He kissed her quickly, and ran for the woods.

38

Salt was glad to see him, no question about it. He nickered and tossed his head so, Matt didn't know how he would live with his own decision. Salt had been petted and cared for his whole life. How would he do, sleeping in the open, not getting enough to eat? How would he behave under the gun? A scared horse might take a rider straight into enemy fire. Would Salt obey, or bolt? He could run as fast as any horse and take just about every fence. But how would he be with Colts going off all around him? For that matter, how would Jesse?

Matt shut his eyes on the thought as he brushed Salt in the Samuels' woods. What was keeping Jesse? He said he'd only be a couple minutes, but it had been more like a couple dozen. Maybe it wasn't true, all this talk about the Feds heading for the border. Some might be hiding in the woods . . . Just as Matt's heart started pounding in earnest, Jesse came rustling through the brush.

"All okay?" Matt asked.

"Sorry, Matt. It was Pappy, he couldn't hardly let me go," Jesse explained, sounding both amazed and sad. "Holding on and telling me, 'Jess boy, I love you like my own.' And he was crying like a baby. Imagine that."

Matt didn't care to imagine it. He took the rolled-up blankets from Jesse and fastened them behind Salt's saddle.

Jesse tied a sack of corn to the pommel. He slung his haversack over his head. Then he said, "When Buck was here last, he planned to take me right then. But Pappy said no. First time I ever knew Pappy to stand up to Ma. He said, 'No, the boy stays here.' That's when Ma started making my shirt."

Matt could think of no reply.

"Let's go," Jesse said.

At the prairie, Matt normally gave Salt the reins. But it wouldn't be right, going at a gallop with all this extra weight, so he kept Salt at a gentle trot. Then he realized he'd already had his last run with Salt, that day with Ma and Sugar. But you ought to know it when it was the last time you were to do a thing. Whether it be riding your horse or fishing with your friend or kissing the girl you liked or sleeping in your room with your brothers. You ought to know it, so you could appreciate it more. Yet this was the last time he'd be with Jesse like this, both the same, both still boys, and he wasn't appreciating it much at all.

"Look at that sky, Jess," he said, bringing Salt up. "Just about every star God ever thought of." He tipped his head back despite his aching neck. "I bet they don't have stars like this in Pennsylvania."

"Well, you'd best keep your mind open about such things. It won't do you any good to go up there with a chip on your shoulder."

"There's truth to that," Matt said, and trotted on.

A waning moon guided them through the woods to the cave. Jesse brought his things inside. Matt tended to Salt longer than he needed to, soaking up the still, hot darkness and listening to the screech owl's mournful whinny.

When Matt slipped through the cave opening, Jesse was sitting on a blanket. The cave was glowing with a candle's light. "Cozy," Matt said.

"Pappy's idea."

"He can't be *too* bad off, then."

Jesse kept quiet a minute, and then said, "When I got there, he was looking all over for the little ones. Calling out for Ma and Lotty, saying he couldn't find the little ones." He tossed Matt a blanket. "I believe Clayton wanted you to tell me something."

"He did."

Jesse lay on his side, propping himself up with his elbow. "I want to hear it all, Matt. Don't leave out a thing."

Matt started with the men on the road and ended with the captain yelling did he want the gun or the rope, and Ma's crying and pleading until the captain contented himself with the carbine beating.

"You'd never want to hear it, Jess," he said, "your ma begging your life from a drunk and crazy soldier—" He cut himself off.

They were silent a long time. Matt just sat rubbing dirt off his boots. Jesse's boots. That afternoon in the barn seemed like a thousand sorrows ago.

"One thing disturbs me." Jesse's words were soft and slow as he stared at the flame. "This boy who was at our place with Buck, he said something peculiar. Said Quantrill can get you to do things you never would have dreamed you'd do. I suppose Buck saw that troubled me. Afterwards, he took me off alone and told me, all serious and big-brother-like, 'Jess, don't worry too much on it. You may have to do some things, but you *can* show mercy.'" He shot Matt a sudden grin. "That sound like how Buck talks to me normally?"

"Not much like," Matt replied, and they laughed just a little.

"He said if your commander's right there you got to follow orders, but oftener he won't be. And he said he's seen Quantrill himself show mercy plenty of times."

Matt took out his knife and dug at the ground. "I wish I was going with you, Jess."

"You're too young for Quantrill," Jesse said briskly, sitting up.

"That ain't so."

"If you're not sixteen, he'll send you away."

"They don't care if you're not sixteen. And besides, how would they know?"

But Jesse paid him no mind. "And then where would you be? Way out there alone and your folks gone away. And I'm taking back my offer of you staying at my place, I can tell you. Not being there myself to watch you around my sister." Jesse was snickering.

Matt flicked dirt at him with the knife blade.

"Every time I think about that day we all went out, how sulky you were, with her all over Ben—"

"Shut up, Jess."

"Sore as a bee-stung bear," Jesse finished, and Matt couldn't help but laugh along.

"I think about her a lot," he said, serious again.

"She'll be all right," Jesse said firmly. "She's a tough girl. And she's with Ma. Ma'll protect her."

"Jess, you reckon it'd be all right if I wrote her a letter or whatnot?"

"Oh, you didn't need my permission to put your hands on her, but you—"

"I did not put my hands on her."

"You ask me, can you write to her from a thousand miles away."

"I did not put my hands on that girl!"

"I know, I know. She told me what-all went on. And I believe her."

"So you believe Susie, but not me."

" 'Course I wouldn't believe you. You're a boy. For real, though, Matt? I don't think it's such a good idea. What if you didn't hear back? Maybe your letter got lost or stolen, or . . . some other reason. Then you'd imagine all sorts of whatever going on back here. Right?"

"I suppose."

"Best to just let it be. That's my thought."

"All right," Matt agreed, though he wasn't sure. He'd have to wait awhile to know what he would do.

Jesse knelt and opened his haversack. He took out his Colt, placed the caps, and laid the gun on the ground. He showed Matt the brush and curry comb; Matt nodded approval. Then Jesse took out the guerrilla shirt, which was crushed into a ball. He smoothed it out on the blanket.

"Don't think I'll get this out till I'm with them awhile. Put it on now, I'd feel a fool: Here I am! With my shirt!"

Matt shook his head, laughing.

"Still . . ." Jesse held it up. "It's a good shirt, isn't it, Matt?"

It *was* a good shirt, as such things went. Deep red, with the four big pockets for bullets and caps. Jesse's ma had fastened metal studs all along the embroidery outlining those pockets and the low-cut neck.

"I guess you'll look pretty tough in that, Jess. I reckon girls'll be singing that song about you."

Jesse frowned, trying not to smile as he carefully rolled the shirt. Then he turned solemn, opening some sort of packet in his palm: "Look, Matt. What Pappy gave me." Matt crawled over to see: morphine. Dr. Samuel had brought Ma some of the tiny crystals when Papa was near the end. "Pappy cut up the grains with the tip of his knife. Says if I'm hurt bad, chew one every few hours. If I'm captured—take it all."

Matt looked up.

"I don't believe I could do that, though. End my own life. It ain't for me to say when my time's over. That's up to God. And if I have to hang, that's His judgment on me for killing other men."

Jesse refolded the packet and stashed it in his haversack. He took out his Bible, found his spot, and read with reverence:

"What time I am afraid, I will trust in thee.

In God I will praise his word, in God I have put my trust; I will not fear what flesh can do unto me.

Every day they wrest my words: all their thoughts are against me for evil.

They gather themselves together, they hide themselves, they mark my steps when they wait for my soul . . .

When I cry unto thee, then shall mine enemies turn back: this I know; for God is for me . . .

In God have I put my trust . . ."

He shut the book and fixed his gaze on Matt to say one last line: "I will not be afraid what man can do unto me."

Matt got to his feet. "Well, damn it, Jess," he said. "Damn it all."

Outside the cave, he leaned against a ghostly sycamore, swallowing his sadness again and again. But he was somehow soothed by the raucous tattling of locusts: *Katy did it! Katy did! Katy did it! Katy did!* In a while, he returned, and said gruffly, "I suppose we ought to get some sleep."

"Right."

Matt lay on the blanket. "How's your back, anyhow?"

"Healing up pretty fair. How about your hurts?"

"I'm all right."

"You reckon we'll get up okay?"

"I'll wake you," Matt said.

Jesse snuffed out the flame. " 'Night, Matt."

" 'Night, Jess."

With the dark came a weariness that sat on his back and shut his eyes. He began to fade. Far away he heard Ma, talking to her father when she didn't know Matt could hear—*I don't believe it's really hit him yet*, she'd said—but now it did. Last night, when he jumped the fence with Ben's gun, he left so much behind: the sound of Clayton milking cows, that first loud spurt of liquid hitting metal. Molly cooing to kittens piled in her pinafore. The soft, warm spot between Sugar's ears. Ben sleepily, dazedly mucking out the stalls. The expected surprise of swallows swooping when the door opened. The corncob battles on October afternoons. The smells of hay and manure and horsehide and sawdust. These things he counted, in place of sheep, until sleep overwhelmed him.

He awoke in darkness. Slowly he stood, favoring his back, holding his neck. He stretched his left arm and splayed his fingers. This would be one long walk home.

Outside, a few birds told him the day wanted to begin. Salt was asleep. Were they up yet at home, with no rooster to wake them? Likely Ben had slept on the tick. Matt wished he could have seen Ben's face when he felt that Kentucky rifle under him.

Then he recalled Ben's worry as he was leaving, Grandfather's grim stare. He'd managed to cause trouble between Ma and her pa after just a few hours. Did they argue when he left? He'd thought Grandfather might have been getting to like him. That was surely changed now. And then, once again, there was

Clayton. Well, the journey should give him time enough to right all his wrongs.

Seven o'clock, Grandfather had told him. And when he got home, he still had to hunt up Papa's buckskin shirt and remember to get his haversack and Ben's gun out of the woods. And he would bring Papa's buffalo robe if he had to carry it the entire way. He had better get Jesse up.

He was about to nudge Jesse's ribs with a boot tip. Then he got on one knee and gripped Jesse's shoulder instead. Jesse opened his eyes.

"Rise and shine," Matt said.

"Hey."

"Hey." He folded his blanket and tossed it to Jesse. "I'll just go and see to Salt."

"All right."

Salt pawed the ground and nickered, bumping Matt when he came near. "Did you have a pretty good rest?" Matt scratched behind his ears and fed him corn. "You'll be going with Jesse now, for keeps. Remember everything I taught you, hear? And learn some other things fast." He brushed and curried Salt until Jesse came out, then blanketed and saddled him. As Matt bitted him up, Jesse began to load his things.

"You won't ever have to put spurs to him," Matt said. "Well, never mind, that's for you to judge."

"I'll be good to him, Matt."

"I know you will."

"I know how you hate to part with him."

"Hell, Jesse." Matt cinched the saddle girth tighter. "It ain't just him."

Jesse tied the sack of corn. Matt fixed the stirrups and checked Salt's feet for stones. Jesse buckled his saddlebag and said, "Well. We best be going."

At the prairie's edge, they dismounted and faced each other. Jesse dug into his pocket. "Here." He reached out a fist. Matt looked at him. "*Here*," Jesse insisted, giving one sharp nod. Matt opened his hand, expecting a rabbit foot—but what he got was Jesse's pa's watch. He frowned. "For safekeeping," Jesse said.

Matt shook his head.

"Please, Matt." Jesse searched his eyes. "I don't want some Federal boy one day telling his friend, 'Look what my brother got off a dead bushwhacker.' "

Matt closed his fingers fast around the watch, and pushed it deep into his pocket. He turned away, adjusting Salt's throat latch.

"I'll be back," Jesse said. "And so'll you. I'll hear you're home, and I'll come out to find you plowing. I'll sneak up and say, 'Hey! Where's my papa's watch?' "

"And I'll say, 'Where's my damn horse?' "

"And *I'll* say—"

They finished together: "—'Don't curse.' " Laughing, they looked away. Matt straightened the brow band and nose band. He smoothed Salt's forelock.

"Well, then, Matt." Jesse put his hand out. They shook.

"You take care, Jess."

Jesse mounted and faced front, pulling his hat low on his forehead. The day was crawling over the horizon in streaks of red and orange. Matt rubbed Salt's neck.

"All right?" Jesse said.

Matt nodded. "All right."

Jesse reached down and Matt reached up. They shook hands once more. Jesse dug his heels and said, "Hee-yah!"

They seemed to start at a fierce run, and were far from him in no time. Jesse took off his hat and waved it in the air. Matt walked backward until they were nothing on the prairie. Then he turned around and headed home.

Author's Note

Matt Howard exists only on these pages, but his friend was a real person.

Jesse James fought with guerrilla bands until word of the war's end reached the western border in May 1865. By many accounts, Jesse, seventeen, was riding toward a Union outpost under a white flag of surrender when he was shot in the chest by a Federal cavalryman. Left for dead, he managed to escape and eventually crawled to a nearby farm for help. That family turned him over to Federal officials. Major J. B. Rogers was so sure the young bushwhacker would die, he paid for Jesse's passage to Rulo, Nebraska, where the Samuel family was living after being banished from Missouri early in 1865. They returned when Jesse, assured by doctors that his days were numbered, begged to be brought home to die.

In Missouri, perhaps more than anywhere else, Civil War grudges died hard. Jesse and his brother Frank—nicknamed Buck—were harassed and threatened by former Union militia after the family returned. While scores of men who had been guerrillas rose above such treatment to become respected citizens, Jesse and Frank, along with some ex-guerrilla friends, chose lives of bank robbery, train robbery, and murder. No one knows why.

Hundreds of books have been written about Jesse James, but almost all concentrate on the outlaw years. Details of his childhood and guerrilla years are few, and mostly anecdotal. Books about Jesse tend to paint him in absolutes: he was an avenging angel who had no faults, or a bloodthirsty devil without a single redeeming quality. The truth must lie somewhere in between.

The Union militia's raid on the Samuel farm and Mrs. Samuel's and Susie's imprisonment have been variously reported, in date and details. The two were jailed for about a month. Mrs. Samuel's daughter Fannie was born in October 1863, and she gave the baby the middle name Quantrill. The hanging of Dr. Samuel resulted in permanent brain damage: he died in an insane asylum in 1908.

Exactly when Jesse became a guerrilla fighter has not been determined, but most reliable sources suggest the date was somewhere between the fall of 1863 and the spring of 1864. Eventually, Jesse ended up in the command of "Bloody Bill" Anderson. One of Anderson's sisters had been killed and another maimed in the Kansas City jail collapse.

On April 3, 1882, in his St. Joseph home, Jesse James was shot in the back of the head by a traitorous gang member. Jesse had a wife and two small children, all of whom were in the house when he was murdered for reward money. He was thirty-four years old.

The issues involved in Missouri's Civil War are still the subject of debate and disagreement among historians and Civil War buffs. Although this story presents a Southern boy's perspective, I have taken care to show that both sides were guilty of atrocities.

Acknowledgments

I have some generous people to thank for sharing their time and expertise. Sally Eckhoff, equestrian, fielded my interminable horse questions with patience and enthusiasm. Civil War gun expert Bob Brecht put the dead Federal's Colt into my hand and taught me what I needed to know.

Roger W. McCredie shared his abiding love of the South and his knowledge of its heritage, history, and culture. MoCSA list members answered questions and provided references, especially at the outset of my research. Particular thanks must go to Scott K. Williams, with a nod to R. Scott Price, Jesse Estes, and Celia Mater. The following folks graciously solved pieces of my nineteenth-century puzzle: Joe Vorisek (shotguns), Dave and Cathy Para (music), Jean Warren (clothing), and Jocelyne Rubinetti (Methodism).

I'm grateful to my first readers: Rebecca Klock, Moira Danehy, Reg Wright, and my mother, Gloria Raccio. Full-service neighbors Barrie and Karen Maguire faxed, FedEx'ed, and calmed. Janice Ward is still listening.

Finally, I want to thank my sons, Tristan and Jesse, for providing distraction and joy when I was submerged in the sorrows of this most tragic war.